Reckless Choices

Emma Batten

To Nigel,
Happy reading,
Emma x

First published in the UK by Emma Batten 2021

Printed and bound in the UK

A catalogue record of this book can be found in the British library

ISBN 978-1-7399854-0-0

Edited by Maud Matley and Michael Golding

Proofread by Sian Herrera-Delgado

Cover painting by Zoe Beardsley

www.emmabattenauthor.com

To Rosemary,
With thanks for the interest you have shown in my writing, for valuable editorial advice, and friendship over the past years.

About the Book

In this sequel to *Still Shining Bright*, and prequel to *Secrets of the Shingle*, I fill in the missing parts of the tale which were necessary to enable the series to flow smoothly.

Having survived the Northfleet shipping disaster, Cora and Emily had settled in Ashford. Twenty years later, we pick up their tale, taking readers from the thriving market town of Ashford to the small town of Lydd, and a remote settlement called Denge on the Dungeness peninsula.

The characters, other than those seen at the royal wedding, are entirely from my own imagination. My readers will know that I do my very best to make the settings accurate, and for this I find myself turning to local history pages on social media where members are pleased to share memories and photos.

The concrete man does exist at Denge! Was he there in 1893? I doubt it, but no one actually knows who put him there and when!

With Thanks

My thanks to Maud Matley and Michael Golding who have supported me in my writing aspirations since the early days and who have edited Reckless Choices, offering valuable feedback.

Also thank you to Debbie Rigden who offered to practise her editing skills and did a fantastic job.

Thank you to Liz Hopkin for her thorough check of the proof copy. Also thank you to Beverley Adams who checked for any errors in the proof copy.

Thank you to Zoe Beardsley for another piece of distinctive cover art. The five Dungeness Saga books are looking fabulous together.

My last three novels have been 'lockdown books' and so huge thanks to my loyal readers who have supported me during difficult times. All your purchases have enabled me to keep writing and publishing books.

Last but not least, thank you to the shops which sell my books. In particular Frances Esdaile from the Chocolate Deli in Hythe, the team at Salts Farm near Rye, Alfie and his staff at Waterstones in Ashford, and Jake Jones and Beth Couldridge at the Romney Marsh Visitor Centre.

Cora's Story
Chapter One
Thursday 6th July 1893

"There's no space in here," Cora objected, her voice sharp.

"It's the same everywhere, love," the stout woman responded. "It's just me and Annie, so you'll have to squeeze up." She lifted a wide-eyed child into the carriage, then placed her own booted foot in the doorway.

"Squeeze up?" Cora repeated. "Look at us! We're like sardines in one of them new-fangled tins!"

Jacob gave her arm a squeeze. "It won't be for long. We're at Orpington – did you see the sign? That's London. The suburbs anyhow." He pulled their daughter, Molly, onto his knees, then slid along the bench to make room while saying, "You can sit on my lap, can't you?"

"I'm getting a bit old to be sitting on laps," Molly objected. "But all right, as I'm here now!"

Cora moved up a little, pushing against Emily. The silent couple opposite raised their eyebrows and glanced at each other. They had resisted making any conversation since boarding the train at Tonbridge, making a stark contrast between themselves and the family group who had chattered almost non-stop, discussing each town and village they passed, and wondering about the day ahead. Seated opposite

Cora and Jacob were two of their sons – Johnny and Frank – both young men now, with slim muscular figures and neatly trimmed fiery-coloured hair.

"I could sit on Johnny's knee if your daughter wants her own space?" Emily offered. At twenty-two years she was tall but slender, and the girl, Annie, looked to be rather stout to perch on her mother's lap.

"You're too big to be going on my knee," Johnny retorted. "You stay there. I'll stand up if I have to."

Emily rolled her grey eyes and turned her attention to the view from the window.

The train gave a jolt, and they continued on their way. Cora shuffled a little. There was no excess flesh on her, and they had already been seated on the hard benches for over an hour while the carriage bumped over the joints in the tracks. She pulled the light shawl from her shoulders and folded it, then manoeuvred herself to push it under her bottom to form a cushion. The movement had caused a hairpin to come loose, so she pressed it back into the bun of faded auburn waves at the nape of her neck.

Looking across at Johnny, Cora caught his eye and they exchanged brief smiles. *What lovely young men they are.* Her thoughts roamed to the eldest brother, William, who had stayed at home with his wife and three young children. *We've had no trouble from any of the boys, but it's different with Emily. I never know what she'll say or do next. It's been a happy life for her, but she seems unsettled.* Cora closed her eyes for a moment. They had been up early preparing to leave Ashford on the 8:35 train to London. *I was a widow by the time I was Emily's age, and she was two years old. Perhaps she'll calm down when there's a husband to care for. But she'll need someone who won't stand for no nonsense!*

"Chislehurst!" Emily announced.

Everyone turned and gazed out of the grimy windows. There was the impression of people surging forward on the platform and guards dressed in black. The images remained nondescript, until a door was opened to offer a clearer view.

"There's no space," Cora and the stout woman called in unison.

The powerful engine let out a blast of steam while gradually building up pace. Brown brick terraced houses, workshops and warehouses lined the trackside, leading Cora to wonder about how the women managed to keep their clothes and sheets clean on washday. They suffered from the filth emanating from chimneys of both trains and factories. Her memories flitted to a shingle headland where her skin had become sticky with the salt carried on the stiff breeze, and locals hunkered down in small cottages of wood with tin roofs. The washing would always have the fresh smell of sea air and never suffer from smut from the chimney, but the locals in that desolate area faced their own difficulties, living far from modern civilisation. *Ashford is a nice place to live,* Cora reflected. *With the shops and the market, and plenty of work. We've got the countryside all around us, and trains to take us places if we want. Although I can't say that I enjoy a train journey. It's darned uncomfortable and I can hardly see a thing through these mucky windows.* She uttered a small sigh.

Jacob gave her arm an awkward squeeze. "Are you all right?"

"I just wish we could see the sights," Cora replied. "I'd like to take a cloth to the windows and give them a good clean!"

"There'll be plenty to see once we are at Charing Cross," Jacob responded. "We'll stretch our legs along the Mall, and there will be so many statues and buildings, you won't know which way to look first."

"Will we stop for a cup of tea?" Emily asked.

"Of course, and hopefully a bun." Jacob smiled at the young woman. "It will be busy though with people like us coming to see the wedding. How about we find a tearoom before we head off towards Buckingham Palace? There's plenty of time."

"Make sure you hold on to your purse, Em," her mother reminded her. "And you, Molly – don't you dare let go of your pa's hand unless you're safe with one of your brothers."

"I'm not a baby…"

"You're twelve years old, and there's all sorts of nasty people out there who might take a fancy to a pretty girl like you," Cora reminded her. Since the plan to travel to the capital had been in its infancy, the dangers of the trip had been drummed into them all.

Molly didn't reply but drew comfort from the smiles offered by her brothers seated opposite. It wasn't easy being the youngest when her siblings had been grown-up for as long as she could remember.

They neared London Bridge Station. "There's the river," Emily announced from her place by the window. "Look at that – Tower Bridge!" The moment was gone before anyone could truly appreciate its splendour.

The station passed with none of those in the cramped carriage able to appreciate the architecture. As the train ground to a halt for Waterloo, to everyone's consternation a couple of lads forced themselves into the carriage, stepping on toes and standing against those already cramped in their seats. They held onto the luggage rack and swayed with the motion of the train.

"It's only for a couple of minutes," Jacob soothed his wife.

“Mind your purse, Em.” Cora shot dark looks towards the interlopers.

No sooner had they crossed the Thames, than the train was slowing to a halt at Charing Cross. Clutching at bags and one another, Jacob and Cora Rose led their family onto the platform. Despite the crowds and the smoke from engines, they all stood for a moment, gasping in awe at the barrel-vaulted roof of ironwork and glass soaring above them. Then the moment was lost, for they had no choice but to be herded with other passengers towards the exit.

“All right, luv?” A cheeky driver stood beside a monogrammed carriage, with two shining black horses between the shafts. He gave Emily a wink.

“Look at them, coming right into the station,” she exclaimed. Separated by a stone balustrade, there was an area for horses and carriages of the wealthy to shelter from the weather.

“Goodness! Don’t you go smiling at any men,” Cora squeaked, torn between looking after young Molly and concerns for her elder daughter. “Johnny. Frank. Keep your sister between you.”

Emily willingly slipped between the young men, her light summer dress of green, with a repeat pattern of tiny flowers, brushing against their best suits. Sandwiched between the hoards, they passed through the ticket barriers and onto the busy city streets. Jacob led them to the Queen Eleanor Memorial Cross – an extravagance of gothic carved stone. They stood for a moment, turning to look back at the Charing Cross Hotel, its ornamental façade rising high in front of the station.

The day was glorious with soft clouds high in an azure sky. Summer sunshine warmed their skin, casting shadows on the women’s faces beneath straw hats. The men removed their jackets but kept cravats in place so as to maintain an air of respectability for the occasion. On this celebratory day, the street scene was busy with horse-drawn carriages and smaller chaises. Family groups and couples in their best outfits all walked in the direction of Trafalgar Square, heading for The Mall. The atmosphere was merry, with those who had ventured to the city in a festive mood, street vendors calling out to advertise their wares, and buskers hoping to fill their hats with coppers.

"It's an hour-and-a-half until the ceremony, but we want to get a good spot," Jacob observed. "Let's go this way," he pointed along The Strand, "and hopefully there's a chance of a cuppa, otherwise we'll find somewhere afterwards."

They joined the ribbon of people, wary of horses moving at a fast pace, and on the lookout for pickpockets. Within minutes, all eyes were on the magnificent Nelson's Column, flanked by lions at each corner of its base. Soon their attention moved to the flowing fountains nearby, and elegant buildings facing the open area.

Molly began to pull her parents towards the bronze lions.

"Later, Moll," her mother protested. "There will be plenty of time after the wedding, and Pa said to look out for a tearoom."

"Ma! Tables on the pavement… and there's a space!" Emily pulled her brothers towards the spot, triumphant in her success.

They secured a table for the six of them and were soon attracting the attention of the waitress who smiled, knowing she'd go home with a purse full of tips that evening. "Here for the wedding, are you?" she asked. "I'd love to see Princess Mary's dress. It's a real fairy-tale wedding."

"We've come up from Kent by train," Cora informed her.

"I hope you get to see some pictures of it," Emily added. "They'll be taking photographs. Clever, isn't it?"

Not wanting to linger over the tea and buttered teacakes, the Rose family were soon pushing back their chairs to make room for the next customers. Once Cora had made sure her daughters were safe, the wonders of Trafalgar Square were left behind, and the wide, tree-lined Mall could be seen extending towards Buckingham Palace.

Moving with the throng, they gazed at the architecture of stately buildings set back behind walls and lawns, often pausing to exclaim over the details or to wonder about the people who lived and worked in such grand places. They had to step carefully though, as trees, some of them surrounded by metal railings, were set within the pavement. To the left, there were glimpses of flower beds and a long lake stretching through St James's Park.

"I'd love to go walking through there," Cora commented. It felt tiresome being dragged along with the crowds, holding her long skirts close, keeping her bag against her, and ensuring Molly's hands stayed tucked through the arms of both parents.

"We'll walk back that way," Jacob told her. "But we won't escape the crowds today, even in the park."

"We can't blame them for wanting to walk there with all the greenery and flowers," Cora conceded. "It's ever so pretty."

"It's fun though!" Emily reminded her. "Being right here, with everyone looking forward to seeing Princess Mary."

Cora looked across at her daughter, strolling along between Johnny and Frank, who had both grown up to be decent and hard-working. She flashed a grin at Emily. "Of course, it is! I can hardly wait to see the bride in her dress. I wonder if she's nervous?"

"I bet she is with all these people that have come to watch," Jacob commented.

"How old is she?" Molly asked.

"The princess?" Cora thought about it. "Twenty-six, I think. I'd married Emily's father, then yours, and become step-mother to you boys, by the time I was that age."

"It's old to get married," Emily reflected. "I'll get a husband before I'm old like that."

"You had better get yourself a nice young man," Frank suggested. "What was wrong with Ernie from Headley Brothers?"

"Oh him! He was a bit boring!" Emily declared.

They approached Buckingham Palace and decided there was no need to try and push any closer. "She'll pass along here to the chapel," Jacob informed them. "Let's just stand in front of this tree and hope we get a good look."

Before long, whispers flew through the crowds and onlookers pressed forward as far as the sombre policemen would allow. Cora, with her family around her, found herself on the edge of the pavement, her neck craned towards Buckingham Palace as the first of the processions advanced towards The Mall. Open landaus, with low-slung sides offering a good view of the passengers, carried members of the Royal household at a stately pace. Dressed in their finery, they spoke amongst themselves and waved to the crowd.

"It's the Duke of York!"

"Here he comes!"

"The groom!"

One of the second group of carriages carried the Duke in full-dress regalia. Onlookers were left with the impression of a smartly-groomed young man, with a neat beard of dark brown hair. His uniform was adorned with medals, and gold braids embellished oversized epaulettes.

The third set of landaus came into view, giving rise to a spontaneous cheer within the crowd, which now surged forward a little, everyone showing their eagerness to glimpse Princess Mary of Teck. Accompanied by her father and brother, she offered nervous smiles, waving her white gloved hand in the direction of the crowds. The satin of her dress shimmered white in the sunshine, and those who were close enough could see flounces of lace within the long skirt.

"Look at that." Emily's voice was low, almost a whisper. "It's like trails of blossom."

"I think it is," Cora replied. "Not real, but silk or satin."

Although the pace of the horses was gentle, and Princess Mary turned a little towards her well-wishers on either side, the pavements were crowded, preventing further scrutiny of the dress. Numerous bridesmaids were seated in the carriages which followed and then, heralded by gasps of awe, Queen Victoria herself held everyone's attention. She was a small but amply proportioned figure, dressed in sombre black. Her smile, however, was gracious as she waved to the adoring masses.

Craning their necks, they watched the landaus turn into the gateway of St James's Palace. "Shall we go and look at Buckingham Palace and then take a stroll through the park?" Jacob asked.

"That sounds lovely," Cora agreed. "And how about a muffin or jacket potato?"

“Great idea, Ma.” Johnny was the first to respond. “There’s street sellers everywhere, so let’s see what we can find.”

Before long, they were tucking into hot buttered potatoes while admiring the architecture of Buckingham Palace. Then a stroll through the park took them past a cart selling ice-cream – an unexpected treat! While it was fun to be amongst the crowds, they decided to avoid the crush as the royal party made their return trip along The Mall, instead choosing to walk past the Houses of Parliament.

On reaching the Embankment, it seemed as if everyone relaxed a little to see the wide street, broad pavements shaded by trees and the river beyond. “I feel better to be away from the crowds,” Cora declared. “It’s been a wonderful treat to visit, but it’s not like being in Ashford. We don’t know who might come sneaking up and try to snatch a purse, or even our Emily.”

“Even our Emily?” Frank repeated. The others frowned, not quite understanding the meaning behind Cora’s words.

“She’s a pretty girl, and who knows what men are lurking about wanting to carry her off with them!” Cora explained, while guiding them to a couple of benches overlooking the Thames. Here a new view came to life – the busy thoroughfare of a river passing through a great city.

Her family exchanged smiles, used to Cora’s lively imagination.

“I’ll only be carried off if I want to be!” Emily objected. She eyed a smart young man walking along the pavement. He gave a nod and a broad smile. “And if he wanted to put me in a carriage to the church then I might not mind!”

"Emily!" Cora exclaimed. "You keep your eyes away from London men. And I wasn't thinking of you being carried off to church. It was being taken and no church that was worrying me."

"That's enough of all this silly business," Jacob interrupted. "We don't want Molly listening and getting worried. And I don't want to regret bringing you all here today."

Cora linked her arm through his and kissed him on the cheek. Her husband always calmed her thoughts which tended to run away with themselves. "I'm having a lovely day. Ta very much."

Full of the wonders inspired by the capital city, the family were soon rested and continued their walk along the Embankment. Both the pleasure and working boats on the murky waters, as well as the architecture, absorbed their attention.

"The buildings are so tall and decorative compared to ours at home," Molly voiced their thoughts. "Even St Mary's Church in the town with its fancy tower would look like nothing special here."

"It's a wonderful thing to visit here today, but we'll be thankful when the train pulls into Ashford and everything is how we are used to," her father suggested.

"Maybe." The girl considered this for a moment, then asked, "Have we got time to go back to Trafalgar Square? We didn't get to see much of it."

Jacob consulted his pocket watch. "I think we have, and then it will be time to head back to Charing Cross."

Within an hour, Cora was again fretting over keeping everyone safe as they strode along the platform. "Let's try down there," she advised, leading them towards the front of the train. "I bet these first carriages are full up with people too lazy to go searching for a bit more space."

Her family smiled to hear her judgements but followed the advice. Several doors were opened only to find there was not enough space for the family of six, so they were forced to keep going.

"What's wrong now?" Frank exclaimed, as he and Emily looked into a carriage, and she appeared to dismiss it. "You're making a fuss over nothing."

Cora frowned. It wasn't like Frank to snap at his sister. He was so placid, despite the fiery hair which carried with it a reputation of having a bad temper.

"I'm not making a fuss!" Emily raised her voice a little.

"I don't know what's got into her nowadays," Cora muttered, as she and Jacob scurried along to see what the matter was. He gave her hand a squeeze, and she pressed his in return while flashing a quick smile at him. "It's been a lovely day, and we'll soon be settled on the train heading home. I appreciate you thinking of it and booking the tickets and... well, you know... everything. It's been a real treat."

Far away from the hustle and bustle of London, in a remote settlement, its landscape bare of any obvious vegetation, a man plodded up a shingle bank from the beach. His hair – a mass of almost-black curls – moved with the light summer breeze, and dark eyes remained on the toes of his worn boots. He had no interest in casting his gaze about the place – nothing would have changed in the past twelve hours since he had been out at sea. Unless... He shook himself, sure there would be no change. Certain she would be there waiting for his return.

On reaching the peak of the stony ridge, the ground now undulated gently, yet beneath his boots the shingle remained. If he were to walk inland, it would be there for a mile or more before intermingling with a meagre covering of soil. He was now amongst a small collection of timber shacks, each with a brick chimney stack and a roof of corrugated iron. His feet guided him to one with a coat of black tar, and a window to the front, its shutters open and sun-bleached floral curtains fluttering about.

"How was it?" His cousin's wife sat at the open doorway. She was a thin woman, other than the swell of her second child protruding under her washed-out rag of a dress.

"All right," he replied. "Can't complain." He waited for her to shift a little, allowing him to enter the home.

"There's been a Royal wedding today!" she announced, a slight lift to her voice, and a nod towards a newspaper on her lap.

"Oh right," he answered. For a moment he reflected that not one of them living here at Denge could read all the words in the paper, but together they interpreted the gist of it. If it gave some pleasure – a time to imagine a life in a different place, a different world – then he was pleased for her. Life was harsh.

Ed Brooks entered the humble shack, his eyes momentarily struggling to see into the dark corners, to the bed cosied up against plank walls. Despite the fresh salt air coming straight from the sea, the room smelt of death. Before he could decipher his mother's features, he heard the rattle in her chest and knew her time on this earth was close to passing.

Chapter Two

"I don't think there's room for all of us," Emily stated.

Cora frowned. They had peered in several carriages and this compartment only had a couple of young women seated on the wooden benches. "Don't fuss," she reacted. "There's plenty of space." She ushered Emily and Molly in first.

Soon they were all settled and exchanging pleasantries with the women who introduced themselves as May and Effie.

"Where are you travelling home to?" Johnny asked.

"Ashford," the brunette, May, told him. Her hair was smooth and glossy, nose pert and her eyes danced. "Then we'll take a trap to Willesborough."

"There's a coincidence! We're bound for Ashford too!" Frank enthused. "We used to live in South Willesborough, but we are near the Canterbury Road now."

"Do you work on the Railway?" the blonde, Effie asked, as she smoothed her dress and gazed at the brothers from beneath the rim of her straw hat.

"How do you know?" Johnny asked. He gave a grin.

"Just a guess," she replied with a shrug. "Half the men in Ashford must work there."

"Half the men we know," May corrected. "Our family do, and lots of the neighbours."

"Well, you're right," Johnny admitted. "Our pa did, but not anymore. And our older brother is there with us."

What lovely young women, Cora thought. *Nice and friendly but you can see they are respectable.* She glanced down at the toes of their shoes peeping out beneath the long skirts and petticoats of their summer dresses. There were many young women who scrimped and saved for a beautiful dress but were hoping the material would hide a pair of worn-out boots. These both wore smart shoes with a low heel. *Properly respectable they are and they speak very nicely to my boys without seeming too forward. It's a wonder these two are not with a pair of young men – pretty girls like them should have a string of admirers.* She looked from one to another, noting their even features, clear skin and hair nicely pinned in place despite it being a long day for them. The stitching on their dresses was neat and she could see they had trim figures.

"Are you sisters?" Cora asked.

"No, cousins," Effie answered. "But we were born a day apart, so it seems like we're twins! May is the oldest."

"And we live next door to each other!" May added.

"Isn't that lovely!" Cora smiled to think of a young Emily trailing after the three boys who became her step-brothers – William, Johnny and Frank. It was lovely to have a big family. She glanced at the elder of her two daughters and received a scowl in return.

The train pulled into London Bridge station, and conversation paused. Doors in neighbouring compartments could be heard opening, then slamming shut. Through grimy windows, they saw indistinct figures moving along the platform, while guards in black uniforms seemed to stand a little taller and prouder than those passengers merely passing though. The call came to say the train was about to depart. Then with its chimney belching clouds of richly smelling coal smoke, the great beast gradually gained speed. In the carriage, conversation turned to the royal wedding, comparing details of what had been seen from their various viewpoints.

While London was left behind and the train passed through the town of Orpington, Cora eyed a picnic hamper at Jacob's feet. It was said that some carriages now featured corridors and it was possible to walk from one to another, then eat in a dining carriage. For the Rose family, and most passengers, this was a luxury which could not be contemplated. However, a hamper might be ordered from the larger stations, and this made a rare treat on a day trip.

"Would you like to share our food?" Cora asked the young women.

Emily, who was reading a news pamphlet, gave an audible sigh, but kept her eyes lowered. Cora glanced in her direction and said nothing to her daughter. May and Effie expressed their thanks while producing slices of fruit cake wrapped in waxed cloth and offering this as a contribution.

"If only South Eastern Railways could provide us with a nice pot of tea, then we could have a proper party," Cora said as she opened the hamper. "Look at this – tongue and ham – thin slices, but it all looks fresh."

"You'd have to go in one of them posh dining cars for a pot of tea," Johnny suggested.

"Gosh! It would spill all over the place," Cora laughed. "Now, put that news-sheet down, Em, and help me arrange this. They've given us six napkins of a good size, so if you share one, May and Effie, and you boys as well…" She glanced at Johnny and Frank who remained boys in her eyes despite having gone out to work for the last ten years.

"What's the cake, Ma?" Frank asked.

Prising open the packets, Cora gave a nod of approval before replying, "Gingerbread and Victoria Sponge. There's a nice bit of jam with the sponge."

They tucked into the feast, and before long the travellers were passing through steep embankments, then plunged into darkness as the train entered a tunnel cut through the North Downs. Sevenoaks station emerged through smoke-caked windows. "That's the posh ones getting off. Look at their parasols and top hats," Cora observed.

"Ma! You can hardly see if they're posh or not, the windows are so mucky!" Molly laughed.

"Oh, I just know about these things," Cora replied, reaching out to put an arm around the shoulders of her youngest child and giving them a squeeze.

The engine proceeded, emitting smoke at an ever-increasing pace as it picked up speed before settling into a rhythm and entering the long tunnel after Sevenoaks. The afternoon was still stiflingly warm and, as they emerged from the long, dark void, the carriage had become unbearably stuffy. Windows were lowered a little and refastened with leather straps. Now they had a snapshot of a brighter world, the view no longer marred by a thin layer of soot. There were hop fields and oast houses, swathes of golden wheat and corn, and fields of sheep and cattle. They spotted clusters of houses, church spires and farms. With her shawl as a cushion between her and the wooden bench seat, Cora relaxed as she had been unable to on the journey up to London. She glanced over Molly's head and gave Jacob a warm smile. "Ta very much. What a lovely day! I know I worried about it, but it's been a real treat."

After the crowds, the noise and the odours of London, Ashford Station seemed strangely quiet when they stepped down from the carriage. There was still steam gushing from the engine's pipes, the slamming of doors and calls from one person to another, but it all seemed rather muted, almost sombre compared to the celebratory mood in the capital city. The Rose family, with May and Effie, moved away from the train and stood for a moment, taking stock of their surroundings. The guard blew his whistle, the great iron wheels of the engine began to move forward and, with a low chuff from the chimney, began to build up pace.

Cora frowned as she gazed along the lines of pointed fascia fronting the canopies, at the trollies lined up for use, and the bridge crossing the tracks. The station buildings displayed adverts for newspapers, tobacco, and places to visit, but nothing was open. "People are at home having their supper now," she realised. "It was different in London with all those street vendors and the tearooms open, and I bet they are still doing a roaring trade."

"Let's get ourselves home," Jacob said. "I know I'm glad of the peace."

They left through the gates and stood on the station forecourt, again noting how quiet it was. "There's our trap!" May exclaimed, waving to a man standing by a stocky horse. "It was lovely to meet you all."

Effie joined her cousin in offering thanks. Then Emily was raising her eyebrows in undisguised disapproval as Johnny escorted the young women to the trap. "Gracious! I thought he'd want to get home and have a nice cup of tea or an ale, not be hanging around saying goodbye to those two."

Cora looked at her daughter but decided to ignore her comment. "Come on, let's make a move and the boys will soon catch up."

The streets of Ashford were peaceful. Most of the women would be in their homes, perhaps preparing the evening meal, sewing or reading. The men might be pottering about in the shed or working on vegetable plots. Whilst walking up the hill from the station, then passing by the silent market, the family saw the last of the workers trudging home. Turning to walk past the Methodist chapel, imposing offices and banks, they approached the heart of the town where medieval buildings huddled low against their taller and more graceful counterparts. Looking over them all, was the parish church of St Mary's, its slim tower embellished with turrets.

"It's so quiet," Molly murmured, used to being in the town centre when the atmosphere was vibrant. "No one comes here when the shops are closed… and the tearooms."

"We walk through this way to go to church," her father reminded her. "And it's quiet then apart from the bells. But there's nothing to bring people here at this time of day. In another hour, the men will be heading for the public houses, but they'll want their supper first."

"They certainly will," Cora agreed. "I'm not complaining about the lack of noise, not after the day we've had!"

Turning again, they walked along North Street and away from the town centre. "I'm getting tired." Molly tucked her arm into Jacob's.

"It's been a long day," he replied.

"We'll have the range going in no time and a nice pot of tea brewing," Cora added.

North Street would eventually transform into a country lane, leading to the village of Kennington, but before the road became flanked by fields rather than houses, they turned into Albert Road, where the family had lived for the past five years. It was a pleasant street, not yet filled with homes and boasting a variety of detached and semi-detached houses. The area offered the Rose family a sense of space lacking in the terraced streets of South Willesborough where they had lived for many years while the children grew up.

Turning onto a red and black tiled pathway, Cora led the way. At the front door she reached through the letterbox and, pulling on the latch-cord, let the door swing open. They traipsed in, and for a moment the narrow hallway was filled with activity while jackets, shawls and hats were removed. Passing by the front parlour, the kitchen was brought to life as chairs were pulled out and the young people flopped down.

This was the room where the whole family congregated at least once a day. In the centre was a large pine table, usually with a teapot in the middle. The modern range with two hotplates was Cora's pride and joy, and there were floor-to-ceiling cupboards either side of the chimney breast. A dresser displayed some of the best pieces of china, but Cora, ever practical, kept nothing in the room that wasn't put to use regularly. Anything purely decorative had a home in a glass-fronted unit in the parlour. The kitchen was large enough to hold two winged chairs set under the sash window, with a small rag-rug placed between them. When the family were at home, footsteps clattered on the tiled floor which was swept daily. The previous summer, Jacob had decorated the walls with a beige paper covered with a repeat pattern of soft pink roses.

While pushing the kettle onto the hotplate and spooning tea leaves into the pot, Cora remembered the years gone by when these young adults were small children. *Look at them all so big now. William has married and gone, but Johnny and Frank are as tall as their pa, and still living at home. Three grown men about the place makes a lot of work on wash day. And Emily, who was so tiny, is taller than me. I wonder where she's taken herself off to. I suppose she'll be back in a minute for a cup of tea.* Cora smiled to see Molly go to the dresser and set out the teacups. *She's a good girl, and I'm thankful for the help she gives me around the home.*

The following Monday was the most strenuous of the week for Cora and young Molly. Before the men had left for work, the fire under the copper had been lit and, as the water heated, soap was grated into it. Molly prepared the porridge that morning, while Cora took the delicate corsets, drawers, chemises and stockings to wash in the warm water. They were set aside to be rinsed, and the men's undergarments were removed from their overnight soak, then placed in the soapy water which was now hot to the touch.

By the time Johnny and Frank were leaving for the Railway Works, Cora had put the men's shirts with the women's aprons in hot water and was agitating them with a dolly. "Have a good day," she called, stepping away from the copper to watch them leave. "Now for the mangle." She noted Molly was clearing away the dirty dishes and turned her attention to a pile of vests and long pants which needed squeezing through the wooden rollers of the contraption.

Jacob and Emily left not long after. He had put his strenuous days at the Works behind him and now took a five-minute stroll along to the nearby cemetery where he took pride in keeping the grounds tidy. Emily worked in a bakery shop near the town centre. "At least Emily's aprons get laundered by the company," Cora muttered to herself, and not for the first time. "I can't complain, not when she's home early to help out."

Cora's arms were aching by the time Molly appeared with some bedsheets, and it was a relief to hand over some of the strenuous work to the girl. "I'll put these on the line while you take over the rinsing," she said, nodding to the clothes in the copper. "And by the time you've put them through the mangle, I'll have a pot of tea ready."

The cycle of washing, drying, and ironing was relentless, lasting two or three days each week. In the summer they benefited from sunny weather and took advantage of this to wash more clothes and bedding. The pitfall was the mammoth pile of clothes to be ironed. In the winter, drying racks hung from the kitchen ceiling and were stood in front of the range, making the room feel cramped. It was a struggle to keep the damp at bay, especially on those days where rain fell steadily. The girls had their smalls airing in the bedroom, it not being right to have them displayed in front of their brothers, and it seemed as if the house was swathed in layers of cotton, linen and wool. During these dark days, Cora did her best to spot-clean clothes, and the sheets only saw soap and water if the weather promised to be dry with a brisk wind.

On the Tuesday evening, Cora was alone in the kitchen with the heavy iron in one hand and smoothing the creases from a shirt with the other.

"Ma," Johnny spoke as he walked into the room. "I've written a note to May. You remember – we met her on the train."

"Of course I remember!" Cora paused and turned to him. "Lovely young woman, she was."

"Would you take it to her?" He offered a small white envelope. "She works in the haberdashery department at Lewis and Hyland. I wanted to ask if she'll come for a walk with me on Sunday afternoon. Don't tell the others, will you?"

Cora slid the envelope into the pocket of her apron. "I'll do that with pleasure," she said, "and I won't say a word. It would be lovely to see you courting."

"Let's see what she says." Johnny gave a grin, while gathering the freshly ironed shirts belonging to him and Frank. "I'll put these away."

Placing the iron back on the hotplate of the stove, Cora stepped forward and gave him a quick squeeze. "I'm sure she was keen on you." There was a patter of footsteps on the tiled floor through the hallway, and Emily entered the kitchen.

All opportunity for private talk passed. "Ta very much." Johnny took the shirts and left.

Cora reached for the pile of aprons, but Emily took them from her arms. "Time for you to sit in the armchair, Ma." She looked towards one of two chairs placed under the back window. There wasn't much of a view, just a narrow passageway between the scullery and the boundary wall, but Cora sank into the cushions with pleasure and took the cup of tea Emily offered. Laundry day was arduous and with four wages coming into the house, as well as the pennies Molly earned from her mornings in the grocery shop, it was tempting to take up Jacob's suggestion of hiring someone to do the ironing. It seemed that Emily read her thoughts. "We can afford some help, you know, Ma. Perhaps even a daily to come in and do the fires and have a sweep around. There's plenty of women who would welcome the chance to earn a bit."

"I thought it was hard work when I had four little ones running about the place..." Cora smiled at the memories. "But at least your clothes were smaller, and it was only your pa out at work getting dirty. Where has the time gone? Now there's four of you grown up, and young Molly not far behind. I'm grateful to have her on a Monday morning though."

That night, Cora thought of Johnny's note to May, now tucked away in her bedside drawer. She would be happy to see him walking out with a girl and smiled to think of the attractive young woman coming to Sunday tea in the front parlour. She reached out and put an arm around Jacob. Life had been fun when the children were small, but she couldn't complain about it now. *It's only Emily who seems to be discontent at times, and if she's in one of her moods, it sends ripples of unease through the whole family. I hope she won't get funny if Johnny does court May...* With these thoughts mulling through her mind, Cora drifted off to sleep.

As the sun set over the hills at Fairlight, and the sea took on a steely grey colour, Ed Brooks dozed in the armchair. He still had the stink of fish on his clothes and engrained in his skin. Waking with a jump, he snorted, and a cough burst from his throat. It was a rude awakening, and immediately he was aware that no sound came from his mother's bed.

"Damn," he muttered, tripping over himself in the rush to take those few steps to her.

No more laboured breaths came from his mother's thin chest. Saddened, but thankful to know she had been released from the toils of her life, he took her blue-veined hand and murmured an inadequate prayer: "Lord, take my mother and give her a better place in heaven than she had on this earth. Amen."

Ed released her hand, allowing it to lie by her side. Then he turned and left the shack.

From a low building of tarred planks, there came the sound of men talking and a disjointed tune from a battered harmonica. The Hope and Anchor welcomed the few fishermen, coastguards, and those oddities who chose to visit the lone outpost and stay in the rooms it offered for paying guests. As he approached, Ed saw his cousin step through the open doorway, tankard in hand. Jake gave a nod, took a long gulp of the ale and threw the dregs on the shingle.

"I'll have to go for the vicar," Ed told his cousin.

"You'll have to get some bloody sleep," Jake replied. "We're out on the boat before dawn, and I can't handle it by myself. If she hadn't taken her time, we could have sent a message with the fish cart. Helen will have to go in the morning – she's got nothing better to do." He referred to his wife – a shadow of the bright young woman who he had met in nearby Camber three years beforehand and lured to the wastelands of Denge.

"All right." Ed turned away, emotionally and physically drained.

Chapter Three

The following morning, Cora set off to the town with a wicker basket under one arm. The sky was cloudless, and the heat of the sun settled on her back and arms. Grinning at a boy with a barrow and shovel, she felt compelled to give him a penny so he could treat himself to a bun later in the day. It wasn't much of a life, scraping up horse muck from the road. He looked no older than Molly. "Ta, missus," he called out, and Cora walked on with a smile on her face. There might be a bit of a whiff from the dirt on the roads, and she could see fumes drifting out of the tall chimneys of the Lion Brewery, but she was grateful to be living some distance from the factories and railway station.

As the buildings jostled against each other, many of them shops with displays outside on the pavement, Cora spotted Emily in the bakery. As she gave her daughter a wave, the double gates to one side opened and a lad came out with his cart. *Now there's a better job for a boy,* she thought. *Everywhere he goes, people will be thanking him for delivering their bread and I bet he gets some stale buns and a loaf to take home to his family when he finishes work.* Turning into the High Street, Cora glanced down to where it widened with the market stalls gaily offering their wares, but today she was heading for the store where May and Effie worked. Glancing at the letter in her basket for the umpteenth time, she ensured it was safe under her purse and string bag.

The row of shops with painted signs showing they were under the ownership of the Lewis and Hyland families, never failed to impress Cora. She had watched the business grow over the years, at first never dreaming of entering such a prestigious store, to more recently when she and Jacob had taken William to be measured for a new suit before his wedding. As she walked on, the road narrowed and these ornate buildings towered above her, with one side of the tallest being emblazoned with the company name. The modern windows fascinated her: great sheets of glass with brown painted frames and displays to tempt shoppers with a few shillings to spare. Decorative supports held lamps – each one with the Lewis and Hyland name paraded on the glass of the shade. Slowing to inspect the displays of men's jackets, trousers and waistcoats, Cora glanced up to the lines of square windows above, recalling the tailors who toiled away in the rooms above the shop.

Stepping off the pavement, Cora side-stepped a ladder supporting a man who was applying a coat of glossy brown paint onto window frames. She avoided one of the smart delivery carts and slipped through a doorway into the building. It didn't matter which door a customer entered – one of the greatest delights of this row of shops was that each segment was linked to the next, sometimes by a small flight of steps, or a ramp if the floors were different levels. Cora was in the footwear department and paused to admire the oak fittings rising from floor to ceiling, filled to capacity with displays of shoes, and boxes of polishes, brushes and laces. Before an assistant had time to approach her, she scurried to the next department, her shoes making a satisfying tap on the floorboards.

Passing through the drapery area, with tempting bolts of cloth in light colours and delicate patterns for summer dresses, Cora stepped into the haberdashery department. Here there was a treasure trove of fastenings, buttons, threads, and so much more hidden away in tiny drawers. It was always a wonder that the assistants seemed to be able to place their hands on the right items. There were racks of pattern books and, in pride of place where the light from the window could beam upon it – a Singer sewing machine!

"Hello Mrs Rose!" May chirped. "How lovely to see you again."

Cora smiled with approval at the young woman. She appeared smart in a dress of charcoal grey, with a paler stripe running through it, and this topped off with a white apron. Shooting a glance towards an older woman, no doubt at the helm of haberdashery, Cora said, "Good morning, May. It's a lovely day, isn't it? I've come to buy some cotton: a beige and some dark blue please."

"There's so many shades, Mrs Rose. I'll bring out a few and you can tell me if any suit," May turned to the drawers behind her and removed several, placing them on the counter.

Cora picked out a couple of reels in beige and held them to the light coming from the window. "I'll take this one please, and now for the blue..." The senior assistant turned away and began to unpack a box of elastic which came in a variety of widths. Cora reached into her basket and slipped the envelope across the counter. "Johnny sends his regards. I'll take this blue; it's for a shirt I'm making for him."

May slid the slim letter into her apron pocket and smiled. "Give him my best wishes, please." She replaced the drawers filled with cotton reels and asked, "Is there anything else you need, Mrs Rose?"

“I don’t think so,” Cora replied. “But I come into the town most days as we live so close. I can always pop back.” She paid and left by the nearest door, rather than stepping from one department to the next.

By the time Cora was leaving the town centre behind her, the basket was filled with flour, tea, eggs and a sugar cone, all served by her daughter Molly who worked in Headley Brothers. Fruit and vegetables would be delivered by cart later in the afternoon.

A week after the trip to London, the Rose family attended their usual Sunday morning church service at the Methodist chapel in the town. For Cora and Jacob, this was precious family time amidst busy lives where the younger generation dashed about between home, work and meeting friends. The chapel, not yet twenty years old, was an ornate building boasting a high roof, and a gothic window under which the congregation entered through one of two doorways. It seemed that wherever a pointed decorative feature could be added, this had been done – over doorways, topping buttresses, and as rows of dormer windows in the roof. Although Johnny, Frank and Emily were fully grown, Cora ushered her family into the church, only pausing to appreciate the newly completed organ gallery and pulpit.

Once back home, the women were busy preparing dinner, but rather than sit with a paper or book, Johnny spent time polishing his best boots and brushing his suit. He retreated to his room, returning with a newly trimmed beard. Emily flashed curious looks at him but said nothing. After they had eaten, he placed a kiss on Cora’s cheek. “Thanks, Ma. That was lovely.” He headed to the doorway, and with “I’m off for a walk…” he was gone before anyone could reply.

"I'd better get on with the tidying up," Cora pushed her chair back, hoping to deflect the interest from Johnny. "Then I'm going to sit in the garden with my crocheting. What about you, Em?"

Emily, who appeared lost in thought, replied, "What's that, Ma?"

"What are you going to do this afternoon?"

"Oh, I got another pamphlet about the wedding. It's got sketches of the dress and the bridesmaids too. They were selling them in the town. I'm going to look at it." She glanced at her sister, "And then you can read it after, if you like?" Molly beamed her thanks.

However, they had barely started the washing up at the scullery sink when Emily revealed her thoughts, "Where's Johnny gone? Out courting?"

"It's not for me to say," Cora responded, her voice a little sharper than necessary. *What's up with Emily that she has to know what Johnny is doing all the time? He's a grown man and shouldn't have to tell his sister everything.*

"Well, I hope it ain't that flighty piece we met on the train. I didn't like the look of her."

"If you didn't, then you were the only one," Cora snapped. "Me and your pa thought she was a nice young woman. They both were."

"I think I'll go for a walk instead," Emily changed the subject. "I saw Jane earlier, and she asked if I wanted to take a turn around the cemetery gardens."

The Ashford Cemetery, with its ornamental gatehouse, expansive grounds and two chapels was only a few minutes' walk away from Albert Road. It was Jacob's job there which led to the family moving to a quieter and less crowded area of the town.

"I've been trimming the yew trees over the last few days," Jacob offered. "It's looking quite smart."

"It's the best park around, despite all the graves," Emily said.

Having matured over the past couple of decades, the landscaped grounds displayed pathways bordered with shaped yew bushes, flowerbeds gaudy with summer blooms and distinctive Monkey Puzzle trees. While the country lanes and riverside paths were attractive, the cemetery offered the people of Ashford a taste of a city park within their own town.

"I'd quite like to take a turn there myself," Cora suggested while putting the clean dishes back in the dresser. "Would you mind, Jacob?"

"I'll be glad to take a stroll with my wife and not be worrying about the pruning and weeding," Jacob replied. "I just wish it was like the parks in London with carts selling ices, but that would be a bit disrespectful, wouldn't it?"

Molly stifled a giggle at the thought of people picnicking amongst the gravestones. "When they make that new park near the watercress beds we can go for an ice, can't we?"

"We can, my lovely," her father agreed. "And if there's a bandstand, like I hear talk of, we can hire a chair and listen to them playing. Wouldn't that be something special?"

"Perhaps I'll go courting and my young man will pay for my seat." Molly's voice was dreamy.

"Courting?" Her parents and elder sister all repeated with varying degrees of horror in their voices.

"Not yet, of course," Molly pacified them. "The park isn't ready, is it? Perhaps in a couple of years?" Before her parents could respond she asked, "Emily, if you're off out, can I read the pamphlet first?"

"All right. It's on my bed." Emily left the room, and they heard her shoes clatter on the stairs. A moment later she returned with a summer shawl and thin gloves. "I'll be back for tea," she said, from the kitchen doorway. "Have a nice afternoon."

The following Sunday both Johnny and Frank polished their shoes and brushed the dust from their suits. They combed their hair and tidied their beards. The brothers made a striking duo with their flaming hair and lean figures as they set off for Willesborough to meet the cousins, May and Effie.

They shared little of the afternoon with their family, but clearly the walk along the river to the old mill was successful, as the next weekend their courting was extended to both days. Having raced home to scrub themselves and change into smart clothes after working Saturday morning, the brothers strode into Ashford town centre to treat the young women to afternoon tea. On the Sunday, they again set off for a countryside walk near Willesborough.

After a month, it was announced that Johnny and Frank were asked to meet May and Effie's parents. "Could we invite the girls here the following Sunday? For tea in the parlour?" Johnny asked as the family finished their cold meat and fried vegetables on the Monday evening.

"Of course you can," Cora answered. "We can pull out the posh table and make room for all of us in there. They're nice young women with good manners. I don't want to be entertaining them in the kitchen."

"They won't mind, Ma," Frank replied. "But that will make it a bit special, ta."

"It will be good to meet them again." Cora was already planning the seating. They didn't have eight good chairs, so the kitchen ones would have to be used but a pretty piece of material over the back of each one would look smart. She could see dainty sandwiches and fairy cakes displayed on the best plates. *I wonder if we have enough of the fancy napkins. I'll have to look in the laundry cupboard and make sure.*

"I won't be here," Emily announced, with a hint of relish in her voice.

"Why not?" Cora asked.

"I've been asked to go for a walk on Sunday, and I'll probably be out next weekend too," Emily told them. "There's no need for me to be seeing May and Effie again when we already met on the train."

"If you're going out with a young man then I hope he'll be coming here to introduce himself," Jacob said. His tone was a little stern, causing everyone to turn towards him.

Emily coloured a little. "Yes. He's coming to knock for me at two o'clock, but he don't need to introduce himself because you see him about the town."

"He can still come and say hello to be polite," Jacob reminded her. "And you've not said who he is."

Emily pushed her chair back and started to collect the empty plates. "Oh, it's just Frederick – him who works in the Cycle Works in New Street."

"I hope you're not going to be riding a bike and showing your legs." Dishes clattered as Cora attempted to hide her concerns. Freddie Barnes was a well-known figure about the town and was a little too cocksure for her liking. There was plenty she had to say about him but would discuss her concerns with Jacob later. "Come on, let's get this table tidied. I've been washing sheets today and there's so much ironing to be done, I'll be lucky if it's finished by Wednesday."

Jacob, seeing her distress, stood and gave his wife a quick squeeze around the waist. She shot him a grateful smile but pushed him away. "None of that.

You men go and put your feet up in the parlour. We don't need you getting in our way."

By the end of July, the summer heat was unbearable. "It would be all right if we had a bit of a breeze," Cora said repeatedly. She opened the front and back doors as well as the windows, but the house in Albert Road remained stifling hot. The sheets dried to a crisp on the line, making ironing more laborious than ever over the three evenings she and her daughters toiled with the flat iron. But even when the laundry was neatly folded and put away, there was still the cooking and cleaning to be done, and washday was soon upon them again. Most tasks involved being in the kitchen near the range, which now received regular scowls as it offered Cora a constant supply of unwanted heat through its iron top and sides.

Serving a full meal not cooked on or baked in the range was against Cora's principles, but finally she gave in and served plates of salad with cold ham and boiled eggs. "It doesn't feel like a proper meal," she apologised, as they tucked into tomatoes and cucumber from their garden, along with lettuce and radish from the greengrocer's. "Here, cut yourselves some more bread." She pushed the loaf towards Johnny and Frank.

"Do you fancy an ice?" Jacob asked Cora, as the plates were cleared. "We've got the weekend coming up, and I feel like treating my wife!"

"An ice?" she repeated, her voice high.

"It might sound barmy, but there's going to be a bloke with a barrow of ice-cream on the High Street in the evenings," Jacob told her. "How about you and I take a stroll and see what he's got?"

"I can hardly believe it, but if you're offering then let's go and have a look." Cora stood to clear the plates. "Glory be! It seems like Ashford is getting a bit of London coming to the streets!"

Within a few minutes, it had been agreed that the younger generation would wash the dishes and Cora was going to change into a floral summer dress. With a straw hat topping her hair, she was ready, and they left arm in arm for the town centre.

"There he is!" Jacob announced with relish, as they turned towards the medieval buildings of Middle Row, and he spotted the ice-cream seller. "To be honest, I could hardly believe he was here."

Swathed in a white apron and sporting a straw boater at a jaunty angle, the rosy-cheeked young man had a queue forming in front of his cart. Nodding a greeting to others waiting, Cora and Jacob stepped behind the line. The barrow held two deep bowls of ice-cream and a basket full of cones. A painted sign offered "Ice-cream – strawberry or vanilla – 1d".

"I'm glad those half-penny licks have been banned," Cora said. They had never reached the streets of Ashford but in the cities, ices had been sold in glass dishes. Once licked clean of the icy treat, the dish was returned to the vendor who, at best, rinsed it in some water before re-using it. Said to be the cause of spreading disease, this way of selling ice-cream had been banned a few years beforehand.

"What flavour will you have?" Jacob asked.

"Oh – strawberry!" Cora replied without hesitation.

The vendor took no time at all to scoop a portion into a wafer cone, then pocket the pennies. Cora and Jacob were soon standing before him and watching as he pressed the soft ice-cream into their cones. They thanked the cheery seller and, in unspoken agreement, passed between a gap in the ancient buildings to take a stroll around the churchyard.

St Mary's was almost crowded by buildings on all four sides. In the early evening, shadows were deep and colours rich. While relishing the sweet strawberry ice, Cora gazed with a deep affection at the church. Her love affair with it had begun on her first visit to Ashford almost twenty years before. She had been drawn to the slim tower topped with turrets, and even now it reminded her of a castle in a fairy tale. Wandering alongside the iron railings bordering the churchyard, the variety of buildings fronting the area provided a wealth of interest in the form of features from many centuries. From the sculptured stonework to orange tiled roofs and walls, and leaded windows, this area told many stories of the town.

Hand in hand, Cora and Jacob circled the church, speaking of nothing in particular, but appreciating the coolness within shadowed areas and the sensation of ice-cream on their tongues. They passed through a gap in the railings, then meandered between the ancient buildings to the High Street.

"It's been a lovely hour – getting out and having a treat." Cora squeezed Jacob's hand. "Ta very much."

Cora didn't so much as glance towards the Man of Kent public house, and if she had then she would not have given a second thought to the lone figure standing to one side of the doorway. He had taken his tankard outside, so as to enjoy a brief break from the smoke-filled bar. His thoughts were on the talk amongst those enjoying a pint or a shot of spirit, but on spotting the trim figure and auburn hair, his eyes followed Cora for that moment before she turned the corner. "Cora Parkins," he murmured. "I'd know you anywhere."

On the road from Lydd to Denge, with his rolling gait giving away the fact that he had spent a couple of hours in the Dolphin, Ed Brooks meandered home. He was wearing his best boots and Sunday trousers, despite it being a Friday. It only seemed right to smarten himself up before he stood at his mother's unmarked grave and shared the week's news with her. Besides, if he was going to the town, there was always a chance – albeit a slim one – of meeting a woman who would look twice at a burly fisherman with a lasting scowl on his face.

It was baking hot and had been for weeks. The ale coating his tongue now tasted sour, so Ed rummaged in his pocket for a mint. He popped the sweet in his mouth, appreciating its freshness, then pulled at his scarf, loosely knotted at his open shirt collar. "No need to look posh now," he muttered. "No one about on this godforsaken road."

He was right. The fish had been whisked away in the early afternoon, and the grocery cart had been to Denge that morning, as well as the dray from Finn's Brewery.

His pace was leisurely, and it took over an hour to reach home. As he neared the settlement, Ed noticed something was amiss. He increased his pace, kicking the ever-present shingle from the road. Upon nearing the home of his late mother, he filled his lungs with salt-air and bellowed, "Jake! What the blazes are you doing?"

With a claw hammer in one hand and iron bar in the other, Jake prised a plank from the wall of the shack. "She don't need it," he called back. "An' no other poor sod is going to want to come an' live down here."

"I bought Helen a news-sheet about the Royal Wedding." Ed pulled the folded paper from his trouser pocket and swerved away in search of his cousin's wife.

Chapter Four

Cora was smoothing the tablecloth while setting out decorative tea plates, cups and saucers, when a movement outside caught her eye. She took a step into the arch of the bay window, remaining partly concealed by the burgundy curtains. *There he is – Frederick Barnes! And on a bicycle! I suppose he thinks he can take Emily out on that contraption. The whole of Ashford will be talking about them!* She watched the young man prop his impressive piece of machinery against the front wall, remove his cap and smooth his oiled hair, then stride up the front path. *There's no doubt he's a looker,* Cora conceded. With his chirpy manner, nicely groomed chestnut hair and smattering of freckles across his nose, it was clear to see what attracted the women to him. *But what Emily needs is a steady young man who won't take no nonsense from her.*

A rat-a-tat-tat on the door was followed by a flurry of movement on the stairs as Emily clattered down, then steady footsteps on the tiled floor from the kitchen to the front door. It had been agreed, with some reluctance on Cora's part, that it would be Jacob who answered the door to Emily's suitor.

"Good afternoon, Mr Rose!" Frederick's tone was chirpy. "Hello Emily. Don't you look a picture!"

From her position in the bay window, Cora bristled.

"Good afternoon, Frederick," Jacob replied, his voice amiable. "Fine day for a walk. Where are you planning on taking Emily?"

"I was thinking of a stroll along to Bybrook Farm. We can follow the stream to the Stour. Then, if Emily fancies it, we could buy an ice from the barrow in the town."

"That sounds lovely!" Emily enthused. "Especially the ice-cream!"

"Make sure you're home for supper and have a good time," Jacob said. "Nice to see you, Frederick. Are you enjoying your work at Onward Cycles?"

"I am! Every year, the bicycle is becoming smarter, faster and safer. I get to try them all out as well!" The passion was clear to hear in Frederick's voice. "That reminds me, Mr Rose, can I leave my bicycle along the side of your house? I don't want to be pushing it about everywhere."

"Of course you can."

"I'll see you later, Pa," Emily said. There was the sound of the movement in the hallway and the men offering their final farewells.

Cora peeped from behind the curtain. She watched Frederick move the bicycle and join Emily at the front of the house. The young people strolled off along the road, offering a charming picture on a summer's day.

"I told her not to be forward!" Cora exclaimed as Jacob stood beside her in the bay window. "Look at that – she's taken his arm!"

"Come on, love." Jacob placed an arm around her waist. "Emily will be fine. Now, we've got May and Effie coming to tea – let's have a nice time with them and our boys."

The afternoon with Johnny and Frank's young women was pleasant. May was a little bolder than her cousin, taking the lead in conversations but always respectful. They both appeared to be fond of the brothers – comfortable in their company and appreciative of the attention received. The dainty sandwiches, scones and fairy cakes were much enjoyed.

As plates emptied, and everyone declined another cup of tea, Cora couldn't help wondering what Emily was doing. Her thoughts wandered from those at the tea table in the front parlour to Emily and Frederick enjoying a romantic walk in the countryside. There was a feeling that if that attractive young man were to place an arm around her daughter's waist or to offer a kiss, then it may well be accepted with an eagerness that was not quite fitting. *She's twenty-two years old and if I made her take a chaperone, then Emily would be furious. I'm just going to have to trust her to behave. Here I am with three boys and never any trouble… and young Molly – she's a good girl. But Emily…*

With these thoughts still running through her mind, Cora gave May and Effie a warm smile when they said their goodbyes on the doorstep. "It's been lovely to see you both again and you're welcome any time," she said.

May tucked her arm in Johnny's and Effie did the same with Frank as they strolled down the street, turning back to wave before they were out of sight.

"Nice young women," Jacob commented. "I think our boys have chosen well."

"I think they have!" Cora agreed. "But I can't help worrying about what Emily is up to."

"I expect she's in the town having an ice-cream – probably strawberry!" Jacob walked towards the tea table and stacked the plates. “Let’s put these in the scullery and go for a stroll?”

“I’ll fetch my shawl!” Cora flashed a grin at him.

A few minutes later they walked along Albert Road in the footsteps of their children. Once on the road to Canterbury, they followed a low stone wall, topped with iron railings, running along the roadside. It was smart enough for any town cemetery but on reaching the gateway, the features upon this wall became lavish with decorative pyramids on top of the pillars. The wrought iron gates were rich with details, and open for Sunday afternoon visitors to stroll through at their leisure. The grey stone gatehouse, to the left, was a prime example of gothic architecture.

“I don’t know how anyone ever thought of putting all those different styles of windows and posh stonework together, and even a little spire on a house!” Cora commented as they slowed to look.

“It’s certainly fancy!” Jacob agreed. “A nice bay window and a red brick house suits me very well.”

Cora squeezed his arm. “Me too!”

The tall Monkey Puzzle trees and specimen firs never failed to impress with their height. As evergreens, they gave a sense of grandeur to the cemetery, as did the rounded yews.

They walked towards the first chapel, another fine example of gothic design, built on a mound, and displaying a tall spire. Having circled the building, the couple meandered along twisting paths, pausing to admire the flowers or to reflect over a gravestone. Next, they passed a second chapel – always a place to arouse curiosity for this was for the souls who practised in the non-conformist churches. As a Methodist, Cora would often wonder, “Why do they give us a different place? We’re all worshipping the same God after all.”

Having murmured her thoughts to Jacob, he replied, as he always did, "I don't know, love."

As usual, a moment was spent gazing at this chapel – as decorative as the last but topped with a bell cote. For a moment, time was spent reflecting on the people who had passed through in the last week. For Jacob, this was a part of daily life: to look on at a respectful distance as he tended the gardens. Next, their wanderings took them to the boundary of the grounds, where brambles and ivy tumbled over a stone wall – a poor relation to the immaculate one fronting the main road. Here they viewed pastureland and fields of newly cut hay. To the west there were clusters of mature trees, glimpses of the Stour and tiny, indistinct figures walking along the riverside paths.

This, of course, reminded Cora of Emily. "I wonder where she is now," she said, tugging on Jacob's arm to guide him back to the more formal areas.

"Probably on her way home," he suggested.

Walking upon neatly edged paths, before pausing once more, this time Cora exclaimed over the roses. "Oh, you've got these looking lovely. Not a faded flower head to be seen!" It had been a long summer, but this part of the garden had been watered and tended daily. The blooms in red, pink, yellow and apricot looked glorious, and Cora was drawn to breathe in the scents from the different varieties.

Cora and Jacob left the cemetery, both pleased with their day: Afternoon tea with their sons and a couple of lovely young women, then a stroll around these beautifully tended gardens made a perfect day. As they returned to Albert Road, the sun warmed the bricks on modern homes in a tidy street, and they both appreciated their small part of the world.

There was something a little reckless about Emily. A little less controlled. Unpredictable. But never in her wildest imaginings would Cora have thought her daughter could stoop to such uninhibited behaviour as they now witnessed. The road stretched out, and there was Emily moving towards them at speed – skirts flowing – ankles *and* calves on display – perched up high on the crossbar of the bicycle! Frederick's arms were wrapped around her waist and his knuckles white as he held onto the handles, desperately trying to keep steady. She was tipped backwards, almost sitting on his lap, laughing joyfully. His face could not yet be seen behind the layers of summer dress and lopsided straw hat.

On seeing her parents, the smile dropped from Emily's face and Frederick, seeming to sense something was amiss, slowed down. Then came the shameful sight of Emily jumping free from this unladylike, albeit side-saddle, position without tripping or tearing her pretty lemon-coloured dress. Her hat fell to the ground and pins came loose, freeing auburn curls. There was nothing Frederick could do to aid her as all his efforts were used to keep the bicycle steady. By the time Cora and Jacob reached this disgraceful scene, Emily was straightening the hem of her dress, and Frederick was dismounting. They stood side-by-side in the centre of the street.

"That was fun!" Emily declared, eyes bright and a grin spreading across her face.

"Thank you for taking Emily out. I think you had better go now." Jacob's face was expressionless and his voice flat.

Frederick adjusted his cap. "Yes, I had better get myself home. See you again, Emily." He pushed the bicycle along the road. By the time he had turned back to give a final wink and a wave, Emily was being ushered through the front door of the family home.

"How was your afternoon tea?" Emily asked once they were in the hallway. "I could do with a cup." She moved through to the kitchen and placed the kettle onto the hotplate.

"It was very nice," Cora replied. "Johnny and Frank have got themselves a couple of decent young women who know how to behave respectably."

"Well, I don't know about that," Emily retorted, still attempting to move the conversation away from her own conduct. "I can't help remembering that May was a bit too forward for my liking. She was chatting away on the train and giving Johnny the eye. I didn't think she was his type of girl."

"It seems like she is," Cora snapped. "And I don't see her or Effie riding about on a bicycle."

"Women ride them." Emily was reaching for the tea leaves now. "Anyone else for tea?"

"They sit on a saddle and make sure they're covered up nicely." Jacob's voice was stern. "You're too old for a smack on the bottom, Emily – far too old. But I'm telling you Frederick Barnes isn't welcome here again."

"They've only been out twice," Cora said. "No need for it to get serious, and I don't expect it will. He's the type to have a different girl on his arm every month."

At this Emily flushed and her body slumped. "I'll make tea just for me as neither of you answered."

Jacob stepped towards Emily and placed an arm around her shoulder. "There will be a decent young man waiting for you. I would like a cup of tea, thank you, and your ma will too. Then we'll wash up the dishes from our tea party. There's cake in the tin if you fancy some."

It's been a funny sort of weekend, Cora reflected, as she walked into the town on the following afternoon. After a long morning moving the laundry between the copper, the mangle and the washing line, she was grateful for the excuse to go to Headley Brothers for a few groceries. *There's Johnny and Frank of an age to marry and courting lovely young ladies, and William settled down with his own family. But Emily – I just don't know when she'll see sense and start walking out with a decent man.*

Passing by the Red Lion Cora remained lost in her thoughts. She gave distracted greetings to those she walked by but didn't notice the man who was at the doorway of the public house. A grin flashed over his face when he recognised her and, unbeknown to Cora, he decided to trail her from a distance. She cornered the junction with the High Street, narrowly avoided a boy tearing along with a barrow, and turned into the greengrocers.

Pausing at the Furley Drinking Fountain, the man made a show of needing water although his thirst had been quenched at the bar just moments before. The cast-iron structure dwarfed him with its great square base rising above his head, despite him being six feet in height. Positioning himself to keep an eye on the doorway of the grocery shop, he glanced up at the decorative lamp topping the fountain, and then examined the huge scrolls of ironwork supports. Finally, he turned to where the water gushed out, cupped his hands and drank.

After shaking excess water from his hands, he took a handkerchief from a well-fitting tweed jacket and wiped them dry. He was smartly dressed from polished shoes to his tailored suit. His brown hair and beard had been trimmed by the town's barber that morning. Although in his mid-forties, this was a man who would turn the head of many a younger woman. There was an air of confidence about him, born from many years of owning a public house and enjoying banter with customers.

Cora, hugging her basket close to her, left the shop and retraced her steps, turning back into North Street. On passing the Red Lion public house, she became aware of someone approaching from behind and turned, instinct warning her of trouble before she saw her pursuer.

"Cora Parkins! It's been a few years, but I'd know you anywhere!"

Flashing a false smile, Cora replied, "James Roberts, fancy seeing you. And it's Cora Rose, as you well know."

"I do, and there isn't a day that passes by when I don't regret not making a move myself. Never thought that old lighthouse keeper would steal you away!"

"You never had any interest in me," Cora retorted. "Full of the old flannel, you are. Have you been to see your parents?"

"I have, and they'll be pleased to hear we bumped into each other."

"Be sure to send them my love."

James Roberts, son of Reuben and Ada who used to run the British Inn at Dungeness, had come into Cora's life one snowy night when she had been staying at the inn. Her affection for the landlord and his wife was strong and had stood the test of time. Yet Cora had never taken to their son, who had been running a public house in Lydd for the last twenty years. Eight years ago, Reuben and Ada had moved to Ashford. Cora saw them regularly, feeling a responsibility to care for the now elderly couple who had taken her and Emily in when they were at their most vulnerable.

"It's been nice to see you," Cora said, keeping her true feelings to herself. "But it's washday and I have to get home to Molly. She's expecting me."

"How old is Molly now?" he asked.

"Twelve."

"How time flies! I thought Emily would be no more than twelve years."

"There you go again!" Cora countered. "Emily's a young woman now. Same age as I was when I came to Dungeness." She began to move away, thinking of Molly struggling with the laundry.

"I'm here for a week," James replied. "I might see you again. In fact, I'll be looking out for you. I never miss a pretty face and a trim figure."

Ignoring these final comments, Cora set off at a brisk pace knowing her every movement was being watched.

"I saw James Roberts in the town today," Cora told Jacob when they settled down in bed that night. "I never did take to him. There's always a feeling that he's out to make trouble."

"I know what you mean, love." Jacob leaned over and gave her a kiss. "Be glad he's in Lydd, and we don't see much of him."

Cora cuddled closer and fell asleep knowing it had been a lucky day when the parents of James Roberts had introduced her to Jacob-the-lighthouse-keeper.

Not far away, in the yard of a terraced house in Beaver Road, James gazed up at the night sky and took a long drag of his pipe. *Cora Parkins – how good to see you again. Just as fiery as ever and not looking a day over thirty!*

Not so many miles away, while the tide ambled about at its lowest point on the beach, Ed's world was consumed by the sea-mist rolling in. He strolled along the high tide mark in search of driftwood for the fire until something caught his eye – a length of wood more substantial and less ragged than those he usually secured.

"Oak!" he exclaimed. "And not too rough."

It could not have been in the water for long, for there was little sign of it having been knocked about by the tide and the surface had not yet darkened. From habit, he looked about him in case Jake were to appear and snatch it as his own. This was too good for the fire but would make a decent shelf or a top for a small cupboard. However, Ed had other plans. The hunt for firewood must wait until it was safely stowed away. At about five feet in length, the oak was picked up with ease. On reaching the top of the beach, he passed Cyril Thoms from Lydd on his way to set up keddle nets. They exchanged curt nods, both men absorbed in their own projects.

The timber remained untouched in Ed's one-roomed home for a couple of weeks. Then one day he gathered sandpaper and a saw, and placed a strong chair outside, its legs bedded firmly into the stones. Finally, the oak was laid across the chair. With a glance towards the shell of his mother's old shack, he said, "Here you go, Ma. I'm going to make you a nice cross, just so you know I'm thinking of you."

Chapter Five

"Isn't this my lucky day?"

Cora shivered to hear James Roberts' voice, despite the day promising to be warm. She was once again in North Street, approaching the Joint Stock Bakery where Emily worked. "It's early for you to be out," she commented, referring to the fact that the public houses would not be open for hours.

"I follow my own times," he told her. "And today I've got a meeting with my solicitor in Bank Street. Perhaps you would like to meet me for a cup of tea and a bun in a tearoom afterwards?"

"No thank you. I've got my housekeeping to do," Cora replied, her tone tart.

"What a shame. I'll say my goodbyes now then. There's been a change of plan. I'm returning to Lydd later this morning and will be back in Ashford next month."

"Have a good journey home."

At that moment, their attention was drawn to Emily who was reaching into the window to adjust the display of fresh bread. She looked up and gave Cora a wave.

"My! Is that Emily?" The appreciation in James' voice was clear. "Look at her all grown up and as pretty as her ma!"

"Yes, that's Emily." Cora moved to side-step around the man who was blocking her progress along the pavement. “Have a good day. Don’t let me keep you.” With that, Cora moved across the road and entered the bakery shop without a backwards glance.

When she left, with a loaf nestled in her basket, there was no sign of James Roberts. *I don’t know what he wants or what he’s up to, but it’s got me feeling all uneasy.*

Before long, autumn would be upon them. In the deep drawer at home, Cora’s thick shawl had seen better days. She decided to turn towards the wide street in which the market was held and to browse in the shops where a second-hand bargain could invariably be found. *Everyone will be looking in another month*, she reasoned. *If I have a rummage now, the best winter shawls will still be there.*

Between tall Georgian and Victorian shops and offices, the area was crammed with stalls and market traders offering their wares. From those selling household goods to clothes and food, each vendor vied for the attention of the customers with distinctive loud banter. Not everyone had a stall: the watercress seller with her basket, the shoe shiner with his stool and leather holdall, and the knife sharpener with his tray all wandered freely.

Giving a chirpy response to their repartee, Cora avoided the market stalls and headed for the brokers’ shops with their tables of clothes and bundles of material set out on the pavement. On entering the shop, she breathed in the dusty staleness of old fabric, allowing her eyes to adjust to the gloomy interior. It was no wonder shoppers were tempted with outside displays, but she knew the winter clothes would still be tucked away.

It took seconds for Cora’s fingertips to alight on a dense knit of the softest wool. The colour was not yet clear, so she carried it to the doorway for a mossy green to be revealed. "Beautiful!" she murmured, allowing the material to fall free and noting the swaying tassels. There appeared to be no flaws or signs of wear in the weave. "I'll take this!" Cora announced to the woman behind the counter. There was a sense of triumph – what luck to find a quality shawl in the first broker's shop.

Back in the street, Cora picked up her pace and headed towards home. After a while she reached into the basket and pulled back the paper wrapping to reveal a little of the green wool. *Emily would love this*, Cora pictured her daughter's face light up if she were offered the soft bundle. Then she recalled the show of ankles and calves amidst the shameful scene of Emily on the crossbar of the bicycle. *I'll keep it for myself.* Cora gave the shawl a loving squeeze.

"Someone came into the bakery to see me today," Emily mentioned as she laid the table for their evening meal. "He had to buy a bun because Mr Alfred wasn't looking best pleased to see us chatting."

"Who was that then?" Cora asked. Visions of Frederick Barnes flitted through her mind. "I suppose it was him with the bicycle."

"It was Reuben and Ada's son, come from Lydd to spend a few days in the town," Emily continued. "I don't know when I last saw him to speak to. Perhaps five years ago? Anyway, he was nice and friendly, but I can't be chatting when there's work to be done."

"Of course, you can't. He must know that." Cora's voice was brittle, and she didn't like it. *It seems like there's one person after the other making trouble for us at the moment. Not a day goes by when I'm not getting myself all in a tizzy about something.* She attempted to lighten her tone, and said, "It's funny you should say that – I saw him when I was walking through the town today, and on Monday. Won't his parents be pleased to have him staying? I expect I'll hear all about it when I call on them later in the week."

"They'll be telling you all the news!" Emily agreed. "Shall I call the others for supper?"

"Yes, please." Cora was already ladling cottage pie onto plates.

Ashford basked in the warmth of the afternoon sun. In the back garden of the house in Albert Road, the lawn was no more than a patch of dusty yellowed grass, and the leaves on the row of apple trees were dry and curling. The rose border, tended daily, still thrived, and the raspberries were plump with sweet juices. Summer was coming to an end though – the evenings had a chill to them, and the sun was setting long before bedtime.

Emily, with her usual energy, came home from work and immediately set about hauling blankets off the washing line. "Molly," she bellowed. "Give me a hand with folding these."

Molly peered out of their bedroom window, and then there came the thud of her running down the stairs. As her younger daughter shot through the kitchen, Cora noticed a slight scowl on her face. It wasn't easy having a big sister like Emily bossing her about. "Ta, love," Cora called.

Through the back window, Cora watched the sisters fold the two blankets and place them in a basket. They walked into the house together.

"Emily's going courting on Saturday afternoon," Molly announced before the basket was placed on the kitchen table.

"That's nice," Cora replied, eyeing the rack hanging above the range and wondering if it could take the weight of both blankets. She wanted to air them for a couple of hours after supper.

"It's with that Frederick," Molly added. "Even though she hasn't seen him in a while."

"Then perhaps it's time he came to Sunday tea and showed us that he's a respectable young man and means to treat Emily nicely," Cora suggested, trying not to let her agitation show. She moved the laundry basket to one of the chairs. It was best to keep busy. "How about he visits us on the following Sunday?"

A huff of despair erupted from Emily. "We're just going out for a bun and a cup of tea, Ma. There's no need to be thinking I'm getting married. There's no harm in going out with a young man and being treated to an ice-cream or a bit of Victoria sponge. It doesn't mean I'm getting soppy over him."

"No point in walking out with him if you don't want to be serious," Cora objected. "It was Ernie last month, and Cedric over Easter time. You're going to get a reputation if you don't take care."

"I suppose it's all right for the boys to go out with those flighty pieces every weekend?" Emily threw at her as she stalked through the doorway.

"Johnny and Frank are serious about their young ladies and treating them with respect," Cora called after her daughter.

"Serious?" Emily repeated with contempt before she stamped up the stairs.

"I hope she meets someone decent soon and gets married," Molly muttered. "Even if it is that Frederick. He's handsome enough and has got a decent job. At least we'll be rid of her."

Despite Emily's assertion that she had no intention of allowing her feelings for Frederick to blossom, she did invite him to Sunday tea in the front parlour. That morning she dusted the dark wooden mantlepiece, carefully moving the carriage clock and figurines. The cushions were plumped, and the lace-trimmed antimacassars straightened.

"I hope she don't get in a huff when the boys are in there reading the papers before dinner," Cora remarked to Jacob.

"She's bound to!" He gave a shrug and a grin. "There's nothing we can do to stop Emily from speaking her mind."

By mid-morning, while Cora prepared vegetables in the scullery, Emily pulled out the mixing bowls and set the scales on the kitchen table. "You can help if you want," she said to Molly who looked on with interest from the doorway. "I'm making gingerbread, and butterfly cakes with jam."

"No, ta," Molly replied. "I'm going for a walk with Ann this morning," She watched Emily for a moment, then added, "But I bet it will taste nice, and Frederick is ever so handsome. I hope he's got good manners and Ma gets to like him a bit."

"That's nice of you, Mol."

Looking through from scullery to kitchen, Cora smiled to see a moment of camaraderie between the sisters. Emily placed an arm around Molly's shoulders and gave her a squeeze, then young Molly scampered up the stairs, no doubt going to fuss over her hair before taking a stroll with a friend.

When the hands on the clock had just passed midday, Cora and Jacob returned from church to find Emily lovingly tending the sponge cakes. Having cut a hole in each one, she spread a thick layer of jam and added the butterfly wings. "Can you pass me the sugar cone?" she asked. They watched as she grated, and a fine layer of sugar settled on the cakes. "I'm putting them on the table now," Emily announced, carrying the plate through to the parlour where the table was already pulled out from the bay window and covered with a cloth.

"You have been busy," Jacob said. "I'm sure we'll have a lovely time."

Cora gave his hand a squeeze, knowing how protective he was over Emily and the words didn't come easily to him.

After dinner, Emily dampened her hair, in an attempt to calm the auburn waves, and plaited it before coiling a bun. "Is it neat enough, Ma?" she asked as she pressed hairpins into place.

"It looks lovely," Cora soothed. "Very posh."

The next time Emily appeared, the loose strands either side of her forehead were bound within twists of rags, and she was wearing an attractive summer dress in a pale yellow with lace trims. She fussed over the tea table, straightening the cutlery, then retreated to her bedroom again. By half-past two, her hair had been freed from the rags and fell in perfect ringlets past her temples to rest on prominent cheekbones. She hovered at the parlour window, frequently stepping forward to look down the street, although Frederick was not expected until three o'clock. As the hands of the clock reached five minutes to three, Emily dashed through to the kitchen. "Ma! Can you put the kettle on to boil?" she called. "Ta!"

Returning to her place at the window, Emily lingered. In the kitchen, Cora waited until quarter-past three, and filled the teapot. "He's bound to be here soon," she said to Molly. "Take the sandwiches through, will you?"

At half-past three, Emily called, "I'll go and meet him at the end of the road." The front door closed behind her with a depressing clunk.

Another fifteen minutes passed, and the thin sandwiches were beginning to dry at the edges. "I'll top up the tea with some hot water," Cora said to no one in particular. "I think we may as well make a start."

Johnny slouched in one of the kitchen armchairs. May was visiting a relative, so Frank had gone courting alone, leaving his brother at a loose end. "I'll go and get Emily," he suggested.

"She'll come back if you ask her," Cora agreed. "And then maybe we can all go out for a stroll. Fancy him not bothering to turn up, but I won't say another word in front of her."

Molly took up the position of lookout at the parlour window, so it was she who announced that Johnny and Emily were returning. "She looks all right," Molly called. "She's holding onto Johnny's arm, and they're laughing about something."

"Glory!" Cora came rushing to the window. "I thought she'd be in a rage. You can never tell how it will be with Emily."

"Ta for coming to fetch me," Emily said as they came through the hallway. "I hope you like the cakes and gingerbread I made, and Ma cut the bread nice an' thin."

The family spent a pleasant hour at the parlour table, with no mention of Frederick Barnes passing their lips. Then they took a stroll along the road towards Bybrook Farm and followed a trail of footpaths leading back towards Albert Road. Perhaps Emily was a little thoughtful at times, but mostly she chatted happily and there was a warm glow to her cheeks. As the day ended, Cora and Jacob relaxed in their bed. "That was a surprise – what a lovely afternoon," Cora said. "Emily seemed more settled than she has been in weeks. I never thought I'd be saying it was for the best he didn't turn up."

No word came from Frederick, and he was never mentioned again in the Rose home – at least not in front of Emily. September came and another weekend passed without Johnny going for a walk with May on a Sunday afternoon. On the following Saturday, he raced in through the front door after his morning's work and bounded up the stairs. Cora had already filled the jug on his washstand with hot water and soon Johnny reappeared looking refreshed.

"See you later, Ma." He gave Cora a peck on the cheek. "Have a nice afternoon everyone."

As the front door closed behind her brother, Molly asked, "Where's he going in such a rush?" She and Emily were repairing clothes at the kitchen table.

"He's off for tea and cake in the town with May," Cora informed her.

"With May?" Emily's tone was sharp.

"Of course! Johnny isn't going to go out with another girl, is he?"

"But he ain't seen her in two weeks."

"She was busy and then had a bad headache, poor girl."

"Oh. I thought..." But they never heard what Emily thought. A slight blush spread over her neck and cheeks while she spread the hem of her dress over her lap before beginning to sew.

"I went into Lewis and Hyland today on my break," Emily announced. There was something about the note of triumph in her voice that set Cora on edge. Her daughter meant to cause trouble, and she was determined not to encourage her.

"It's lovely in there," Molly commented. "Imagine working in a place like that. I'd like to be in drapery with beautiful materials, or haberdashery with all the bits and bobs needed to make a dress."

"May works in haberdashery," Johnny commented. "She could let you know if a position comes up."

"No, she don't!" Emily blurted out. "Not anymore." There was a moment of silence at the table before she continued. "I needed to go and get some… well, it was ladies' unmentionables. Not something to talk about in front of the men. And there she was – that May! She was there as bold as anything working amongst all those… those things I can't talk about. It's not decent – her being an unmarried woman and being with all them frills and fancy bits."

Johnny said nothing but his skin flushed, and he scowled at Emily for bringing this news to their supper table. Frank looked down at his empty plate, his neck reddening.

Cora took a sip of tea. "I'm sure there was a good reason. It must have been an emergency and they called on her."

"She was there on Thursday last week as well," Emily added. "I happened to mention it to Jane, and she saw her when she went shopping with her ma. It's not decent. Her coming here and sitting in our parlour, and us thinking she's a respectable woman, and all the time she's working in that shop seeing all sorts of things I don't want to imagine. It's not right – is it Ma?"

"No. It's not respectable," Cora admitted. "But…"

Johnny stood, pushing his chair back so it slammed into the dresser. The china quivered. "You weren't even here when May came to tea. Don't you go talking about respectable when you were out God-knows-where with that lad who had a different girl every month. I don't know what's got into you, Emily." With that he left the room and seconds later the front door was heard slamming behind him.

Jake Brooks' gaze followed the cart laden with baskets of fish wending its way to Lydd. "Look at us," he snarled. "A couple of bloody fools! We'll never get rich – it's this lot who make the money from our hard labours."

"I'm thinking of rebuilding my smoking shed," Ed offered. "That will at least give us food for our bellies when we can't go out on the boats."

"Smoking fish!" Jake snarled. "Fancy yourself as the next Cyril Thoms, do you? Going to set yourself up with a little business, are you?"

"I didn't say that." Ed turned to walk away. With the toes of his worn boots, he kicked viciously at the shingle. He reached the ridge at the top of the beach and paused between two boats hauled beyond the high tide mark. Standing tall, Ed breathed in deeply, finding time to appreciate the salty tang in the air. The sea was barely breaking on the shore, it rolled to and fro with none of its usual energy. On the bank, in the shadows of the wooden hulls, Jake's parents and Aunt Ida were pulling at the nets, removing strands of seaweed. Ed gave a curt nod and set himself to pulling out a tangle of net.

There was no sign of Jake who had not followed to help. "He's up to something," Ida muttered in response to words left unsaid by those toiling on the beach.

Chapter Six

As upholder of the family's morals, Cora left the home when the breakfast dishes were cleared away and the floor swept. As always, the wicker basket was hanging from her arm awaiting the necessary shopping. With her free hand, she lifted her skirts to keep them away from dusty roads. In recent weeks, there had been barely any rain to wash the streets clean.

Glancing towards the cemetery, Cora noted a sombre gathering moving into the gateway and she lowered her head a little while walking on. Her attention was drawn to straw gathered in swathes on the ground of nearby Hardinge Road – an indication of another funeral procession passing by in the last day or so. The clatter of horses' hooves had been deadened by softening their path. *I wonder who that was*, she thought. *I hadn't heard of anyone…*

The first days of September passed, and there was no break in the sunny weather. Where leaves had been lush and flowers bright, small front gardens had now lost the youthful vigour seen in spring and early summer. Ashford looked to be weary of summer, yet it was too early for the leaves to change to their autumn colours and bring an alternative warmth to the town.

When she reached the junction with Somerset Road, a wagon from the sawmills lumbered by and was overtaken by a smart gig pulled by a grey mare. A light breeze lifted the dust from the wagon; it settled on the hem of Cora's dress. With an audible tut, she brushed it off. All her thoughts were on the task ahead, and her pace was brisk as she passed shops, public houses and offices.

Emily saw her mother go by the Joint Stock Bakery, with not so much as a glance through the window. Now in the High Street, Cora almost marched along, turning into Lewis and Hyland, and striding past a portly woman with a tape measure around her neck and a notepad to hand. A short flight of wooden stairs took her to a discreet room where women could peruse the styles of undergarments on offer and be fitted for new items.

The area where Cora found May working was no larger than the parlour at home. With only a small window looking out to yards and outhouses behind the shops, Cora's immediate thought was that this was a miserable place for a young woman to spend her day. How much livelier it was to be looking out on the street. Yet she wasn't here to pity May. It was time to find out exactly what the young woman was doing amongst all sorts of undergarments, and some of them not at all suitable for the eyes of a respectable person.

A deep counter ran along two sides, and behind it a woman of about Cora's age eyed her from beneath an abundance of dark curls, cascading from a high knot on top of her head. The countertop was glass, as was the front, giving glimpses of trimmings, rolls of stockings, folded bloomers and intricate fastenings. Pictures on the walls depicted the styles on offer – shapely sketches under the quivering flames of gas mantles in elaborate holders. Shafts of daylight filtered through leaded windows, past the layers of summer's dust on almost opaque glass. They settled on the curves of three mannequins, on May's brown hair and her outstretched arms as she stood absorbed with adjusting the bones on one of the corsets displayed on a model.

Turning on hearing Cora approach, May's mouth opened into a round 'O' and she dropped her arms. "Hello Mrs Rose! How nice to see you."

Cora noted that May lowered her eyes a little and a flush rose through her neck.

"I thought you worked in haberdashery, May?" Cora cut straight to the point.

"Oh! Yes – I do! At least I did…"

"You're here permanent now?"

May raised her eyes, gazing past Cora towards the doorway, then flicking her attention to some open boxes on the counter.

"No. Not permanently. Mrs Browne – who works in haberdashery – says it helps if we get experience in other areas. They needed someone here, and so I changed department."

Cora considered this for a moment. *What kind of experience does a young woman gain while working amongst ladies' delicate undergarments?* "You're just here for a few days then, or a couple of weeks?" she queried.

"I… Perhaps a little longer," May admitted.

"To learn about…" Cora paused and allowed her eyes to follow the line of the counters, before settling back on May and the mannequins. "To learn about intimate things."

"It will help me give advice on fastenings and ribbons… and lacy trimmings," May told her. The flush rose to her neck. "So, when I'm back in haberdashery I can be more helpful."

"*When* you are back in haberdashery," Cora stated. But when exactly would that be?

"Can I help you with anything, Mrs Rose?" May interrupted her thoughts.

"No. Ta," Cora's reply was brisk. "I'll let you get on."

"All right. I've got to get these fancy chemises unpacked." May gestured towards the boxes on the counter.

"Goodbye then, May."

"Give my best wishes to Mr Rose."

With visions of bloomers embellished with lace and ribbons, Cora turned on her heels. Leaving both the back room and the shop, her mind raced as visions of May dealing with ladies' unmentionables raced unhindered. *What sort of ideas will it put into a young woman's head when she's handling all those flimsy bits and pieces? I don't know. I really don't know. She might get notions that she has to dress herself like someone who's not quite as respectable as she ought to be. And how does Johnny feel about it? I'll have to tell his father to have a word…*

Cora's basket remained empty, while the need to talk through her concerns drove her to walk briskly along Bank Street and towards the railway station. Barely noticing the elegant façades, once so fascinating to her younger self, she was soon leaving the town centre behind her and passing the gates to the livestock market. Now she slowed, finding herself to be tiring in the heat of the day. Glancing across, Cora noted animals crowded into wooden pens, men in country tweeds and the building where the official business was carried out – a simple structure with sweeping roofs covering verandas. There were wagons and carts, boys on bicycles, and ragamuffins walking about with a scoop to pick up the muck which inevitably was being excreted from the rear ends of the livestock. As the heat of the day increased, the air would be rich with animal droppings – a country smell which Cora didn't find offensive. The market was a lively place filled with noise and movement. On another day, Cora would linger as she passed, and to see the Romney Marsh sheep herded through the streets was a pleasure to her. Now, although taking in the scene, she kept moving towards the railway station and Beaver Road.

Once the publicans of a beerhouse at Dungeness, named the British Inn, Reuben and Ada Roberts lived in a cosy terraced house. Snug between two other homes, they were spared the harsh winds so prevalent on the Dungeness headland. With a row of shops providing for their daily needs just a few paces away, and The Locomotive public house close by, they found themselves pleased with life in the town. If they wanted a taste of the countryside, the watercress meadows were a pleasant place to stroll, and occasionally they would follow riverside footpaths in the direction of Buxford Mill and Great Chart.

Delighted to have two of the people she cared for so deeply now close at hand, Cora's shoes tapped on the pavement, and she gave cheery greetings to those she passed. The house was a typical red-brick style with a bay window to the front room. There was a shallow front garden, and a short path to the door which Cora rapped on before turning the handle and entering.

"Hello! Anyone home?" she called from the narrow hallway.

"Is that you, Cora?" Ada's voice wafted from the kitchen, before she appeared in an apron with a feather duster in her hand. Years of trekking across the shingle at Dungeness and helping her husband run the British Inn had kept Ada in good shape, although her skin was weathered and her hair now an iron grey. Straight-talking and brisk, her affection for

Cora was deep. "What brings you out so early? Nothing bothering you, I hope?"

"There is," Cora admitted, following Ada into the kitchen. "But I know you'll talk some sense into me." Making herself at home, as she always did, Cora set about preparing a pot of tea. A few minutes later, they were seated opposite each other at the small kitchen table and Ada was hearing about the concerns over May and the influences of working with the frills and dainty items to be found amongst women's undergarments.

"What exactly is worrying you?" Ada asked.

"I'm worried that people will think May is a bit flighty. Perhaps that she'll be a bit loose with her morals." Cora considered this for a moment. "That when the neighbours or the men at Johnny's work hear of this, they'll think it's not very respectable, and he'll get a ribbing for it."

"And do *you* feel May is not quite as respectable as you would wish for Johnny?" Ada asked.

Again, Cora paused to reflect on her feelings. She gazed out of the small back window to the brickwork of the scullery and privy, then up to the slate roof where a blackbird perched.

"She's a nice young woman. Confident and talkative. I know Emily doesn't like that about her, but Jacob and I are becoming fond of May. And Johnny… he seems very attracted to her."

"As I see it, what Emily doesn't like is anyone being close to Johnny. He's always been a favourite, hasn't he? Right from when she was a scrappy little two-year-old."

"But they're all grown up now," Cora objected. "She should want him to meet someone decent and get married."

"I just wonder..." Ada said no more, instead returning to Johnny's affection for May. "It sounds as if she's a lovely girl and like they are getting serious. But I can't help wondering what she sees when she spends all day amongst those bits of frill and lace. It might give her ideas of wanting to dress up a bit indecent. And if May is full of confidence like you say, maybe she'll be getting ideas about flirting with other men?"

"Johnny wouldn't like that..."

"Of course he wouldn't. I don't know her, but I can't help thinking she should never have taken the job when she had a good position in haberdashery."

Cora took a sip of her tea. "What am I going to do about it?"

"How old is he?" Ada asked.

"Twenty-six."

"Twenty-six – there's nothing you can do, is there? Johnny will have to make his own mind up. I suggest that you have a quiet word with him. Don't tell him what to do. Just ask how he feels and does he think this is a suitable occupation for his young woman."

"Don't go rushing in?" Cora asked, with a grin.

Ada, who knew Cora so well, reached over and patted her hand. "That's exactly right!"

They spoke about other matters over two cups of tea, and by the time Cora was giving Ada a hug on the doorstep, she felt much calmer, knowing her decision to speak with the older woman had been the right one.

That evening when Johnny returned from work, Cora shooed Molly from the kitchen. "I want to speak to your brother in private," she said. Johnny slouched in the armchair untying his heavy work boots, but Cora knew she held his attention. "I went to see May this morning," she began.

"Oh?'

"She's working with ladies' delicates, like Emily said."

"Emily is making trouble." His gaze remained on his boots.

"I won't deny that."

Johnny pulled his boots off and straightened his socks. "I didn't know she wasn't in haberdashery," he admitted.

Cora pulled out a chair and seated herself near him. She loved Jacob's three sons as if they were her own. Together with Emily, and later Molly, the children had enjoyed a safe and happy upbringing. William had married a lovely woman. Cora had no qualms that both the younger boys would also make the right choice. With his red hair and blue eyes, Johnny's looks were striking. Tall and well-groomed, he would usually receive a second glance from a young woman, and he knew how to treat them with respect. Now, it seemed as if the freckles across Johnny's nose had paled, and his eyes looked weary. May's bold move from haberdashery to ladies' undergarments was playing on his mind, and Cora didn't want to say anything to cause further distress.

"It was a nice job she had in haberdashery," Cora observed. "Just the thing for an unmarried woman. How do you feel about her working with… with… well, you know?"

"I don't know what to think," he admitted. "I feel like I can't ask her about her day… about her work. It wouldn't be right, would it? I can't ask her about all those… those things."

Cora said nothing but allowed him to ponder upon his thoughts.

A moment later, Johnny spoke again, "I've got very fond of May, but I can't help feeling this isn't respectable."

"I'm not sure if it's permanent," Cora told him.

"But how long will she be there?" he asked. "How long before the men at work have heard about it and they're all making a joke of it? How long before she's getting ideas about dressing up all fancy herself, and she's not my May anymore?"

"Perhaps you need to ask her?" Cora suggested. "When you see her at the weekend?"

Johnny stood. "Is there some ham on the cold shelf?" He reached for the bread. "I'm going to make a sandwich and go there right now. I can't wait till Sunday."

Throughout their evening meal, and afterwards while the women laboured over the ironing, Cora deflected the girls' questions about where their brother had gone. "It's his private business," she replied, refusing to be drawn into any gossip.

By the time they heard the front door open, and he stepped into the hallway, the sun had set, leaving streaks of pale yellow and grey in the sky to the west. The family were now relaxing in the parlour, and only Molly was upstairs in her bedroom.

"I've got some news!" Johnny announced from the open doorway. His eyes shone and skin glowed. "Where's Moll?" He turned to stand at the bottom of the stairs. "Molly! Come down here. I've got some news and I want you all to hear it at once."

When he had assembled everyone, Johnny stood with his back to the fireplace. "Right everyone – there's been some talk about May. You know what it is. So, I've come up with a plan to sort it out. I've asked May to marry me, and she said yes!"

There was a moment's silence as the news was digested. Frank was the first to stand up and shake his brother's hand. "Congratulations! I had no idea you were thinking…" He took the words from the mouths of the others.

Cora felt a contentment flow through her. *I liked May from the moment we met, and Johnny is ready to settle down. He's got a few pounds in the bank so they'll be able to find some decent rooms somewhere. She can get herself a job working a few hours a day before the little ones come along. Maybe Lewis and Hyland will keep her on, and even if it's with those women's delicates, it won't be so shocking once she's married.* She stood to give Johnny a hug, but one glance at Emily stopped Cora in her tracks. Her elder daughter looked stricken – her face pale and eyes wide. *I knew she wouldn't be happy, but what's all this about?* Torn between going to Johnny or reaching out for Emily, Cora watched as Emily stood up. In a flash, she had left the room, and a moment later the front door slammed behind her.

Stepping into the one-room timber shack he called home, Ed let the door swing back. It knocked gently against the wall, and he kicked some stones, so it held in place. His gaze fell upon the prized piece of oak driftwood. "I've neglected you for long enough," he murmured, picturing the unmarked grave in Lydd Cemetery.

A box of tools was pulled out from under the bed and Ed ran his eyes over the contents, never trusting Jake not to come rummaging about, taking things which were not his. Everything seemed to be where it should be. He put the tools on the ground outside, pushed the base of an old chair into the stones until it held steady and placed the wood on the seat of the chair. Then, with a saw in his hand, Ed stood back to survey the dimensions of the wood.

Two hours later, he once more considered the oak. Now it was in the form of a cross, held together in the centre by three strong nails. He had smoothed the surface and edges, working with the grain and gaining pleasure from the golden glow. The end of the longest stretch of wood had been shaped to a point, ready to sink into the soft earth.

"I'll carve your initials tomorrow, Ma." Ed picked up the cross and propped it against the wall inside the home. "Not your whole name – best to do a little and take care to get it right."

Emily's Story
Chapter Seven

So, I've come up with a plan to sort it out. I've asked May to marry me, and she said yes!

Emily pulled at the folded shawl placed on a shelf below the coat hooks. This was Cora's new one – the much-coveted square of soft green wool. It could have been any old rag and was just a case of grabbing whatever came to hand. Trailing behind, as Emily opened the front door and almost tumbled out, the shawl caught on the latch and tore. *Drat!* Emily acknowledged the damage to the beautiful garment, but her remorse was short-lived. Her thoughts were all on her own anguish.

So, I've come up with a plan to sort it out. I've asked May to marry me, and she said yes!

Johnny's words screamed through Emily's head, as she allowed the front door to slam behind her, and the gate was left to clatter against the wall. She raced along Albert Road, instinctively turning towards the town centre, only pausing when the buildings became taller, crowding against one another.

Leaning against the red brick wall of a house, Emily bent forward slightly, holding her side and breathing deeply. She straightened herself and reached to her tumbling curls, pressing hairpins into place. Then, before continuing, Emily wrapped the shawl around her shoulders. Her pace was still brisk, but where before she plunged on with no thought, taking no notice of her surroundings, the young woman now became aware of how dark it was and all that was familiar had changed.

Well-known features of medieval, Tudor and Georgian buildings had become indistinct and, in their place, it was a shaft of light through a window or shutter that caught Emily's attention. The pavements were now free of housewives and delivery boys. Instead, men congregated around the pubs, or lurked near alleyways. They glanced towards the lone woman, alerted by the brisk beat of her shoes on the pavement. A courting couple passed by. Scowling, Emily noted a protective gesture as the man guided his sweetheart through the dark streets, his arm around her waist.

So, I've come up with a plan to sort it out. I've asked May to marry me, and she said yes!

Emily glanced towards St Mary's Church, noticing the silhouette of the turreted tower against the starlit sky. In the quiet times, when she could indulge in her dreams of her and Johnny being together, she had visualised them marrying within the ancient walls of the parish church. *Stupid thoughts. Ridiculous. It would be at the Methodist Church. But it won't be. It won't be anywhere. How can he do this? How can he think of marrying that May when we've always been so close, and it would all be perfect? How can he think she's the one for him? He only met her on the train two months ago. Two months and a week or so.*

Drawn to the church, thinking nothing of the practicalities of navigating the medieval heart of the town, Emily took the twisting route around jettied and rendered buildings at the end of the wide High Street where the market was held. Breathing deeply, tobacco and ale filled her senses. Emily could taste the bitter tang on her tongue. She could hear the men laughing and discussing the events of the day. They spilled into the narrow streets, which held onto the smells and sounds between ancient walls. She scuttled into an alley and was alone again. The narrow route between buildings was navigated at speed, and the church, with its decorative tower was before her – a dark bulk of gables, buttresses and coal-black leaded windows.

It wasn't the most straightforward path, especially at night, but by taking it she passed places which were part of the story of her life. St Mary's Church had been a favourite for Cora, who admired the architecture and used to take her small daughter there to listen to the clock chime. Emily recalled learning to count to the melodic strike of the clapper on cast bronze.

Moving on, now at a slower pace, through the churchyard, and past the homes fronting it, she turned onto a street with terraced houses and the red-brick police station. There was no memory of it, but she knew this was where her mother had learned of her father's death. Another chapter of their life together, which in turn gave rise to the annual visit to his grave in a lonely churchyard on the hills above Folkestone. The glow of light at the windows of the police station made Emily wonder how often a young woman had sat at an ink-stained table to be told the tragic news of her husband's death. *She was the same age as me, and I've lost Johnny like Ma lost Pa. Only it's worse because my pa would never have chosen to leave us. But Johnny did. He left me on purpose.*

Filled with a renewed sense of loss and fury, Emily began to run again. Vicarage Lane passed through areas of allotments and open land. It was rough underfoot, but the stars were bright, and she could keep up a good pace, skipping over dips in the ground and piles of horse manure. The next memory came as she turned onto Marsh Street, a main thoroughfare leading to the railway station. In one of the substantial houses, she and Cora had lodged for a few nights before moving to rooms in Willesborough. It was here they had their first experience of an inside water closet – something which Cora often remarked on over the following years.

Not having encountered anyone since the town centre, Emily now became aware of several workers emerging through the gates of the station. At first, she considered the late hours kept by those who had to make the steam trains safe before returning to their homes, but thoughts of others were swiftly overtaken by her own dilemma. *Where do they go? All them trains? Hastings – Folkestone – Maidstone – Canterbury. I could go anywhere. Anywhere. And then he'd be sorry. He'd miss me and know it was me he loves and he'd have to tell that floozy May that it was all a mistake.* Emily – impulsive and unreasonable – thought nothing of how Johnny could possibly find her with all these possible destinations open to him.

No longer able to sustain a steady run, Emily now moved at an erratic pace, alternating between jogging and walking. The terraced houses of Beaver Road loomed either side and she turned at speed onto a path, turned the handle of the front door and entered without knocking. Stepping into the hallway, Emily called out, "Ada! It's me!" Then she paused for a moment in the dusky darkness.

The parlour door opened, and a golden light beamed into the hallway bringing with it the comforting scents of beeswax and lavender. However, the figure at the doorway was not Emily's beloved Ada, nor the steadying influence of Reuben. This was a younger man – someone who did not hold such a firm place in her affections.

"Oh… hello. I didn't expect…" Emily hesitated.

A grin spread over the face of James Roberts. Cora would have been antagonised by this – seeing a man who relished the drama of a young woman arriving unannounced and clearly in trouble. Emily had no ill will, but his appearance caught her off-guard and she uttered no more in defence of her tumultuous arrival. He said nothing in reply, but merely waited. Perhaps he was pausing for the young woman to catch her breath and declare why she was in his parents' hallway. Or perhaps – and more likely – he was appreciating the unexpected sight before him.

Emily had never looked so beautiful: her eyes shone – although those who knew her best would have seen fear and desperation in them; her face was flushed and cheekbones prominent; glorious auburn waves tumbled loose, having freed themselves from the pins. Beneath the pale-yellow summer dress, gentle curves of her slim body were accentuated by a corset and her breast heaved from the race through the town.

James smiled. He had always found the spirited Cora attractive and here was her daughter looking both vulnerable and tantalising. It was rare this man missed out on an opportunity and he had never forgotten that he had not acted swiftly enough with Cora before her head was turned by the lighthouse keeper. Perhaps the daughter was a greater prize?

Movement at the head of the stairs caused them both to turn. Ada was there, wearing her housecoat over a nightgown. Reuben stood behind, an indistinct figure in the darkness.

"Looks like I need to put the kettle on," Ada commented.

"I'll do it," James stepped forward.

"No, you'll sit in the parlour with your pa, and Emily and I will have a chat in the kitchen." Ada took control as she came down the stairs and put an arm around Emily's shoulder. "Come on, love."

Emily felt warmth and gratitude flood through her, knowing she had come to the right place. *Ada will understand. She always does. She'll know that Johnny's done something foolish and how to work it out. Then everyone at home will see sense.* The kitchen door was closed behind them, and Emily blurted out, "It's Johnny! He's going to get married to May. It's all gone wrong."

Wrapping her arms around the vulnerable young woman, Ada murmured soothing words, as she had since Emily was two years old. For that moment, she gave none of the sensible advice which was to come, only offering love and compassion. Tears flowed and the words from Emily were disjointed as she attempted to calm herself.

"There, there… you'll feel better for a good cry," Ada whispered. Reaching into the deep pocket of her housecoat, she pulled out a clean handkerchief.

After a few minutes the sobbing subsided, and Ada extracted herself from Emily's arms. She busied herself with preparing the tea and listened as the story unfolded.

"I saw your ma only this morning," she said, after hearing how Johnny had raced out, not even waiting for dinner, and returned to announce his news to the family. "She told me about this business with May working in ladies' delicates. Do you think she spoke to Johnny about it?" Recalling her talk with Cora, Ada was piecing together the events leading to Johnny's proposal of marriage, while cautious of betraying any trust shared.

"I know Ma wasn't happy. It's not right working with all those frills and lacy bits."

"But Cora likes May?"

"She did like her," Emily admitted.

"And we don't know of May ever doing anything improper?"

Emily pondered on this for a moment. She considered May as being a little too confident for her liking, especially the way she seemed to find it easy to make conversation with everyone. On two occasions Emily had been in Lewis and Hyland and watched May serving customers. Reluctantly, she had to admit there was nothing to fault in the other young woman's dress or manner.

"Well…" Emily attempted to avoid the question. "I don't really see May much. Johnny and Frank go walking out with May and Effie in Willesborough. But Johnny… he didn't go for a few weeks, and we went out for a lovely walk. Me and him. He was kind, and he was always special – since we were small."

"And you thought his feelings for you might grow to be romantic?"

Emily took a sip of the tea. "He's not my brother!" her voice rose, and she continued, "You know that!"

"But you were all brought up together," Ada stated. "Johnny loves you as a sister. The same as Molly."

"I wanted it to be more…" Memories of Johnny trimming his beard and brushing down his clothes before going out courting brought fresh anguish, and new tears began to flow. "It's not wrong, you know. Not dirty or anything."

"It's not *illegal*," Ada conceded, "But I think it would make people, and especially your family, feel a bit uncomfortable."

"But if we loved each other…" Visions of her and Johnny together flooded her mind – she pictured them taking countryside walks hand in hand and cuddling up on the settee in the parlour on a rainy Sunday.

"Emily." Much as Ada loved her, she was not someone to pander to foolish dreams. "Johnny has made it clear he loves May, and if you try to cause any more trouble, the whole family will suffer for it. It's not nice when families start to fight. Think of your ma and Jacob and try to keep yourself calm."

"Go home and watch him getting all soppy with that May? Planning their wedding and God knows what else?" Emily looked at Ada in horror.

Ada met her gaze. "Yes, that's exactly what you need to do. And when you're feeling miserable you will come here and tell me, but when you're at home you will try and look happy about it all."

Emily said nothing in reply. Instead, she took a sip of tea and turned her attention to the flamboyant floral pattern on the china. She contemplated the rambling roses, wondering what pattern to choose if she were setting up home. There was a tiny chip on the rim of the saucer, and she ran her fingertip across it. It was several minutes before Emily spoke again, "I can't go back now. I can't face it."

"No. You'll stay here and sleep in the spare bed. James can make do with a chair in the parlour. Then you'll have to leave early to go home and change into your work dress. I don't know what you're doing in your Sunday best."

There was no arguing with Ada. Besides, she was right. Emily murmured her agreement and chose to remain in the kitchen while Reuben and James were told of the plan. Before long she was being ushered upstairs to the back bedroom. While Emily drew back the curtains and gazed out at the stars, Ada was rummaging in the chest of drawers in her own bedroom. She returned with a cotton nightdress. "It will go round you twice," she announced, "but better that than sleeping in your chemise."

"Ta." Emily gave a weak smile. She closed the curtains and sat on the edge of the bed.

Before long, Emily was curled up within the swathes of Ada's nightdress and a fresh handkerchief in her fist. Exhausted from the race through the town, her sleep was deep for several hours. When she woke in the early hours, not long before sunrise, memories of Johnny's supposed betrayal flooded her mind and she sobbed quietly, reliving and embellishing every moment.

As the working men of Ashford started early shifts at the railway, the brewery, iron foundry or flour mills, and the women brought the kitchen ranges to life, Emily slipped out of bed and crept downstairs. She opened the back door, conscious of every small noise and ventured out to the privy. From the yard, she moved into an alley and, with Cora's shawl wrapped as a shield around her, started the walk home.

The town was awakening just before dawn. Coloured in shades of grey, the only blasts of light came from a lamp at a window or an open doorway. Before long it would all change as the sun rose with spectacular showiness, giving warmth to the orange bricks of the houses, and a vibrancy to autumnal flowers and trees. As Emily left Beaver Road, the knocker-upper walked past at a brisk pace, a pole over his shoulder. One of the few people on the streets, Emily kept her head down, not wanting to encourage a cheery greeting. She passed the railway, noting figures moving towards the station buildings and workshops, and continued up Marsh Street towards the town centre.

On turning into the wide High Street, Emily was bathed in the sun, now making its dramatic appearance, and with it came the clatter of market stalls being set up. The people of Ashford no longer whispered to each other in apologetic tones but called out, wanting to make themselves heard. The young woman persisted in hiding away beneath the shawl. She plodded on, neither looking nor speaking to anyone.

Just as she had left the terrace in Beaver Road by the back, Emily entered the family home through the scullery. Cora was standing before the range stirring porridge. The tea was already brewing. "I'm sorry, Ma."

Cora barely glanced at her daughter. "It's your brother you need to apologise to."

"I know." Emily, whose spirits had lifted during the walk, felt a heaviness descend.

"You'd better get changed," Cora stated. "I don't know what you were doing in your best dress."

I wanted to look pretty for Johnny. I wanted him to notice me. Emily, still standing, poured a cup of tea and took a couple of mouthfuls before leaving the room. No more was said between the two women. *I bet she saw I took her shawl.* Remorse hit Emily as she recalled the soft garment tearing on the door catch. *I'm going to be saying sorry all day long.*

In the hallway, Emily had no choice but to face Johnny as he descended the stairs. She stood, eyes lowered to the bundled shawl in her arms. "I'm sorry, Johnny," Emily forced the words out, her voice rough as they caught in her throat. He paused, and she repeated. "I'm sorry. I'm sorry I was jealous of you and May. It was unfair of me."

Johnny now stood beside Emily and placed an arm around her. "I hope you cheer up, Em. You need to calm down a bit, and you'll soon meet someone decent."

She shrugged, unable to reply and they parted, he with no idea of her true feelings. Half an hour of awkward apologies followed before Emily left home, the small portion of porridge weighty in her stomach.

Set apart from the low shacks and the rambling British Sailor, there stood a terrace of four brick-built homes, partly rendered in a grey-brown concrete. The walls of these cottages were all straight; the doors and windows matched one another. Inside they offered a standard assortment of rooms, while outside they shared brick-built earth closets and an outhouse with a copper. These properties made a striking, almost absurd, contrast to the other buildings rising from this wasteland. The men who lived in them were coastguards, rather than locals of Denge – their time in this remote place would be short-lived.

While the men had work to occupy them – albeit a lonely vigil over a bleak coastline – the women suffered from their homes being a long trek from Lydd. They struggled to adapt to their purchases being restricted to whatever was offered for sale on the grocer's cart, and their company was limited to the other women living in the terrace.

Jake Brooks, standing outside the British Sailor as the sun sank low in the sky, finished his fourth pint of ale. "I've been thinking of ways to make a bit more money," he confided to Ed. At that moment, one of the coastguards left his cottage and began his amble towards the public house. Jake sneered in his direction. "But it's not for their ears – meddlers the lot of them."

Chapter Eight

"Good morning, Mrs Farrow. A cottage loaf, is it? Shall I pop it in your basket?" Emily wrapped the bread in thin paper, then leaned over the counter to place it on top of the other items wrapped in brown paper.

It wasn't too hard to retain a cheerful mask while busy serving customers. She fixed a smile on her face and prepared to welcome the housewife who was next in the queue. However, movement in the doorway caused her attention to wander and cheeks to flush. James Roberts stood there – a reminder of Emily's shameful flight from home the evening before. Having blustered her way through serving, she prepared to face him.

"Good morning! How can I help you?" Her voice rang clear, giving no hint of the nerves trembling within.

"I'd like a fruit loaf as a treat for Ma." James flashed a friendly smile, then lowered his voice. "How are you today?"

"Fine, thank you very much." Emily knew her response sounded overly formal, but it would be frowned upon if she were to pause and chat over the counter.

She turned to take a fruit loaf from the shelf behind her, unwittingly giving James a chance to appreciate her slim waist, and the apron ties cascading across her shapely bottom.

"I know you're working," he said, while handing over the money. "But I'm here for a few more days. Come and see us if you can. Ma will want to know you are all right. We're all worried."

"Oh… ta. I'll come and see Ada tomorrow after work." Then she recalled leaving early that morning by the back gate. "And say thank you to her please. I had to leave early, you know."

"Of course, you did," he reassured her.

Emily watched him go. *He's very understanding. Fancy a smart man like him having to sleep on the settee and not being a bit cross about it. Instead, he comes here to see how I am.* Visions of her family encouraging Johnny and Frank's romances with the cousins from Willesborough flitted into her mind. *I don't know what to make of them anymore. All they do is fuss over those flighty girls who should know better than to be chatting up men on trains and working with delicates. It's like I don't matter anymore. I have to count my blessings that I've got Ada and Reuben, and even their son is more interested in me than my own family are.*

The following afternoon saw Emily once more at the kitchen table in Reuben and Ada's home. Recollecting the trips to Dungeness over the years, the shared memories brought pleasure to them all.

"I couldn't believe it when we could come all the way by train!" Emily grinned. "When was that, Reuben?"

"1883!" he announced with delight. "Didn't that make life a lot easier for us? Ada and I could get in a coach and be in Lydd within minutes. It was a darned awful trudge over the shingle to get to the town before that."

"They were good days – running the British Inn. Everyone knew each other and we all pitched in together if someone was in trouble," Ada recalled, "but it was hard too."

"Always windy!" Emily reminded them.

"But plenty of fresh fish." Reuben took a long sip of tea, draining his cup.

"And milk from goats!" Emily's voice rose into a squeal. "Can you imagine what the people here would say about that? Having goats wandering all over the place, and milking them?"

"That would put an end to all them fancy flowerbeds people like to have!" Ada laughed.

"I'm glad you live here now," Emily said, feeling her body slump a little. "But it's been years since we visited – there's no reason now, is there?"

"Not really, love." Ada reached out to place her hand on Emily's slim wrist. "We're making new memories."

Before long, Emily was buttoning up her coat and receiving a hug from both Ada and Reuben. At the front gate she forced a smile, while they waved her off. The warmth of the kitchen, the affection flowing between the three of them, and the childhood memories were lost with each step along Beaver Road. At home, Cora would be preparing supper and then the boys, Johnny and Frank, would be back, and with them the reminders of May who would be joining the family within no time.

Emily glanced towards the distant church tower of St Mary's and a dart of self-loathing shot through her. *Foolish dreams – thinking that me and Johnny could be married, and it would be me and him getting all soppy in the parlour. Me and him going for an ice and taking a walk around the churchyard or over the watercress meadows. But we could have been. We could have been if it wasn't for May…*

Tears threatened and Emily clenched her fist around the bag she carried. She barely noticed a man approaching directly in her path and had to pull herself up before they collided. "Sorry," she muttered, moving aside.

"Come on, Em. Where's that lovely smile of yours?"

The cheerful voice caused her to start and focus on the present. "Oh, it's you, Mr Roberts!"

James Roberts, as dapper as ever from his polished shoes to his slicked back hair, gave a guffaw. "Mr Roberts? I thought I was James! Now what's that glum face for?"

"Sorry James. I was miles away thinking about… thinking about all sorts of things."

"How about I buy you an ice? It's a lovely day and there's a cart all set up in the town."

"Before supper?" Emily queried.

"Before supper!" he agreed. "No harm in having a bit of something sweet to cheer us up."

"You don't look like you need cheering up," Emily retorted, as they fell in step beside each other.

"I will if I don't get a strawberry ice!"

All her pessimistic thoughts flew away as James swept Emily along with his cheerful banter, and before long she was telling him about the talk around the kitchen table with his parents.

"I don't know that there is much to miss about Dungeness," he responded. "A load of old stones and a few shacks – there's nothing much there to go back to."

"There's people and memories," Emily told him.

"Maybe, but you were lucky you didn't have to grow up there," James reminded her. "I did, and I can tell you that living at the Brit wasn't much fun. Now Lydd – that's a great place. It's got a smashing High Street with everything you need in the shops. There's the green, and the train down to the coast at Littlestone, and some decent pubs… and hotels too." They were nearing the town centre now and a smart gig passed by at speed. James placed his hand on Emily's elbow, guiding her away from the kerb. She appreciated the gesture.

"I spent a few years in London and could tell you some stories about that!" James continued. "But Dungeness – there's no point in getting all dreamy about it. When I was a child there was no school and no shops. I was glad to get away. Fifteen I was when I left!"

"Fifteen!" Emily considered this for a moment. "And here I am twenty-two and still at home with Ma."

"Well, Em," James spoke slowly, as if considering his words. "There's no reason why you have to stay, is there? It's not as if your mother needs you. Not like she's sick or anything. You could go anywhere you fancied and get lodgings, and a smart young woman like you could a get a job easily."

"I… I never thought of that…" *Well, only when I was tearing past the station the other night. But I never thought about it otherwise.*

The ice-cream cart was in sight now, and they quickened their pace. The conversation turned to the wonders of the icy dessert being produced, then sold in the street. It was only as they crunched on the last of their cones that James broached the subject of Emily clearly being unhappy at home. "It's none of my business, but there's something making you upset at the moment," he began, "and I don't like to see it. Not just me – I'm sure my parents don't like to see you like this."

"I don't want to talk about it." Emily felt a heat rise in her neck. She turned to face towards North Street. "I've got to go home now."

"Of course, you have," he agreed. "I'm going back tomorrow, so I won't see you in a while. But if you do decide to have a new beginning somewhere then you could always try Lydd. You just come and look me up at the Dolphin, and I'll take care of you."

"Oh! Ta. Ta very much," was all Emily could manage before tears began to well up again. She turned away, and no more words were exchanged. The unexpected kindness left her feeling both warm and shaky all at once. As she walked, Emily knew he was watching her every step, but she didn't dare look back. *If he sees me crying, he'll think I'm a right soppy fool, and I don't want him running up to comfort me. Best I get home and get on with the chores and stop getting all tearful.*

"Is that your ring? Can I have a look?" Molly's voice rang out, high and filled with eagerness.

Although Emily stood in the bedroom, the door was open, and she pictured the scene unfolding in the hallway. Johnny would be there, tending to May's every need – taking her shawl and gloves, offering to brush the dust from the bottom of her long skirt. Frank would be following suit with Effie, and perhaps wondering if he too should be making a proposal of marriage. Then – and as if the hallway wasn't full enough with her brothers and their fancy pieces – Molly was crowding in upon them. The girl would be looking at May and Effie's dresses, commenting on their hairstyles and of course fussing over the ring.

"She's forgotten she has a sister of her own," Emily muttered and scowled at herself in the mirror. She had been twisting her hair and pinning it in place for the past half hour, knowing that her face might be a little thin and her nose pointing upwards a little too much for her liking, but her hair shone like burnished copper and the natural waves were envied by women who suffered from their hair falling straight after hours of being twisted in rags.

The voices downstairs moved from the hallway to the parlour and Emily could hear her mother now. She pictured Cora holding the teapot, placing it in the centre of the table, then taking her turn to admire the ring.

I'd better go down and help, otherwise Ma will be looking all disappointed. Emily glanced at herself in the mirror, attempted to turn her grimace into a smile, and stepped out of the bedroom. Once in the hall, she called out a brief greeting and went straight to the kitchen knowing there would be plates of sandwiches, fruit cake and shortbread to carry through.

Although the sun still beat down upon Ashford, the evenings were drawing in and Emily dreaded the thought of colder days ahead. The ice-cream cart, having enjoyed a roaring trade just a week before, was no longer, but would reappear soon in a new guise as a stall selling roasted chestnuts. In the households, men assessed their supplies of wood and coal, and began to replenish their stocks. In the gardens, apples and pears were gathered and stored on boards in sheds, preserving the fruits for the months to come. Women, still wearing thin dresses and light shawls, checked the stocks of winter vests and chemises, socks and stockings.

Serving the bread and sweet treats from behind the bakery counter, Emily reflected on the weeks and months ahead of her. *They don't want me at home anymore. Ma is saddened that I am not married yet.*

Johnny and Frank are embarrassed by me, and even Molly has no time for me now that May is fussing over her. I am a disappointment to the whole family. Emily remembered the scene in the street when Frederick Barnes had allowed her to ride on his bicycle. Shame coloured her cheeks. *If only I could start again, in a place where no one knows me.*

Customers came and went. Emily wrapped bread, took their coins and smiled politely. She remembered none of the conversation shared, or if the loaf wrapped was a wholemeal or fruit bread. A plan was germinating – the seed of an idea. Not so long ago, Emily had looked at the railway station and rashly considered running away. Now she knew there was one destination where she would be made welcome.

Once the decision was firmly planted in her mind, Emily was determined to act upon it straight away. It would be expected that she should give one week's notice to leave her employment. *But then if Ma were to come in – not if, because she is here most days – then she'll know about it in a flash and be asking all sorts of questions. If I'm going to go, then it must be now, and it won't do me no harm because James will vouch for my good name, and I won't need no letter of recommendation. And now I've decided I don't even want to work till the end of the week.* Emily considered the precious packet of coins she would be given in two days' time in return for a full week of work. She needed that money and had worked four days of the week. It was quiet at the end of the day, with most of the bread sold and just the shelves to wipe clean before going home. A young waitress came in and bought a loaf. Emily left the cash register open after giving the change. A moment later she slipped her hand into the drawer and removed two florins, three shillings and some pennies – a generous allowance for working part of the week.

Once I'm settled, then Ma can pack up my things and send them on. The bag stashed in the garden shed the evening before held a pitiful amount of Emily's belongings. The basket now placed on the kitchen table held a pair of smart shoes, and her purse, covered by two shawls. In the semi-darkness, she cut a thick slice of bread and a chunk of cheese, then wrapped them in greaseproof paper. They were joined by an apple and some fruit cake. She stuffed them under the shawls. Cold tea lingered in the pot – Emily grimaced as she took a few mouthfuls. Her heart was pounding, and she felt sick. *Time for an adventure. No need to get all wound up about it. I'll be all right once I'm out of the house and away from this lot.*

Picking up the basket, Emily thought of her mother and the times they had shared. Fragments of confused memories came to her: of being on a lifeboat, three boys with red hair, stones underfoot in all directions, and visits to a grave on a lonely hillside. *I'm not leaving forever. I'll get settled and then I can write and tell them how well I am doing. I'll tell them about my new job and the rooms I've found to live in. Then I can get on the train on a Sunday and go to visit them…*

Emily left through the scullery and then the back gate. With the carpet bag in her hand, and the basket in the crook of her arm, she scurried through the streets with her head down, giving no passing greeting to those who shared the pavements with her.

Once at the railway station, Emily considered the early hour. Appreciating that James Roberts would keep late nights in his role as landlord, it seemed wrong to appear early in the morning. In her mind's eye, she would arrive late morning, not while he was still in his nightshirt. Casting her eyes around the decorative iron supports, the wide canopies and along the tracks to the engine sheds, she realised that it was possible to stay right here in Ashford for a while and no one would take any notice of a young woman with a travelling bag. The cold tea had left a bitter aftertaste in her mouth – when the café opened, she would welcome a warm drink.

A couple of hours passed. Emily found herself absorbed by the comings and goings within the station. The rhythm of trains, porters and passengers soothed her troubled thoughts. Breathing deeply, she didn't mind the tang of smoke, instead relishing anything which filled her senses with something out of the ordinary. Eventually a great clanking engine drew to a halt at the platform, Emily checked with a porter that the train was bound for Lydd, then hauled herself and her baggage into a carriage. Seated on the bench, she found herself to be eager for the journey and her arrival in Lydd.

It had been many years since Emily had last travelled on this line and once the train had left Ashford she turned and pressed her face on the grimy windows, keen to spot familiar landmarks. After a steady decline, the train burst free from the woodland and clattered across open fields intersected with winding drainage ditches. Before long, the red brick station at Appledore could be seen and here Emily changed to a branch-line train.

Now in one of only two coaches pulled by a sturdy tank engine, the chuff of smoke from the chimney gave a steady pulse to Emily's journey. Through the murky glass she watched fields shorn of their crops, and pasture with sturdy Romney Marsh sheep, slip by. There was a golden stone arch and ruined walls of a bygone religious monument, then the town of Lydd could be seen in the distance, with its slender church tower, and the sails of two windmills rising above slate and tile rooftops.

Memories flooded back as Emily stood to drag her bag off the luggage rack before the engine had ground to a halt in the station. As a porter opened the door, the guard was announcing, "Lydd. Lydd. All alight for Lydd. Next stop New Romney." Then Emily and her belongings had spilled out onto the platform, and she stood for a moment to familiarise herself and admire the pretty brick building, with its pointed canopy and the tubs of autumnal chrysanthemums in yellow and orange.

A feeling of belonging swept over her, which was odd as for most of Emily's life Lydd had simply been a place to pass through. Now it was her destination and the thought of making a home here sent a ripple of excitement through her. "Ta very much!" She flashed a grin at the ticket collector and passed through the gateway in the picket fence. Taking no notice of the weighty bag or cumbersome basket, she straightened her back, pointed her chin upwards and walked away from the station.

Rather than follow the main road to the town, Emily chose a side street and a path through the cemetery. *As long as I can see the church then I can't go wrong.* The tower of All Saints was ahead, and she was confident it would guide her.

"There, Ma. I hope I've done you proud." Ed stood back to study his handiwork. The oak cross was bedded in at the head of his mother's grave. It was peaceful in the cemetery and Ed was not inclined to leave. Instead, he leaned against the gnarled trunk of an elm tree.

Ed's thoughts drifted from memories of his mother to wondering what hardships the coming winter would bring. A young woman entered the far end of the cemetery, and he watched her progress along the central path. Her frame was slender, back straight, and head held high – this was not someone bowed by the harsh winds that pummelled the coast. In one hand there was a carpet bag, and in the other a basket. Ed recalled hearing the usual clatter of an engine arriving not long before and realised this newcomer must have arrived by train. A breeze whipped through the cemetery, and the woman's headscarf slipped back to reveal auburn curls tumbling about on top of her head. She dropped the bag, shoved the scarf in her basket and flashed a quick smile towards Ed. In return, he could only stare at this woman in awe.

Chapter Nine

I might not be posh, but I still have my dignity and won't be starting my new life in Lydd by going into public bars. Emily stood before the Dolphin Hotel – a two-storey rendered building, dating back to the previous century. It fronted a short side road and was the last building before the Rype – an area of open land with short grass, a handful of stunted pines and sturdy holm oaks. *The Dolphin Hotel – I didn't know that – I thought it was just a public house. Well, that makes it a bit more respectable, but I won't go knocking at the front door.* To the left of the hotel, the neighbouring houses were adjoining, but to the right there was a yard and stabling for horses, as well as further outhouses. *There will be a kitchen door around here somewhere.* Emily set off to discover the rear of the property.

On rounding the corner of the building, Emily came face to face with a scrawny woman enthusiastically brushing the back step. She paused on seeing Emily approach and busied herself with pinning stray strands of thick dark hair back into her bun.

"Hello, I've come to see Mr Roberts," Emily announced.

"It's a bit early to be checking-in if you're after a room," the woman replied, eyeing the carpet bag. "And this is the kitchen door."

"I can't go knocking at the bar door!" Emily declared. "And I'm not after a room – at least I didn't think I was. I'm just here to see Mr Roberts, like I said."

"You'd better come in." The broom was left propped in the doorway, then Emily was led through the kitchen and into a bar area.

It was dark in the recesses, but sash windows were pulled open, giving a contrasting blast of sunlight across the room. The air still smelt sour with the remains of the previous evening's tobacco smoke, and dried beer spills showed on the floorboards. At first there was no sign of James, but someone could be heard rummaging about behind the wooden counter.

"There's a woman here to see you, Mr Roberts," the housekeeper said. Then, as an afterthought, she turned back to Emily and asked, "What's your name, Miss?"

"Emily Parkins," Emily responded.

At this, James Roberts instantly appeared. Gone was the air of the well-groomed gentleman who strode about the streets of Ashford and frequented the bars when on business in the town. Here was the landlord of the Dolphin, swathed in a coarse apron, preparing the bar area before opening time. Clearly distracted, he barked, "Where's the potman, Hattie? I want this floor cleaned." Then a frown flitted across his handsome face, swiftly replaced with a smile. "Bless my soul! It's Emily!"

"She's come to see you," Hattie replied, unnecessarily. "And I'll give Alf a shout. He's fetching the coal in."

"Bring us some tea, will you?" James was untying his apron to reveal a shirt and waistcoat, both well-fitting. "You don't mind sitting here, do you?" he asked Emily. "We open at noon." He led her to a dark oak table and pulled out a Windsor chair.

Emily was still taking in the details of the room: exposed ceiling beams; elaborate mirrors behind the bar, reflecting an array of bottles and glasses; a hint of furniture polish not quite masking the smell of stale tobacco smoke; on the walls, a variety of paintings – dark and, as yet, not revealing their stories to her. "You said I could come," Emily told him, "and it seemed like a good idea. No point in spending all my time behind that bakery counter when there are other places in the world to see."

"Of course! You are more than welcome!" James looked towards the kitchen door, and called out, "Come on Hattie, my throat is parched!" Turning back to Emily, he grinned, "You're special to me – you and your ma – I remember finding the pair of you living with my parents at the British Inn. What a time of it you had been through, but I could see you'd be all right. Now, did you tell anyone where you were coming? Am I going to have Jacob coming here and checking that I'm treating you right?" He leaned over and gave her arm a squeeze.

"No, I just came," Emily replied. "They're all so busy fussing over May and talking about Johnny's wedding that they probably won't notice I've gone for a day or two."

"When you're settled, you can send them a letter," James suggested. "There's no rush, is there?"

Hattie bustled in at that moment and placed the tea tray on the table. James and Emily gave their thanks. As she left, a short, stocky man shuffled into the bar area. He dragged a broom behind him.

"That's Alf," James informed her. "Don't worry about him. He won't listen to us, and if he does, he won't remember a thing." Alf turned and ran his eyes over them. His gaze lingered on the teapot. "You can have a cuppa when you're done in here," James told him. "Now mind you don't go brushing dust over my young lady friend. She's from Ashford and has been brought up decent."

Young lady! Well, I never did! How nice to be treated with a bit of respect – I've done the right thing coming here. Emily gave the tea a stir and poured milk into the china cups.

"So, it's Johnny's turn to get married, and I bet his young woman isn't a patch on you! I've never seen someone with such beautiful hair – apart from your ma, of course. You've got spirit too – I like that!"

Emily, unused to such praise, felt a glow of contentment within her. She was safe here with Reuben and Ada's son, and it seemed as if he was happy to help her out. "Yes, he's getting married, and they all seem to like her," she admitted.

"That's good for Johnny, but someone has to look after you," James declared, further adding to Emily's feeling of satisfaction. "I'm going to be opening up in ten minutes, so I'll take you back to Hattie, and she can show you up to your room. Then perhaps you can go for a walk – get to know the town a bit better. You'll find it small after being in Ashford, but I like it well enough."

"My room?" Emily's voice was high, and she felt her heartbeat quicken. "I wasn't expecting… I didn't think. I've got some money… for rooms…"

"There's no need to worry about that."

"But it's not decent, is it?" Emily felt the heat begin to rise. "I mean for me to be staying here."

James grinned and merely shrugged his shoulders as he stood up. "This is a hotel, Emily. The Dolphin *Hotel* – did you see the sign? I've got four rooms for paying guests, and it's rare they are all filled, so no reason you can't have one, is there? Hattie has her room up in the attic, and Alf has his space above the stables. It's all respectable – I can promise you."

Gazing around the bar, Emily could see that it was indeed a well-run establishment. Now Alf had swept and mopped the floor everything appeared orderly. The paper on the walls was freshly applied, although, like the ceiling, it had already taken on the amber hue of tobacco smoke. The brass pumps behind the bar gleamed and the rosewood countertop shone. Emily considered James Roberts: *a proper gent, always keeping himself smart. He wants to treat me nice and take care of me, but how can I afford to stay in a hotel?*

"I can't afford a hotel room. It's good of you, and perhaps for tonight, but I'll have to look for a place somewhere," she voiced her fears.

James let out a guffaw as he stood and began to gather the teacups. "It won't be like that. I'm not suggesting you have a room with Hattie waiting on you, doing your laundry and cooking all your meals. No – it will be like living at home. You pay me a few shillings a week by way of rent, but it's up to you to clean it and change the bedding and empty the chamber pot. There's a hot meal in the back room at two o'clock every day when the bar has closed. You can eat with us, or if that doesn't suit, Harriet can keep it warm. You can do some chores about the place to help pay your way as well. How does that sound?" He began to walk to the kitchen.

Through the front window, they could see customers gathering. Emily knew she had to decide quickly, or James would be busy tending the bar for the next couple of hours. "Ta. Ta very much!" she replied.

In the kitchen, Hattie was peeling potatoes, her hair now covered by a mobcap. "Leave that for a moment," James ordered. "Emily will be staying here with us, and I need you to show her to a room – one at the front. She's a family friend and isn't expecting you to go running around after her. In fact, she'll be helping you out a bit, so that should put a smile on your face!"

Then he was gone, and Emily was left alone with the housekeeper. "Sorry to inconvenience you," she said. There was a bowl of potatoes to be peeled, as well as cabbage to prepare. On the large central table sat a substantial pie. *Hattie must be making a meal for several people,* Emily realised. *I wonder who else lives or works here.* No sooner had the thought crossed her mind than a young whippet of a man shot through the back door, removing his coat as he progressed. He called out some form of unrecognisable greeting while catapulting into the inner hall.

"That's John," Hattie informed her. "He works in the bar, and his sister helps with the washing-up." She nodded towards the scullery and a capacious sink, then recalled Emily's earlier words, "You're not troubling me, Miss. You look as if you have some sense in your head, and I won't object to a helping hand around here."

"I need to find a job," Emily told her. "And when I know my hours, you can tell me how I can help."

"You're staying for a while then?"

"Yes!" Emily replied, and she couldn't help feeling excited about the prospect. The welcome at the Dolphin Hotel had been encouraging.

Minutes later, Emily was standing at the threshold of the room which was to be hers. It was a decent size – square, with an attractive cast iron fireplace. A closet and a chest of drawers stood against one wall, while a washstand topped with a bowl and ewer was in the corner. A chair, placed under the window, offered a spot to overlook the street below. The bed was unmade, but Hattie had pointed out the laundry cupboard on the landing. "Help yourself," she had instructed. "There's sheets and blankets, and if we need kitchen towels, you'll find them there too."

Hattie left and Emily immediately moved to the window. "I've done all right here," she whispered to herself. "I could sit all day watching people coming and going." Her room was at the front of the hotel and if she leaned forward, to the right she could see the hotchpot of shops, offices, public houses and homes making up the centre of the town. Some were tall and substantial – such as the Town Hall and George Hotel facing the High Street. Others were low cottages – perhaps dating back to medieval or Tudor times, and, in the mix, short terraces of brick-built homes. It was fascinating to be looking at the backs of some of the properties, knowing when she examined them further there would be so much to be revealed about their history.

Emily levered the sash window open and craned her neck but couldn't quite see the church. Below her, customers loitered at the entrance to the Dolphin. Suddenly conscious of being seen, she retreated but left the window ajar. New sounds began to drift through on the air – that of youngsters calling out to one another – and, curious, Emily returned to the window, this time looking to the left while refraining from leaning out. Small groups of children were tearing across the Rype. The school was out of sight, but she recalled an attractive stone building with tall, mullioned windows. *It must be them going home for dinner. James said that we eat at two o'clock when the pub closes, so I'd best go and see if Hattie needs a hand, and if not, I'll go and look in the shop windows to see if there's any cards saying that there's work going.* She looked at the basket and carpet bag abandoned by the bed. *No rush to unpack these.*

Stepping onto the landing, Emily could hear the hum of voices in the bar and saloon below, but upstairs there was a feeling of serenity. She studied all the panelled doors and speculated about the guests who would stay for a few nights in the numbered rooms, and what lay behind those with no numbers. There was a further staircase – Emily took a few steps towards it. *This must lead up to Hattie's room in the attic. I wonder if there's anyone else living in?* A creak of a door caused her to start and then smile to see a tabby cat padding towards her. "Hello," she said. "You must live here too…" Quizzical as to what lay beyond the part-open door, she couldn't resist peeping into the room, so tiptoed towards it. To her surprise there was a lofty space before her, set out with a table to one end as well as a long central table with chairs lining each side. *Oh! Some kind of meeting place… and there's someone there!* Emily retreated, creeping away to the head of the stairs. The figure of an elderly man bending over some paperwork had startled her. *Well, I be! There's all sorts of folk here, and I suppose I'll learn who they all are in a day or two.*

Back in the kitchen, Hattie was sitting at the table with her feet propped up on a stool and some darning on her lap. "There you are!" she said when Emily appeared at the doorway. "Friend of Mr Roberts, are you?" Her eyes narrowed and, although the older woman's manner was in no way unfriendly, it was clear she was surprised by the arrival of a newcomer in their midst.

"When I was a girl – not much more than a baby really – we lived with his parents, me and Ma," Emily began to explain. "It was when they ran the British Inn.

Then we moved to Ashford, and a few years later they moved too – they're like grandparents to me."

"You were at Dungeness then!" Hattie exclaimed. "And you seeming like such a smart young thing. You look like you've lived in the big town all your life!"

"I have really," Emily admitted. "We weren't at the beerhouse for long."

"And now you're here in Lydd," Hattie stated.

"Now I'm in Lydd." Emily was not going to give away her reasons for being there. "I fancied a change and I like it here – at least I think I will."

"You're going to be looking for work, you said?"

"I need to find something straight away," Emily admitted. She glanced towards the back door, hoping to take a walk before dinner time. "I'm going to go out looking to see if there's any cards in windows, if there's nothing you need a hand with…?"

"No, you go," Hattie gave her approval. "But I'd be grateful for a hand with washing up after dinner. That Alf is a clumsy oaf, and he can be put to better use doing jobs for Mr Roberts. Young Sarah will be here by then and she usually does it, but I want her to do some extra cleaning today."

"I'll be glad to help you." Emily gave a big smile. "Ta for making me welcome. Ta very much!" She left by the kitchen door, rounded the corner of the building and stood, allowing her gaze to roam across the green to her left, then towards the town. Once more, a feeling of wellbeing swept through her and she turned towards the square named Wheeler's Green, eager to see what was on offer for a young woman seeking employment.

Ed stood poised, his hand on the door of the New Inn, when a movement further along the road startled him. There she was – the young woman who had caught his attention earlier. *She's lovely!* The heat of the summer had passed but the stranger still wore a light dress of pale grey with a dainty floral pattern. The coat she had been wearing earlier was now replaced with a feminine shawl. *Where has she left her belongings – her bag and coat?* Now all she carried was a handbag.

While Ed stood transfixed by her slender figure and mass of auburn waves, the woman also paused – as if taking in the scene for the first time. For a moment, they both stood – he absorbed with her, and she barely aware of him standing there. Then she hurried away along the street. He willed her to look in his direction – wanting to hear her voice as she offered a 'good afternoon', but she seemed intent on whatever was ahead of her that day, not inclined to glance at a ragged fisherman.

Stepping back from the doorway, Ed Brooks decided to drink in the Dolphin instead.

Chapter Ten

With so much to view, Emily lingered at the corner of Wheeler's Green to absorb the scene. It wasn't so much of a town square as a triangle with a variety of shops and cottages. Several of them clearly dated back several centuries, and they stood at all angles, some up against the pavement and others with a small patch of land in front. There was a rural feel about this setting – none of the buildings could compare with the grandeur of the tall, elegant buildings fronting the High Street and Bank Street in Ashford, but it seemed as if Lydd boasted a good selection of shops and this was all before the main road had been reached.

In the centre of this area there was a piece of fenced land, bare of grass and dusty with dry earth. Not worthy of the name 'green' it was perhaps an area to pen animals. Emily glanced towards nearby stables and considered the use of this patch, but in this busy place she was soon distracted.

Loud chatter from a doorway on a side street caused her to turn her attention to the butcher's shop, where rows of pheasants and rabbits hung from a pole below the upstairs windows, and larger carcasses were lined up beneath. *Now there's a job I wouldn't want – having to hang up all that meat!* Emily grinned. She already felt safe in the knowledge that James Roberts would keep a careful eye on her and wouldn't allow her to take on any unsuitable work. *I wonder if that's where Hattie buys the meat?*

A woman with a pram and cumbersome basket bustled by, causing Emily to step aside. *Time I stopped dawdling.* Her attention turned to a show of material in a shop window. *Now this looks like a nice place. I wouldn't be sorry to see a card asking for an assistant.* She scanned the front of Hutchings General Store, awed by the large windows, clean paintwork and impressive displays, but saw no vacancies advertised. *No harm in asking but I'll have a proper look around first.*

From Wheeler's Green, Emily found herself at the end of the High Street, which was again fronted by buildings of all eras and sizes, most of them butting up against one another. All Saints Church was overlooking them all, its tower plain but dignified. Nestled by the churchyard gates sat the local post office, with its bow front windows. For the first time Emily considered her family and felt a brush of remorse. She scowled. *I can send them a letter in a week or so when I'm settled. They'll hardly notice that I'm gone, apart from when there's ironing to be done!* The church clock struck the half-hour. *Half-past twelve already and I'm still dawdling!* She quickened her pace, putting her back to the church and setting off along the street.

Glancing in windows as she progressed, Emily was again admiring of the selection of small shops. At the bank – Curteis, Pomfret & Co – she recalled a small leather-bound bank book snug in the bottom of her carpet bag. Cora had been given a charitable donation of five pounds when her husband, Emily's father, died. Many years later, two pounds of the money had been put in an account in her name. *I'll never go short all the time I have that book, and there's a branch of the bank nearby.*

Two buildings on the High Street stood out as being taller and grander than the others. The writing displayed high with the dormer windows on an ornate section of rendered wall revealed the function of the first building: George Hotel. The second showed a crest and flag, leading Emily to conclude this was the centre of the town's business and most likely the town or guild hall.

Before long, there were more houses than shops. Interested in the architecture, Emily slowed her pace, marvelling at the details of the windows and doors, weathered stone and peg tile roofs. On reaching a low wall, she spied a large house set back from the road. Its brickwork and tiles were a mellow orange, chimneys stood tall, and it seemed to ramble this way and that, having been added to over the centuries. There was a gardener tending the lawn and someone cleaning the casement windows. "Vine House," Emily read. "And very nice too. But I think I'd fancy a modern home – not that I'd be complaining if a gent came along and offered me somewhere to live like this!" She turned to study the house opposite, admiring the stretch of orderly sash windows, but frustrated by the high brick walls concealing any view of the gardens. "There's some nice houses here, and perhaps I could be a housekeeper or help with the children. But I think a shop would suit better."

Beyond these properties the homes crowded the road less. Emily spotted cottages and short terraces, but it was time to turn back. Retracing her path, and still absorbed with the details, she strolled along. At times the side roads were tempting, but she remained in the High Street, conscious of the dinner hour approaching. On passing the George Hotel, her attention was drawn to a card in the window:

'Respectable, hard-working woman required for general duties.
Uniform and meals supplied.
Enquire within.'

Emily looked down at her neat dress and polished boots. Her hair needed attention, no doubt, and she ran her fingers across it, pressing the grips in place. Then she peered through the part-glazed front door and pressed on it, stepping into an entrance hall with a reception area and staircase rising to the first floor. Aware of a small crowd gathered in the nearby bar, Emily rang a brass bell and waited by the counter.

A woman appeared from a doorway, brushing down her immaculate apron as she walked. "How can I help you?" Her tone was pleasant as she slipped behind the reception desk. A bunch of keys hanging below her hip swung about and settled.

Emily, conscious of her tangle of waves and admiring the woman's glossy coils of blonde hair, replied, "I saw your card in the window and came to enquire about the work." *Enquire! I do sound posh and I'll have to be if I'm to work in a hotel.* "I'm Miss Emily Parkins, just arrived from Ashford."

"Pleased to meet you. I am Mrs Tatin. My husband owns the hotel. Are you experienced in hotel work?"

"I'm not." Emily felt her spirits slump. "I've been working in a bakery – serving the customers, keeping the counter area in good order, and making sure the delivery boys have the right orders."

"You're used to dealing with people then, and that's important," Mrs Tatin observed.

"I am!" Emily felt encouraged, and continued, "And I'm used to helping out at home. There's three boys older than me, so I have to do the ironing in the evenings after washday. There's always jobs to do around the home, isn't there?"

Mrs Tatin smiled and nodded her agreement. "You are a hard worker – I can see that. Tell me, Miss Parkins, have your family moved to Lydd?"

"No. Just me!" *Oh Lord, here we go… she's going to start asking all sorts of questions…* "I am staying with Mr James Roberts," she informed the older woman. "He is a… well, like an uncle to me. I have a room at the Dolphin Hotel, but I'm not there to work – I need to find a job and pay my way."

"I am looking for a general help – someone who can help in different areas as necessary…" Mrs Tatin proceeded to describe Emily's day if she were to be offered the position. It would start with cleaning the guest bedrooms and changing the linen as needed, as well as keeping the water-closets and upstairs areas clean and tidy. For the rest of the day, she would help when required with laundry, ironing, washing up or cleaning. "We have maids for all these tasks," Mrs Tatin explained, "But their afternoons off vary, or there may be a reason for extra help in a particular area." She studied Emily for a moment, then continued. "You would have a uniform and a selection of aprons, depending on the task. And how would you feel about greeting hotel guests on reception? You could wear your own day dress for that."

"Oh!" Emily's eyes widened, as she imagined herself standing behind the counter with the guest book before her and greeting people who may have travelled some distance to stay in this hotel. "I would like that very much, Mrs Tatin. I have neat handwriting and enjoy meeting people. You wouldn't regret it!" *I'll have to mind how I speak though – I don't want her thinking I'm too common.*

"Let me show you the guest lounge and dining area, and a couple of the bedrooms." Mrs Tatin glided from behind the reception and beckoned Emily to follow.

Twenty minutes later and they were descending the stairs on their way to the entrance hall. It had been agreed Emily would return to the hotel on the following morning to hear if she had been successful. "Please bring your character references with you," Mrs Tatin smiled as she gave her parting words.

"Yes, of course!" Emily managed to keep the encouraging expression on her face until her back was turned. *My 'character' – I didn't think. How stupid to have never even thought about it. I won't get a job without a 'character'.* However, it was never long before Emily was coming up with one scheme or another and she had no intention of being defeated by the small issue of a few lines on a piece of paper. *I'll have a chat with Mr James, and he is bound to come up with a plan!*

The afternoon meal at the Dolphin was an informal affair. Emily was introduced properly to Alf-the-potman, then to brother and sister, John and Sarah, who worked at the bar and the scullery sink respectively. The sixth place at the table remained empty until after the pie had been served, and then they were alerted to light footsteps on the staircase. She recognised the balding newcomer as the gentleman spotted in the upstairs room earlier that day. He was introduced as Mr Blackmore, but no clue offered as to his role within the hotel. *I'll find out soon enough. I wonder if he lives here or is he working for Mr James?*

The pie was superb, and Emily thanked Hattie before offering to tidy up.

"I'd appreciate that," the housekeeper replied. "If you could give Sarah a hand, I can take a stroll to the shops."

However eager to show she was keen to help when possible, Emily's mind was also on the likelihood of work at the George Hotel. "Mr Roberts…" She thought it best to address him in a formal manner while with his staff. "Can I have a word with you after I've helped out here?"

"I'll be in my private lounge," the landlord answered. "First door, straight ahead as you go up the stairs."

As the church bell chimed three o'clock, James was sitting at a writing bureau with a piece of headed paper in front of him. The script along the top stated 'Albert Joint Stock Bakery' yet had been copied at this very desk using a sheet of carbon paper, so as to produce the effect of being one of many sheets created in an office. He wrote without asking Emily for her input, and passed it to her, having completed the reference with an impressive swirl of a signature.

Emily read out loud: "To whom it may concern, Miss Emily Parkins has been in my employ since January 1889. Her responsibilities include serving customers, keeping the shop clean and preparing deliveries. Miss Parkins is punctual, tidy and trustworthy. Mr Robert Anderson – Master Baker and shopkeeper."

"What do you think?" James asked. "I imagine Mrs Tatin will be happy enough with that."

"It's very good," Emily agreed. "You've a neat hand, and whoever that Mr Anderson is, he seems happy enough with me!"

"And now for a personal letter of introduction!" James took a further piece of paper, this time embellished with the header 'Dolphin Hotel. Lydd. Proprietor Mr J. Roberts.' His writing took on a different style as he created the second reference. This time he read aloud while putting pen to paper, "I have been a friend of Emily Parkins' family for twenty years. I know Miss Parkins to have a friendly character, and to be both hard-working and trustworthy. Her family are held in high regard and have good morals, being regular church goers. Seen as part of my own family, Miss Parkins is residing at the Dolphin Hotel. I have no doubt she would work hard for any employer and be a valued member of staff." The completed paper was handed to Emily.

"Lord above! What lovely words you have to say about me, Mr James!" Emily gushed. "But twenty years – I only met you properly a couple of weeks ago."

"Oh no – it's not like that at all," James reassured her. "My parents think the world of you and your family, and even if I have hardly seen you over the years, it feels as if I have always known you. They speak of you so much! It is as if you are a favourite cousin. And see what firm friends we have become – there's not one untruth about it!"

After this speech, Emily felt quite overwhelmed by the trust shown in her by the landlord, and the welcome she had received in his home. Tears began to threaten when she thought of her lovely bedroom and the delicious dinner served by Hattie. James stood and put an arm around her shoulder. She allowed herself to lean into him for a moment, liking the musky smell of his waistcoat and the crisp cotton of his shirt.

"Ta very much," Emily managed to say, as she moved away.

“This is my private lounge,” James told her. “But, like I said, I see you as family and you can use it any time. No need to ask. I’m in the bar during the evenings anyway.”

“Ta,” Emily said again. She stood at the doorway. “I’m going to go and unpack now. Fancy leaving everything in my bag! Then I’ll see if Hattie needs a hand with anything.”

“Hattie has a doze in her room at this time,” James informed her. “You do as you wish! After all you could be a working woman again by tomorrow.”

“I hope so!” Emily flashed a grin as she left.

That evening, as Emily settled into her room at the Dolphin Hotel, she imagined how different her life would be now. Of those who would become her family, most were not related to one another and some didn’t even live in the hotel, yet they would come together during different times of the day and spend time alongside each other in different capacities.

The bar opened again at six o’clock in the evening, and supper was a disjointed affair at eight o’clock – with James, Alf-the-potman, and young John flitting between the oak table in the dining room and the bar areas. Sarah was still there, but she returned to the family home – a cottage on the Rype, she had said – after clearing away the supper dishes. It seemed her role within the hotel was more on the domestic side, rather than washing up the pewter tankards and glasses from the bar.

Then there was the elderly man who Emily had seen in the upstairs room when she first arrived. He spoke little yet seemed to command respect from the others. Was this due to his age, or did he have a senior role within the running of the hotel? Emily could not be sure if he lived there or not, as the gentleman had appeared at both mealtimes, but nothing further had been mentioned about him.

I'll learn in good time, she reflected, while climbing the stairs. *It's like my whole life has been shaken up – dinner at two o'clock in the afternoon and supper at eight – and all these new people. I'm not complaining though. Everyone is kind and I've got a lovely big room all to myself.* She crossed the landing and entered her bedroom. It felt a bit chilly after being downstairs with the fire burning, but far too early in the year to light the coal in her ornate cast-iron fireplace.

After setting her lamp on the bedside table, Emily placed her dress over the back of a chair and her corset on the seat. She changed into her nightdress and, as the church clock chimed ten, drew back the curtains to view the street scene. The sky was partly overcast, but the moon was full, giving a dramatic outline to the clouds and casting its magical light on uneven rooftops. A fox came from the direction of the Rype, and Emily watched him progress along the pavement. He jumped up and balanced on a wall, before finally dropping down into a garden.

From the bar beneath her, there was a steady murmur of voices, accompanied by the occasional shout or heckle filtering through. She could hear the scraping of chairs and imagined men standing at the bar, their ale slopping over the wooden surface and a haze of smoke wafting above their heads. From her vantage point, she saw someone leave the hotel and slope off down the street towards the town.

Letting the curtain drop, Emily turned towards the bed. Her foot nudged the carpet bag. *I'm letting my standards slip. Better put this away.* As she opened a trunk, Emily recalled seeing the bank in the town. *There's all sorts of people coming and going in a hotel. It's best I find somewhere to hide my bank book.*

Not only did this contain the two pounds compensation for her father's death, but Emily had added to it over the years and there was now three pounds saved. She placed the bag on the lid of the trunk and felt around inside the folds of material, aware it had been emptied earlier but she must have missed the small book.

Emily frowned and took her time to search for the slim leather clad book again. There was no sign of it. She recalled gathering her belongings in her shared bedroom with Molly. Squirrelling clothes and precious items away in case her sister should appear and start asking questions. At one point the bank book had been hastily pushed under her bedcovers when footsteps were heard on the stairs. *But I'm sure I took it out. I'm sure I packed it.* There was no choice but to abandon the search. *When I write home, I can ask them to send it,* were her last thoughts on the matter as she slipped between the crisp sheets and appreciated the luxury of the soft mattress.

The muted sounds from the bar continued, but soon they mingled with Emily's dreams. It had been a long day – hardly credible that it was the same one as when she had crept away from her family home at dawn and taken the train to Lydd. She stirred as last orders were called and voices in the street told of men leaving both the Dolphin and the nearby New Inn. "I'm going to like it here," she murmured in a half sleep, as the bolts were drawn on the front door.

As he donned his apron and started clearing up the last of the tankards, James Roberts smiled with some satisfaction at the thought of the attractive young woman sleeping in the room above.

The same full moon which bathed the streets of Lydd in its light, guiding the men home from the public houses, shone upon the remote coastal settlement on the Dungeness peninsula. Jake Brooks tumbled out of the Hope and Anchor, then began his wandering route home. Like a cat who checks on his territory, sniffing out the familiar places and leaving his scent, Jake lurched towards the embankment at the head of the beach. He stood, partly concealed by the two fishing boats, and surveyed his patch of the coast. The sea was rolling in at the lower reaches of the shingle bank, and he watched for a moment, swaying with it. Then, scanning the coast, his gaze settled on the shape of a bulky vessel. "Steamer," he muttered, with contempt in his voice. This distain meant nothing – there was no reason for it. Jake Brooks scorned and mocked everything other than his own meagre success.

A low light shone at the window of a coastguard's cottage. It disorientated Jake's alcohol-fuelled body as he staggered towards his home, and he stumbled over a clump of withered sea kale. "Bloody coastguards, poking their noses into honest people's business. They'll be sorry. I tell you, they'll be sorry." But no one was there to listen.

His wife was lucky that night – Jake fell asleep on the rug in front of the dying embers of the fire.

Chapter Eleven

"What are you going to do today?" Hattie asked, as they sat together over a companionable cup of tea. Breakfast had been just the two of them, with the housekeeper explaining that 'Alf just comes and takes a crust of bread or a bowl of porridge whenever he fancies it – but don't let him talk you into frying him a piece of bacon' and 'Mr Roberts stays in bed until gone eight o'clock because it's past midnight before he's given the bar a bit of a tidy and logged all the takings.'

"I have to go to see Mrs Tatin at the George Hotel this afternoon," Emily replied. "And before that, I want to have another look in the shop windows to see if there are any other vacancies. First, is there anything I can help you with?" But before Harriet could respond, Emily spoke again, voicing something she had been wondering about, "Are there any guests here? I mean paying guests in the hotel rooms?"

"There's only Mr Blackman – him who was here eating with us – and he comes regular. He is treated as a guest and I'll do him a breakfast in the dining room shortly, but Mr Roberts has him eating his main meals with us because he's a friend going back many years."

"Oh..." Emily was none the wiser about who Mr Blackman was or why he stayed so often. "Does his room need cleaning, or the bed making?" she asked.

"No, he's a very private person. We change the bedding and give it a clean when he leaves. Unless he has a fire and then he'll say what time suits him. And Alf does the chamber pot."

"Does Alf do all the guest's chamber pots?" Emily enquired.

"Just Mr Blackman's," Hattie responded. "You'll do your own, as you're living here."

"I don't need no one waiting on me!" Emily drained her tea. "Now how about I do this washing up, and you tell me if there's anything else I can do…"

An hour later, Emily decided to walk part-way around the Rype before exploring some more of the town. It was a strange, bleak patch of land – not at all like a village green with a cricket pitch and perhaps a stone memorial, or an ornate sign hanging from a post. This was more like an area of heath, with sparse, tough grass and thin soil. There were a few bent pine trees, and a dense holm oak. What seemed incredible to Emily – used to the ordered streets of Ashford – was the size of the Rype. "It would take me an hour to walk the whole of it," she surmised. "I'll start here, and go so far, then cut through the middle. After all, I need to spend my time looking for work, not strolling about for no good reason!" Then she laughed at herself for talking out loud, and set off to navigate the north-eastern end, the closest extremity to her viewpoint on the street corner by the Dolphin Hotel.

The day was bright, with clouds high in the sky, and a brisk breeze from the west. Emily strolled along, conscious of uneven paths underfoot, taking care while rounding the narrowest point and facing the great length before her. A distant smock mill marked the far end. "No time to go all that way," she murmured.

Ambling in no great hurry, Emily was pleased to exchange a greeting with those who passed by and to absorb the details of a farmhouse, terraced houses and finally the huge tithe barn – its thatched roof a great cape over broad shoulders and the walls barely peeping from beneath it.

Here she judged herself to be almost halfway along the length of the green, and so it was time to cross and proceed with the business of the day – seeking out work opportunities.

On leaving the Rype, Emily found herself once more in Wheeler's Green. It was mid-morning, and the square was busy with women buying their groceries, while delivery boys trundled carts about. A pair of horses clattered through, causing those who strayed from the pavement to jump out of their way. Emily avoided an old man with his shovel and pan picking up the horse droppings, choosing to explore Park Street which seemed to run behind the High Street. After passing some stables, she came across the rear of the George Hotel and pondered upon what was beyond the windows that were less regular in shape and size compared to the elegant frontage.

I wonder what Mrs Tatin will have to say when I go back with my references? It's a bit early now, but after I've had another look about, and a cup of tea with Hattie, then I'll return.

Park Street offered more shops, but no cards offering job vacancies. When she reached a smart coaching inn, Emily decided it was time to slip through to the High Street and head back towards the Dolphin. With her mind so full of what Lydd had to offer – the ancient buildings, numerous side streets still to be explored, the people to meet and shops in which to browse – Emily had thought little of her life and family back in Ashford. On spotting the post office, she felt a sharp pang of remorse. *It wasn't fair what I did – leaving without a word.* She thought of her lovely room in the Dolphin and the welcome offered by James and Hattie. *But I know Ma didn't think much of Mister James and I can't think why. She would have stopped me from coming here – I know it – so best I write when I'm nicely settled, and she won't have so much to grumble about.* With this resolved, Emily glanced across the churchyard – *I'll have a look there later and must ask Mister James about where the Methodist chapel is, or perhaps I'll go wherever he attends* – and she turned back towards Wheeler's Green, then the Dolphin.

Emily gave her best shoes a final polish, taking care to push the cloth beneath the small buttons, then she replaced the tin of shoe polishes, brushes and cloths on the scullery shelf. She ran upstairs to fetch her soft grey shawl and handbag, with the precious references inside, then returned to the kitchen. "How do I look?" she asked Hattie. "Will Mrs Tatin approve?"

"I'm sure she will," the older woman stood and studied Emily. "You look a picture." Then eyeing the lightweight dress, she said, "I hope you've got a winter outfit with you. We suffer from harsh winds here – there's nothing between us and the coast."

"I've got a thicker one in brown, and a plain work dress," Emily told her. "I couldn't carry any more. And my coat is a good one, but the shawl will do for today."

"And no doubt your family will be sending a parcel of your things?"

"Yes! It won't be any trouble for them, and then I'll have another winter costume, and I've got some pretty ones for next summer."

"You'll be staying permanently then?" Hattie gazed at Emily, her thoughts unreadable.

Emily, who hadn't thought much further than the next week or so, responded, "Yes. Yes, I think I will. If Mr Roberts wants the room or it's a bother to have me here, then I can always look for lodgings. I think I'll like it here in Lydd."

"I don't think Mr Roberts will object." Hattie turned away – the pans on the hotplates needed tending.

"You are presentable, Emily," Mrs Tatin surmised, looking up from the references, "and friendly. It seems as if you are willing to work hard, and I can tell you want the job. I am looking for someone who can learn several different roles, and I think you could do this." Emily listened, alert to the clues that she had been chosen for the job. Mrs Tatin had certainly seemed impressed with her character references. "How would you feel about working here on a week's trial and if it suits us both, then you will continue? The hours vary, but I expect you to start at eight o'clock in the morning and work until the bar closes at two. Then you will either continue here in the afternoon or return in the evening. We are open seven days a week, of course, and that means working Saturdays and sometimes on a Sunday too."

"I understand," Emily replied, "and I don't mind when I work, especially as I'll be doing all sorts of different jobs. A week's trial would suit me very nicely."

"Excellent! We have rooms for live-in staff," the older woman said, "but you would have to share."

"I'm nicely settled, thank you." Emily thought of her large room at the Dolphin, and how already she was beginning to feel as if she was part of one large family of characters who lived or worked there. She had shared a bedroom with Molly for many years and relished having her own now. "And you mentioned meals before, but if I finish at two o'clock, then I could go back to the Dolphin and eat there with my family – at least they feel like family!"

"Just let cook know your plans," Mrs Tatin appeared to be pleased with the arrangement. "Your time is your own for an hour at two o'clock, or for longer if you are working in the evening."

"I'll be in the hotel area, not the bar?" Emily suddenly felt anxious. It wasn't right for a young woman to be serving beer and spirits. *Or tucked away with ladies' unmentionables.* She shook the dark thoughts from her mind. *You're here to make a fresh start, Emily Parkins.*

"I would never ask a respectable young woman to serve in the bar," Mrs Tatin replied, making it clear she ran a decent establishment. "Now, are you happy to start tomorrow? Come at 8 o'clock and you can begin with the bedrooms. You and I will work together, so you can see just how I like everything to be done. "

"You and I?" Emily echoed, noting her employer's spotless dress and flawless hairstyle.

Mrs Tatin gave a smile. "You will find I work as hard as anyone else, Emily. I don't ask my staff to do anything I would not do myself. Now let us go up to the laundry room and find your uniform and aprons."

Emily had never seen such a space before: at the George Hotel, a small room was given over to racks of sheets, blankets and towels, all folded into perfect bundles. Then there were dresses and aprons and starched caps for the maids. Trousers, shirts and waistcoats for male staff. Mrs Tatin pulled out a plain black dress, allowing the material to fall so they could see if it was the right length and fit. She frowned. "You are quite tall. I will pick another, and you can choose between the two of them. The bedroom opposite is vacant at the moment – try the dresses on and be sure to show me each one. I'll select your aprons."

Before long Emily had her work dress and four aprons: two for dirty work and two for serving in the dining room. She was reminded to bring one of her own outfits to wear while working behind reception.

That evening in the interlude between supper and bedtime, Emily decided to write a letter home. She was about to spend her second night away from the family and could not deny, however hard she tried, that they would all be worried about her. At the top of the stairs she faltered, recalling James' kind offer that she may use his private sitting room. She would not sit at the desk but recalled a small gate leg table - the perfect place to write. Having collected her leather wallet of paper, pens and ink, she settled down.

Although brimming with stories of the past days, Emily stalled after writing the address and initial greeting. Should she start with an apology and explanation, or launch into her news, or begin in some other way, as yet undecided?

I'm sorry I went off without telling you... but I'm not sorry - not very. I've got some good news. A new job in a hotel – much better than the bakery. It's really posh and called the George - George Hotel. I'm not just a cleaner or a maid or someone washing up the pans – I do a bit of everything. Even working on the reception! Oh, that's no good. No good at all...

Emily's attention moved to the room which James Roberts used. A pale grey striped wallpaper adorned the walls – *very classy*. The fireplace, not unlike her own, was cast iron, and the mantelpiece sported a stylish carriage clock flanked by a couple of vases. The pictures on the walls were masculine – hunting and rural scenes, yet there were hints of a feminine influence in the form of cross-stitch samplers in decorative frames. Emily had never considered that James Roberts may have a female love interest in his life but draped casually over the back of the sofa and falling into a pool by the turned wooden leg, was a lacy shawl. From her seat at the small table, Emily pondered this finery and wondered who it belonged to. *Not that it's any of my business – he's a proper gent and deserves to have a nice lady friend.* She picked up the pen, refreshed her ink and set about writing the letter home – a suitable mixture of apologies, positive news about her new job, and details of her living arrangements.

I won't write too much this time, she decided. *There will be more to tell in a week or two and by then they will have got used to me being away from home*. As Emily reached the point of signing her name, the door opened and in came James, his initial surprise in finding her there soon replaced with pleasure that she had accepted his offer of using the room.

"How perfect to find you here!" he exclaimed "I didn't think you would."

"I'm writing a letter home," Emily told him, her pen poised over the final words in the letter.

"They'll be pleased to hear from you," he said. "But I wonder..."

Emily scanned the words she had written so carefully, ensuring each line was even, each loop and tail regular. They had seemed so right just a moment before. Now the sentences were ungainly, offering nothing to pacify her troubled parents.

"It's hard to know what to say," Emily admitted. "It seemed like the right idea to move away. Making a fresh start. But they won't be happy, will they? "

"If you were to wait... If you were to wait just a few days, there would be more to tell wouldn't there?" James walked to his bureau and began to search through a pile of paperwork, allowing Emily time to consider his words.

"There is nothing to tell yet, is there? I mean I am happy here but there's nothing to say to make them pleased for me. In a few days, I can tell them about my work," Emily realised. "It will be much better to wait."

"I think you are right, "James agreed. "If it was my mother, she would want to know all the news... All the details. Starting work – that's not enough, is it? Wait until you have more to tell them."

"Ta." Emily screwed up the paper and wiped the nib of the pen clean.

"I am sure they will be pleased for you when you have proper news to tell." James stood behind Emily and placed his hands on her shoulders. "Think of how proud they will be to hear about you working in the George Hotel – better than a bakery, isn't it?" He began to massage her shoulders gently. The rhythmic pressure was soothing – offering a comfort unknown to Emily since she was a young girl. Not that anybody had ever massaged her shoulders, but it reminded her of warm moments: sitting on Jacob's knee as he read her a story; her mother's hands cupping hers as they learned to beat cake mixture and knead dough together; wrapped up in a shawl after her bath by the fire – Emily and the boys all clean and scrubbed. When had those moments ended? It must have been as they all grew up, or was it when Molly was born? A warm fuzz of contentment filled her whole being and Emily couldn't bear to think of this moment ending.

"You know I'll look after you, don't you, Em?" James murmured. "You know you're welcome here. For as long as you like."

"Ta for helping me think about the letter," Emily whispered. "I didn't know how to get it right but talking to you makes everything clear."

James stopped massaging her shoulders and for a moment his hands remained there. Then he brushed his fingers tips up her slender neck to the wisps of hair behind her ears. Emily felt a shiver of pleasure - his touch was mesmerising. This was an affection unknown to her before. Warmth and wellbeing cosseted her.

"I think we will be very good friends, you and I," James stepped away, leaving her feeling lost and empty. "I had better get back to the bar. Sweet dreams, Emily." He left without taking the papers he had apparently been searching for in his desk.

Brandy loosened the tongue of the young coastguard, newly arrived from Ramsgate. He couldn't help but express his surprise at this lonely outpost – why was there a need to have four coastguards' cottages when there were more to the east at Dungeness, and to the west at Galloways, he asked? Stirring up this young man's interest in dark happenings and ghoulish matters, his colleagues baited him with stories of smuggling, shipwrecks and the shady characters who inhabited the small scattering of wooden shacks.

The landlord of the Hope and Anchor listened and smiled to hear the newcomer's declaration that there would be no illegal business going on during his watch. Having run the beerhouse for years, the older man was wise to the ways of Denge. There was nothing much to do here but fish from the beach or drink at the bar. The drink would win, and this young rut would soon be closing his eyes to anything unsavoury.

Jake Brooks, sitting alone with his tankard of strong ale, was not so tolerant. He resented their easy companionship and sneered at the youngster's ignorance.

I'll show him the coastguards hold no clout around here. Give him a shock to wipe the baby fluff off his chin.

No one noticed when Jake left the beerhouse. They didn't see him remove his fishing knife from his belt, creep up the stairs to the lookout and slash the throat of the coastguard who slumbered on his watch.

*

"What the hell is this?" Ed snapped, as he swung himself into the boat and stumbled across something lying along the hull. The soft light of dawn was creeping across the sky, not yet strong enough to reveal the contents of the vessel.

"Fish food," Jake replied with relish. "Now make yourself handy with the oar."

Ed's cousin stank of ale, and there was something else – an odd metallic odour about him. *How does he do it – stay up drinking all hours and drag himself out to the boat at dawn?* At only twenty-eight years, Ed was already weary of life. With his back to the open sea, he set to with the oar, dropping into a steady rhythm.

They were some distance from the coast, when the commotion began on shore, yet the shouts – the horror – could still be heard. Ed, by now fully aware of what, or who, his feet were resting on, glanced across at Jake. His expression was blank, all his attention being on the dip and pull of the oars. With little warning, vomit rose in Ed's throat, and he lurched towards the side of the boat, releasing last night's fish supper into the sea. There was no reaction from Jake – he merely paused for a moment before the outward journey was resumed.

By the time the sails were raised, Ed could only imagine the chaos erupting on the shore, in the lookout, and amongst the cottages. Not long after that, the body of the blameless coastguard was slung overboard. Ed watched him slip away, while Jake busied himself with the nets.

Chapter Twelve

News of the murder swept at speed across the shingle wastelands to the nearby town of Lydd. It was the talk of the men in the bars of the Dolphin and the George, and no doubt every other inn and beerhouse. Emily heard whisper of it while she cleaned the bedrooms, the long landing and elegant staircase under the guidance of Mrs Tatin. There were opinions aired and stories to be told once she was in the scullery, stationed before the deep sink to wash up under Cook's watchful eye. Later, when she donned a frilled apron and prepared to serve dinner to the hotel guests, not a word about the death was uttered within that well-proportioned room with its tall windows overlooking the street.

Having completed six hours' work, Emily walked back to the Dolphin, both invigorated and exhausted by the new experiences. Over a week had passed since she first arrived and there was much to learn. Whereas in the hotel rooms of the George, the subject of the unfortunate coastguard's death had been spoken of in hushed tones, it had been a different matter in the bar of the Dolphin. With James Roberts at the helm, every last detail had been picked apart and discussed. So, when Emily returned for dinner, the news was old and barely worth a mention at the table.

There were five to dine – Mr Blackmore had left the hotel for the time being, and Emily remained none the wiser as to what his role was during the time he spent at the Dolphin. However, it was clear that the elderly gentleman was treated with the utmost respect by everyone from James Roberts to Sarah the maid.

It was Alf, seemingly so absorbed with his cottage pie, who suddenly observed, “If the rain hadn’t lashed down so hard last night, they could have followed the trail of blood...”

“Trail of blood?” Emily blurted out.

“They never found the body, and they couldn’t see where it had gone.”

This put a whole new perspective on the scene. Whereas the story had been of a coastguard murdered in his lookout tower, for no known reason, now it seemed there was no body. Emily frowned and questioned those sharing the table with her, “Someone was murdered but there is no body?”

“That’s right,” James replied. “You’ve heard about it then?”

“I heard about it before I had cleaned the first bedroom,” Emily stated. “But I imagined…” She stopped there. *No need to say what I thought – when you hear of a murder you think there is a body. And if there isn’t, how do they know?* “If there was no blood – how did they know he had been… you know…”

“There was blood,” Alf was keen to elaborate. “All over the place: on his chair, the desk, down the stairs of the lookout, but that was it. There was a heck of a lot of rain last night.”

Emily considered the time when she had woken and listened to the water lashing against her windows. “Yes. Yes, I suppose there was.”

“I think that’s enough for the dinner table.” Hattie’s voice was sharp, and the words directed at Alf.

Nothing more was said of the unfortunate matter, at least not until the table had been cleared, and Emily was working alongside Sarah at the deep scullery sink. As she scoured the baked-on morsels of meat and potato from the dish, she finally voiced her thoughts, "It's bad enough to be dead, but fancy having no body to bury. It don't seem right."

Sarah glanced towards the open doorway into the kitchen, and to Harriet who was rummaging about in the dresser. "It's no surprise. What sort of people live down there with no soil under their feet, and not even a path to their front door? They don't know how to act civilised."

Emily had never been to Denge, but she had lived for a short time in the nearby settlement of Dungeness, and it was where her beloved Ada and Reuben came from. She didn't quite see what impact a lack of soil and no paths had on the characters who lived there. "It's fishermen, isn't it?"

"Just a couple of boats." Sarah was dismissive. "Nothing much. They've got nothing else to do, you see…"

"Nothing else to do?"

"Well, they probably got bored and that's why he was killed."

Pausing to digest this further information, Emily then reflected on her companion. At seventeen years of age, Sarah was thin, her cheekbones prominent and her eyes a pale blue. Her hair, pulled back into a bun, was almost colourless. *It's as if she's spent too long in the wash!* Emily thought, likening the girl to a faded rag. What makes her say all them things? *Ma would say she's heard them from her parents, and I reckon she would be right.*

"I'd like to go there and see it for myself," Emily suggested. "See what sort of place it is."

"Not while there's a murderer about?" Sarah questioned, her hands busy with the drying cloth.

"Oh! Perhaps not yet..." Emily hadn't thought that he – or she – might strike again. "I suppose they put him under the stones. The coastguard, I mean."

"They'll find him soon enough then." Sarah spoke with a confidence, belying her actual knowledge. "They're always shifting about – the stones are."

It was a Saturday and Emily had the rest of the day off. For the first time since arriving in Lydd, she was uncertain about how to occupy herself. Memories of Jane, her stalwart friend and confidant, came to mind. *What must she think of me going off and not a word in over a week*? A tight knot of remorse pressed itself against Emily's throat. *I could write to her – tell her not to say a word.* But already the opinion of James Roberts was vital to Emily, and she knew he would suggest she wait a little longer. *He knows best of course. When I write to Jane, I want to be able to tell her all about my work. It will be a good long letter when there is plenty to tell. Perhaps she will be able to come and visit – it's no distance.* She pictured the two of them in their best dresses parading up and down the High Street and stopping somewhere for afternoon tea – maybe in the George itself!

Well, I haven't got a friend to go walking with or out for tea, but I'm sure to get to know people soon. She left the scullery and went to her bedroom. Before long, her plain black dress – the uniform she wore while working – was discarded and Emily had slipped into the summer dress she had been wearing on her arrival in Lydd. She spent some time coiling and pinning her hair in front of the mirror, then picked up the lighter of her shawls and walked down the stairs, leaving by the back door as usual.

On a mission to buy some yarn for mending her winter shawl, Emily walked with purpose to the High

Street and to a small haberdashery shop she had noticed. She crossed the road, having to jump onto the pavement as a boy on a bicycle appeared at speed, precariously swerving around debris on the road and narrowly missing Emily. At this moment, as she regained her balance, the door of the barber's shop opened and a man stepped onto the narrow pavement, not seeming to consider there may be someone else in his path.

They both stopped and Emily took a step backwards, as they were close enough for her to smell the scent of the barber's oil on him. Appearing to be confused by her being there, he faltered and muttered, "Oh. Sorry. I didn't think..." His dark eyebrows were almost knotted together as he frowned at her.

"It don't matter. I landed here all of a rush because of that boy on his bicycle. He nearly hit me!" The words flew from her and as she spoke Emily noticed the frown left his face, leaving him to be almost handsome. His clothes were a little ragged, but clean. The newly groomed black hair and beard looked smart, without following the latest fashions. He was tall, she noticed – almost a head taller than her – and his frame was muscular, perhaps honed by labouring hard throughout his working day.

"Are you all right?" He still didn't smile, but there was a hint of concern on his face.

"Oh yes. It was just a bit unexpected." Emily flashed a grin and stepped aside, walking around him to continue on her way.

The smile remained on her face as she continued along the street before arriving at the small shop where she hoped to find a matching wool for the shawl closeted in her basket. At the doorway, she glanced back down the street. He was standing where she left him and gave a slight nod of acknowledgement.

Don't you go smiling at strange men, Emily Parkins. Cora's voice rang out in her daughter's mind. *I'm not smiling – just looking,* Emily replied to herself. *I know he ain't educated or wealthy, but I can't help it if I like the look of him. You never know what's going to happen next in Lydd – I wonder if I'll see him again.*

Encouraged by her encounter on the High Street with the tall, dark stranger, and happy to have secured some brown wool to match her winter shawl, Emily decided that she would venture into a tearoom and be bold enough to sit on her own. Opposite the Guild Hall there was a lovely old establishment and, to her delight, the table at the window was empty. "This looks respectable enough," she murmured, pushing on the door. Her entrance was announced by the tinkling of a bell, and Emily was soon seated at the table of her choice with a good view along the High Street.

"I'll have a pot of tea and a slice of ginger cake, please," she said to the young waitress.

Emily spent a pleasant half-hour watching the people of Lydd stroll by, or pass at greater speed on horseback, by cart or bicycle. As she drained her second teacup, the waitress hovered nearby and Emily asked, "Is there anything interesting I could look at in the town? I'm new here, you see. Staying at the Dolphin Hotel." There was an emphasis on the word hotel.

"Anything interesting?" the girl repeated. "There's the tithe barn on the Rype, where they sometimes hold dances – but there's not one now. And the Guild Hall has some paintings and fancy furnishings – but you can't just go in. Not without good reason." She paused and pondered on the matter. "Part of the church is Roman – but that's not interesting, is it? It's only a bit of old wall."

“I’d like to take a look,” Emily replied, much to the surprise of the waitress. “I wonder if I’ll be able to see the old part.”

“There’s bound to be someone who can show you,” the girl responded. “I’ll get your bill, shall I?”

As the clock struck four, Emily entered the churchyard and gazed up at the slender tower before her. At the base there were two doors, side-by-side, and above them a substantial decorative window. *This all looks too tall and straight to be Roman. Not that I know what Roman walls look like…* To the right, the churchyard was surrounded by old cottages, and to the left was the main road. The properties varied in style and size, tempting the explorer to head in that direction. No sooner had she set off on the narrow path trailing through the neatly mown grass, than a series of stone faces high up on the window surrounds caught her attention. *I wonder what these are all about – some of them look like real people and some look as if they are there to scare me.*

Each one was so different, and many were worn, requiring extra concentration. They were carved from a beige coloured stone, whereas the main body of the church was of ragstone, typical for the area. With each medieval window being adorned by two faces, and as high up as the eaves on a house, Emily had to tread carefully around the headstones and uneven ground, to study them as closely as possible. *You need sturdy boots for a task like this – but I wouldn’t have wanted to sit in that tearoom with boots on!*

After contemplating the last of the carvings, Emily stepped backwards and turned with the intention of joining the path. It was at that moment she realised she had not been alone while engrossed in her studies. Someone had been watching her.

"Oh, it's you!" Emily blushed – knowing her words were both rude and overly familiar. "I'm sorry – I mean... I didn't know there was anyone else here."

"I was wondering what you were looking at..." the man with the freshly barbered hair and beard began. His voice was deep and, as his words trailed away, it gave the impression he was unused to talking for the sake of making polite conversation.

"All them heads..." Emily raised her arm to indicate the row of carved faces decorating each window. As she did so, the stranger was unwittingly given the opportunity to admire her slim waist and the curve of her breasts under the light grey dress with its pattern of tiny white flowers.

After looking up and scanning the line of windows, the man answered, "I'd never noticed them before."

"Are you visiting then?" Emily had assumed he was local.

"I've been here all my life – never travelled further than Rye."

"I've been there! On a daytrip once." Emily smiled to think of the narrow streets and ancient buildings.

"Not here exactly," he embellished. "Not here in Lydd. I live at the coast, in a place called Denge."

"Fancy that!" Memories of the cottages at Dungeness came to mind. "I used to live near there, at Dungeness. That was when I was a small child."

"I'm surprised I haven't seen you before."

"I'm surprised you haven't seen these carvings before!" she countered.

He smiled and seemed to relax. "I wasn't looking."

"I was told that part of this church is Roman," Emily changed the subject a little, "but I don't suppose you know which bit."

"I do know," he replied with a touch of pride in his voice. Then he turned and walked back to the path, setting off with long strides, leaving Emily to catch up.

They swept around the eastern end of the church and along the north side, with Emily lagging behind. When he finally paused, they were almost back at the tower, but now faced a wall which differed slightly from the rest. "I'm Emily," she said, as she studied the stonework which, although the same shade of grey and rising to the full height of the adjoining walls, appeared more weathered and featured some blocked-in windows with a door.

"Ed," was his brief reply.

"Ta for showing me the Roman parts, Ed." Emily stepped forward to allow her fingers to trail along the line of a lost doorway. *I wonder what those Romans were doing here and what would they think if they were to come here today and see their wall still standing. There's nothing fancy about it. It looks a bit scruffy really next to the rest of the building, but as I know it's old, really old, that makes it interesting.*

When she turned to share some of her thoughts, Emily noticed that the stranger, Ed, had moved away and was now leaving the churchyard. She followed in his tracks, rather pleased about how the afternoon had unfolded.

That evening, as Emily sat repairing the hem on her shawl, James Roberts entered his sitting room. She started, expecting him to be busy in the bar, and let the material drop into her lap. He didn't go to the desk, as she thought he would have, but pulled up a chair and sat, their knees almost touching.

"You mustn't worry if you hear stories of police officers being in the bar," he said.

"Would I hear that?"

"It's a different life – not like living in Albert Road. All sorts of things happen when you live in a public house."

"Or a hotel?" Emily thought of her mother, still seeking her approval.

"Of course – a hotel!" he gave a brief grin. As if reading her mind, James continued, "Best let this fuss die down before you write home. No one in Ashford or off the Romney Marsh will have heard of Denge, so they'll say the murder was in Lydd, won't they? It makes sense."

"I don't want any fuss," Emily agreed. "No need for them to come running to save me. I wasn't going to write yet anyway, not until I'm settled in my work."

"That's for the best."

"Is that what you came to say – about me not writing home?" *How strange that he must be busy down there in the bar and suddenly he comes up to tell me that. Nice though – nice that he cares about protecting me.*

"No. We had already agreed about that, hadn't we? I came to say not to worry if you hear about officers in the bar. You know how Alf talks without thinking, or even John. They won't be in uniform – the law – they'll be trying to mix with the men, hoping to hear something."

"Hoping the drink will loosen their tongues?"

"That's it! And it will if there is anything to tell. The police will be doing their rounds of all the bars."

James stood up, pushing the chair back, and went to stand at the window. "It's lovely having you here, Em. I like talking to you, and I like the fact that you have settled in so quickly. It's only been a week, but it feels like you belong here at the Dolphin."

No one ever said that before – that they like talking to me. He came up here to share the news. No one ever shared news especially with me before. They just told everyone around the table or as we passed by. "Ta for telling me. It's interesting how the police are coming to mingle and are hoping to hear something."

"I'm glad you find it interesting. Not scary." James turned and his eyes met hers. "Come here, I want to show you something." Emily moved her mending aside and went to join him at the window. He had pulled the curtain back and they looked out onto Lydd at dusk. "That murder – it was miles away by the coast, not here in Lydd. It's not Lydd business."

Emily scanned the rooftops, the darkening shapes of the walls and trees. She gazed at the swathes of grey-blue clouds, and the soft yellow hue remaining after sunset. Cushioned by the protection given to her by James, she said, "I feel safe here."

He put his arm around her waist, his hand resting on the curve of her hip. "I'm glad you do."

She leaned into him a little. It was good to feel both appreciated and cared for. The moment lasted seconds before James was pulling at the curtains and heading towards the door, then Emily was once more moving the thread through the wool of her shawl, making it good for the cooler days ahead.

"Don't just stand there gawping. Help me get his trousers on!" Jake barked. "He ain't going to do it himself."

Ed stood at the doorway of his home, surprised to find his cousin there, but astounded to discover a wire man-shaped frame lying on the floor. Jake had clearly spent some time perfecting this figure from the broad shoulders to muscular thighs. It lay on Ed's bare floorboards as if on its front - legs and arms both slightly bent, almost appearing to be in a restful slumber. Jake was kneeling at the legs, tugging at the trousers.

This is why he was dressed in his long johns and shirt, Ed realised, thinking of the dead coastguard lying in the hull of the fishing boat.

"Why did you take his uniform off?" Ed asked. Although even as he spoke it was clear Jake had a plan to make some form of life-size model of the murdered man.

"Damn, I forgot the bandages," came Jakes answer. He yanked the trousers away from the ankles of the wire man, reached for a roll of bandage, then started wrapping it around the leg. "Do the other one." He nodded towards the small pile of bandages.

It took a while to dawn on Ed that the wire man had no hands or feet. "Don't need them getting in the way," came the reply when Ed queried the lack of body parts.

Within an hour, the frame, now bandaged from head to wrist and ankle, and dressed in the coastguard's uniform, was ready to be filled with concrete. "But we won't do it here," Jake told Ed.

"He'll get too heavy. We'll fill him out there, then add his hands and feet.

"Out where?" Ed asked.

"You'll find out soon enough. But now we best go to the pub, or they'll be wondering where we are. Got to act normal, haven't we?"

Ed shrugged and trailed after his cousin.

Chapter Thirteen

A month had passed since Emily first arrived in Lydd. Autumn had settled upon the town, taunting the townspeople with hints of the harsh days to come. First, rain fell for several days, not the welcome softness of summer waters, but sharp, bitter drops almost piercing the skin. Leaves, once a crisp golden brown, became sodden and slippery on the pavements and at the roadside. Then the clouds dispersed, and the last of the leaves tumbled in a glorious manner – caught up with the westerly squall, dancing as they were whipped along the streets.

Emily wondered what had possessed her to arrive in a summer outfit – it was now washed, pressed and folded for the following spring. She purchased a length of brown tweed and a pattern from a small drapery shop on the High Street. During the afternoons and evenings, when she was free of work, she sat cutting and stitching the fabric to create herself a winter dress. James lit the fire in his private sitting room and encouraged her to use the space, not minding about any stray threads falling upon the thick rug. In an afternoon, he was often there with her, reading or writing in companionable silence.

Fully intending to send a letter home, Emily knew shortly after it was received in Ashford a package with her dresses and other belongings would arrive. Until that time it would do no harm to make another dress. *I should keep myself busy. No need to have idle hands.*

Emily justified the stitching of the garment. She felt settled in her new life – more so than she could have imagined in such a short time – and it almost seemed that her family in Ashford were from another age, another time. *But I will write home. I'll do it soon. Like Mr James said, no point in writing until there is plenty to tell them. Plenty to make them proud of me.* Yet the making of the dress hinted at a different story – one of a young woman estranged from her family and unlikely to contact them in the near future.

In the Dolphin Hotel, Emily found herself accepted as part of a new family – albeit not one as she had known before. Hard-working Hattie was always kindly and dependable, seeming to appreciate any help on offer. John and Sarah were both friendly characters, she usually reserved, as if a little shy. They dashed here and there – he most often behind the bar, and she in the scullery, at the copper, or the washing lines in the yard. Sarah went home to their family after supper, whereas John worked until closing time before setting off for the cottage on the Rype. Emily knew little about them, and they did not pry into her life, which suited her very well. Alf bumbled about in his good-natured way, from bar to woodshed, to stables, often needing a prompt or hand with something. The only enigma was Mr Blackmore, once more staying as a guest in the hotel, and appearing to be absorbed in some business which Emily knew nothing about. Then there was James Roberts, who treated Emily as if she was a member of his family, continuing to be as welcoming and helpful as on the day she arrived.

The first time Emily heard of the body on the shingle, she and Sarah were toiling over pans at the scullery sink, while Hattie sat with her cup of tea after the Sunday roast.

"There's a body lying about at Denge," Sarah informed her, keeping her voice low. She nodded towards the housekeeper in the kitchen, indicating that this was just between the two of them.

"A body?" Emily echoed, a thrill of horror running through her. She glanced towards Hattie who seemed to be absorbed with flicking through sewing patterns. "A dead body?"

"Not exactly…"

"Not exactly dead?"

"It's not a real body. It looks like one and it's given people an awful shock," Sarah elaborated.

"A monument?" Emily frowned, thinking of her trip to London last summer.

"More like a warning!" Sarah whispered. "You see it's wearing the uniform of that dead coastguard."

"Oh Lord! But it's not him – it's not his real body?"

"No! Someone must have gone and given him a prod or something – anyhow, it's definitely not a real body. Not that I've seen it, of course," Sarah stopped scrubbing for a moment. "Not yet…"

Emily, taking her drying up cloth and running it around the rim of the roasting tin, repeated, "Not yet! Are you going… going to see it?" This sounded like an adventure, and one her parents would not approve of!

"Me and John are. After I've done here, I'm going back to the cottage to get a thick coat – you can be sure it will be darned windy down there – and then we're off." Sarah placed the last pan on the drainer and pulled the plug on the huge Belfast sink. She gave the sink a cursory wipe.

"Can I come?" Emily asked.

"Of course, you can! It's quite a walk though. You'll need to wear some sturdy boots if you have them and a warm coat. I'm off now. Follow after me as soon as you can, and we'll wait for you by our cottage."

Within minutes, Emily left by the back door, suitably attired as instructed by Sarah. They met in front of a short terrace of cottages, of which the middle one was the home of John and Sarah, then walked to the western end of the Rype. From here, they took a rough rubble track leading to the coast.

The land on either side was bleak, with stones prominent amongst bare soil, and a scant covering of grass on the pastureland. Field boundaries were in the form of fences and dykes, with trees being sparse. The wind blowing in from the sea came unhindered, and already a tang of saltwater and seaweed hung in the air.

Long before the coast or the humble dwellings at Denge appeared in sight, the soil and grass had petered out and shingle banks undulated, one after the other on each side of the track. A drainage channel followed the line of the road, or more likely the ditch was there first, harking from a time when the sea flowed deep along gashes into the expanse of the stony promontory. Along the edges, reeds and bulrushes stood, colourless and ragged from being thrashed about in the wind.

"Thank goodness for this track!" Emily said, recalling there being no paths through the nearby settlement of Dungeness, and having to battle with flat boards, named backstays, into which her boots slid.

They walked mostly in silence – it seemed that John saved his banter for the bar, and Sarah never uttered many words. There was no awkwardness though, and Emily was thrilled to be viewing the landscape, seeming so familiar, yet she had never ventured along this particular road, nor been to the beach at Denge.

As they neared the tarred collection of shacks squatting haphazardly beyond the ditch, they slowed down, and for the first time Emily felt a little uncomfortable – she had not considered that the people of Denge would be eyeing them as they intruded upon their settlement. There was a young woman, heavy with child, and a toddler at her feet. Nearby, a couple of older women, swathed in shawls, sat on benches by their doorways observing the strangers with suspicion. *It's not much of a place – I thought there would be more – more homes, more people.* The beach was still not in sight, but closer to the coast there stood a row of cottages – far more substantial than the wooden homes – and what seemed to be a lookout tower.

"It was there he was murdered," Sarah announced. "Up in that tower."

"I know." Emily was both compelled to look and repulsed by the thought of such horrors.

"And they took his clothes – they must have done to make the model of him."

"It's a funny sort of thing to do," Emily observed. *And it's funny how Sarah don't say much, but she's got plenty of information about this.*

"That's what they do around here!"

"Murder people?" Emily asked, feeling herself tense. "Do you think we should... perhaps we shouldn't go any further?"

"No, well not often – I'm just saying that they keep themselves to themselves and don't want any interference."

"Come on, Sarah!" Her brother interrupted. "They won't mind us coming – the Brooks family drink in the Dolphin and won't be bothered by us walking out here. They just don't want men in uniforms, and especially them lot with their look-out seeing all sorts of things that aren't their business."

The watercourse came to a sudden end, appearing now to take its path underground, and John led the way to the other side, bringing them uncomfortably close to the homes. Emily offered awkward smiles to the young mother, and elderly women. They gave no response. Now heading back in the direction of Lydd, the shingle was clear of any vegetation and, as soon as they were free of the buildings a human carcass could be seen sprawled on the stones. Emily's heart gave an unpleasant jolt – *I'd swear that was a real body if I hadn't been told otherwise. He's lying there like… well, like a dead body.*

Standing before the lifeless form, the three of them braced themselves against the force of the wind racing from the coast. It caused the bell-bottomed trouser leg of the uniform to flap about erratically, and their own clothes to whip about in the same manner. In silence, they studied the muscular legs and torso dressed in a thick navy woollen cloth, and shoulders beneath a wide collar edged with traditional white piping, the material also lifting with the gusts. Emily could imagine a row of brass buttons settling within the stones, but none of these ornamental details could be seen, as the figure lay on his front.

On closer inspection, the face, mostly hidden by a cap, was no more than a shape covered in a grubby cloth, with the feet and hands being similar. Whoever created this had not been skilled enough, or had not allowed the time, to sculpt these features.

"He's here as a warning?" Emily frowned. Most people would approach Denge from the road, as they did, but if you were then to wander from the coast or small settlement, this figure would certainly come as a shock. *It looks real enough until you get close, and it gave me a scare even though I knew what to expect.*

"He's here to tell incomers to let the locals get on with things in their way, and not to go interfering," John replied.

"In their way?"

"Like smuggling. It doesn't bother anyone if a boat lands here with some tax-free liquor and tobacco, does it?"

Emily tried to visualise this unexpected scene. "No, no. I don't believe it does."

"And it makes life a bit easier for the people who live here."

"They put this here as their way of saying to the coastguards, 'Look the other way or else you might be sorry'." Emily tried to understand. "So perhaps that man who was murdered… perhaps he saw something he shouldn't."

"You would think so," John agreed. "But there's no sign of any smuggling going on that night. It's a mystery as to why someone decided to get rid of him."

Emily stared out across the rolling ridges of stones towards Dungeness and the lighthouse where her stepfather, Jacob, used to work. Suddenly she had spent enough time here looking at the concrete man dressed as a coastguard and began to walk away. With unspoken agreement, John and Sarah followed. "Can we look at the sea?" Emily asked. "I've not seen it in ages. Ma and I go to Folkestone every year after we've gone to see my pa's grave. But that's different – it's a town beach."

They turned back, past the shacks and the rambling Hope and Anchor beerhouse, then the bay was spread before them, with Dungeness Point to the east and the vast sands at Camber to the west. Here was a working beach for fishermen – with none of the frills associated with a day at the seaside. The only place for refreshments was the Hope and Anchor, and it seemed unlikely that this catered for women. *You'll never get a penny ice here* – Emily grinned to think of an ice cream seller in a white apron, pushing a cart to the high tide mark. *Not that there is any beach to speak of, but I expect there will be a strip of sand when the tide is low.*

A couple of fishing boats were being winched up onto the bank, just beyond the high-water mark. As men turned the handle, and women paved the way for the boats with smooth planks laid on uneven stones, the gulls circled and screamed their glee. Emily became aware of a cart trundling along.

John, noting her attention turning to the road, said, "It's the cart coming to take the fish back to Lydd. Most of it will travel by train inland."

Emily nodded her understanding, but now her attention turned to one of the younger men engaged with hauling the boat in. She recalled the short conversation with the dark-haired man she had met in the churchyard. *He said he lived here in Denge! But I didn't think – didn't think about him being a fisherman. I don't know what else he might have done though. No wonder he looks so strong if he has to work this hard.* Ed toiled with his shirt sleeves rolled up, pushing on the handle of the winch. Even from a distance, his trousers were clearly stained and well-worn. His boots appeared to have a hole in the toe, and this was confirmed when he bent over to pick a stone out, then tossed it across the beach.

Before Jake bellowed for his cousin to 'get on with it', Ed spotted the onlookers on the beach and flashed a grin at Emily. She hadn't the time to respond before the moment passed, and his attention returned to the boat.

"Come from Lydd, have you?" The voice came from behind them and there was the young woman who they had seen while walking past the shacks. She was slim, despite it being obvious her pregnancy was well-established. Fair hair was scraped back into a bun, but her grips were no match for the sea winds, and there was as much flying about as secured at the nape of her neck. Her beauty came from large grey eyes – showing a peaceful nature in the face of the hardships endured living by the coast. "We don't get many women coming this way," Helen said. Her words told of a lonely existence. Then she offered a brief smile to John, "'Scuse me, sir, I know you ain't a woman!"

"I'm not!" he responded. "We've just taken a walk down here from Lydd. I've come with my sister, along with Emily who is new to the area and living at the Dolphin." He gestured to his companions.

"And what do you all think of the man lying there?"

"He's very… very life-like," Emily ventured to comment. "Gave us a bit of a shock, even though we was expecting him."

"It's like a warning, isn't it?" the woman suggested.

"A warning?" John asked, despite this being something they had discussed not long before.

"Like a 'mind your own business' warning." Her words were said with no aggression – it was as if she were resigned to the ways of Denge.

"Come and help with the fish, won't you?" The voice coming from Jake Brooks was part roar and part snarl. He was now back in the boat and handing crates to Ed.

Lord! I wonder if she's his wife, and if she is then I bet it's not an easy life for her. Emily watched as Helen scuttled away with no more words shared between them.

They watched the fish being unloaded for a few minutes before John suggested it was time to walk back. It was three miles to Lydd and the track was rough underfoot – suddenly all enthusiasm for the escapade was over and Emily had no wish to retrace her steps with nothing new to see. "We had better get on with it," she said. "I don't want to be stuck out here once it starts getting dark."

It took a few minutes to scramble across the stones before reaching the end of the track where the cart awaited the fish, and then they set off at a fair pace, soon putting Denge behind them.

Back in Lydd, James Roberts paced about in his upstairs sitting room. He had asked Hattie several times if she knew where Emily had gone with John and Sarah, but the housekeeper could only repeat the same declaration that she knew nothing of their plans, only that Emily had set out for a walk with them. James sought out Alf, who was snoozing on his bed under the eaves of the stable loft and asked if John had shared his plans. It was all in vain – there was nothing to be learned and nothing to be seen from the sitting room window, or from the corner of the street overlooking the Rype.

"I'm worried about her – I feel responsible," James explained to Hattie, but it made no difference.

As afternoon turned into early evening, and the last of the sun's rays shed a golden light through the front windows of the Dolphin Hotel, James poured himself a whisky and pulled a chair up to the window to await Emily's return.

In the remote settlement by the coast, Ed's body felt light, and he had an urge to allow a great grin to fix itself upon his face. He knew to be cautious though, not to allow Jake to see how this young woman – Emily – had caught his interest. She was the reason why he pressed down on the handle of the pump with enthusiasm, sloshed the sparkling droplets over his face, then plunged his hands and lower arms into the water.

What brought her here today? Denge of all places? Who knows where she might turn up next and I'll not have her thinking I stink of fish. He took a moment to pick the dirt out from under his fingernails. *Wouldn't do any harm to cut these nicely.*

He bounded over the cumbersome stones, past the tall narrow shed he had just erected as a place to smoke fish, and back home. Outside his front door – the only door – Ed glanced at the basket of fish which was meant to be sharing his home for the night. *I can't carry on like this – no one at the Dolphin would sleep with a pile of raw fish, or any fish, stinking away all night.* He removed one for supper and placed the remainder in his empty smokery. Then, rather than eat supper and head for the Hope and Anchor, Ed set off along the top of the beach in the search of precious driftwood and wondering what Emily would think of his new venture of smoking fish. *It might be the thing that keeps our bellies full through the winter.*

Chapter Fourteen

"I was worried about where you were – of course I was," James explained, having ushered Emily up the stairs and closed the door to his sitting room behind them. "But my fear was that Mrs Tatin would hear of this trip to Denge with my barman."

"Mrs Tatin?" Emily felt her skin turn cold. "Do you think?" But she wasn't quite sure what he might think. The walk back had been long – her legs ached and her throat was parched. Now James had rushed her upstairs and Emily was struggling to put her thoughts in order.

"I hope no word of it reaches her ears. I know how important her good opinion of you is – how she expects you to behave respectably at all times."

Emily thought of the hours spent sitting behind the reception area with the hotel guest book before her, or arranging the cut flowers in the hallway, guest lounge and dining room. These were all tasks which depended on Mrs Tatin's goodwill. Without that, she could be assigned to the thankless chores of ironing, scrubbing or sweeping out the grates.

"Was it wrong to go for a walk?" Emily asked, but the answer was already clear in her mind: there was no harm in going for a walk, but to trudge miles to see a concrete image of a dead man could raise questions as to the suitability of this destination for a young woman.

"I believe Mrs Tatin keeps a… a…let us say 'motherly' eye on the women in her employment, and I am certain she would not approve of you courting a barman!"

"Courting?" The word gushed out almost as a squawk. "Courting? Why would you think that?"

"Hush, Emily." James placed a hand on her shoulder. "I did not think… A beautiful, intelligent woman… You could do better, and John is no more than a boy. These are not my thoughts. But perhaps Mrs Tatin would think…? She doesn't know you as I do."

"But we were with Sarah."

"As chaperone?"

"No! No! She was just there. We went together. I never thought…" Emily walked to the window. Lydd was now in near darkness, and it horrified her to see how close they had been to returning after sunset. Oil lamps gave a warm light to the room, and flames licked around coals in the grate. Suddenly, she remembered and announced with some triumph: "It was Sarah who invited me! Sarah, not John."

"Well, let's hope that John didn't think anything, and that Mrs Tatin hears nothing of it." James turned away, his gaze falling on a tray he had placed on the table some time before. "Tea!" he announced, taking Emily by surprise. "I bought tea for us – for you – it will be past its best though."

"I don't mind if it's cold *and* stewed," Emily declared. "Shall I pour?"

The pot was still warm, and the process of adding first the milk, then the tea, had a soothing effect. She stirred the sugar for longer than necessary, liking the way the liquid swirled about in the delicate china cups. James' concern had caught her by surprise, and she needed to consider his reaction. Having passed him a cup, they sat in silence for a moment before he spoke again.

"Let's not worry any more about it. There is no harm in you going for a walk with these young people who are part of our household – although if you wanted to go walking, I am sure there are places a young woman would prefer."

"It was a long way," Emily admitted.

"A long way and nothing much of interest at the destination," James commented, before returning to the subject of her companion. "While John is good enough as a barman, I know you would never consider him in any other light. Why, he must be a year or two younger than you, and he has nothing to offer other than a cheerful nature."

"I never thought of him as a... as a..." Emily blushed. "A love interest." *Love interest – what a thing to say, Emily Parkins! What a thing to be talking about with Mr James!*

"Of course not!" James spoke with assurance. "I should never think such a thing. You have some learning and know a little of the world – why you travelled to London only recently! A boy like John would be no good at all. But be careful, Emily, for you are both beautiful and intelligent, and I would not care to see you with some scoundrel."

There he goes again – praising me! I've had him all worried, but Mister James is still kind to me. He's right – I must think carefully and not do anything else to upset him. It's a wonder that he isn't settled with a wife, and I see no sign of him courting anyone. Emily recalled the woman's lacy shawl she had seen draped over the back of the sofa the first time she had been in this room. *I wonder who that belonged to? It would be nice to see him married, but perhaps he doesn't meet many suitable ladies, and it must be difficult to go out courting when he has the hotel to run.*

"It's very kind of you to look out for me," Emily said, replacing her cup on the tray. "I won't be going walking all the way to Denge again."

"I think that's wise." James stood and reached for the tray. "I'll let you freshen up before supper. And, Emily, I know you would never consider John in a romantic manner but be sure not to encourage him. It's easy to be overly friendly when we are all here together, but he is my barman, whereas you... you are a friend of the family."

"I'll be careful." Emily watched him leave, and then walked through to her bedroom. Bedraggled after the walk in brisk coastal winds, she ran her tongue across her top lip. It tasted of salt, and she smiled, recalling the moment when she had stood at the head of the beach to watch the fishing boats being pulled in. Then she hung up her coat and picked up the jug from the washstand. *A wash won't go amiss before supper. I probably look like I live in one of them shacks rather than here with this posh room all to myself!*

Emily was a little on edge the next morning as she emptied chamber pots, swept the hearth, and made the beds in a room let for five nights to an elderly woman with her spinster daughter. She sighed to see a trail of dirt where the odd job boy had topped up the coal and, kneeling with her brush and pan, she swept the large square of carpet in the centre of the room. Before leaving, she ensured the curtains were hanging straight, and enjoyed the moment when she glimpsed a snapshot of life in the small town. The figures of the delivery men, the errand boys, and the women going to work in the shops were becoming familiar. The next time she looked, having completed another room,

Emily would see the children running along to school, and later it would be the housewives with their shopping baskets.

Moving into the next bedroom, it was the hearth that drew her attention first. *No point in making everything nice and then raising dust,* Emily could almost hear her mother's voice. In her mind she countered, *I'm doing all right Ma, I've got myself a good job and a lovely room. And I'm not going out with good-for-nothing rascals like that Frederick Barnes.* She smiled to think of the fun to be had on Frederick's bicycle, but this was quickly followed by the shame of him not appearing for the Sunday tea which had been so carefully prepared.

Next, Emily turned to the bed and hauled the covers off, moving them to the side before stripping the sheets and pillowcases. These were placed in a huge basket on the landing, and crisp white replacements were lifted from the shelf in the laundry cupboard. The floor was swept and finally the woodwork polished. Before she left the room, Emily made sure everything was in its place, and allowed herself a moment to look out of the window onto the street scene below.

The sheets were deposited with Fanny in the wash house, where the copper boiled not only on a Monday, as in a normal household, but all other days apart from Sunday. Walking through to the kitchen, Emily noted the large brown teapot was in its usual spot in the centre of the table. She gulped down a cup of slightly stewed tea and returned to Fanny and the piles of steaming towels, bedding and uniforms.

"Shall I take a turn on the mangle?" Emily called to the perspiring laundry maid.

"Ta!" Fanny replied, her voice lacking the energy you would expect from a sixteen-year-old.

It was while the washing was being pegged onto one of the long lines that Mrs Tatin approached.

"Emily, I was in room four and noticed the chamber pots were..." It was unlike Mrs Tatin to pause for dramatic effect, but this sin warranted it, "...full."

Emily's cheeks burned. "Oh larks! I'm so sorry. There's nothing worse than..."

"You're right – especially for a guest to find someone else's..."

"I'll see to it now." Emily faltered. Was there to be some punishment for her negligence? Perhaps a docking of her pay or worse – suspension from her duties behind the reception desk.

"Don't look so worried. I treat my staff fairly and in return they work hard. You are no exception, and I am pleased with your work. Occasionally a mistake happens."

"Thank you, Mrs Tatin." Emily remained subdued. "I'm very happy here, and I won't let it happen again."

"I'm sure you won't."

Emily was about to step away when Mrs Tatin spoke again, "You must miss your family?"

Emily considered her place in the Albert Road home: the unmarried older sister to Molly; the unpredictable daughter; the younger sister to the boys, now fully grown-up. Without her presence, life would have continued just as before. It was Monday – wash day – meaning that Molly would be at home with Cora. They would have the smalls out to dry by now and perhaps be scrubbing at any dirt on the shirts, frocks and trousers.

"I do miss them," she replied, feeling cautious. "But I'm nearly twenty-three and am glad to have the chance to live in a new place, meeting different people."

"When you want to visit, Ashford is no distance at all by train," Mrs Tatin commented. "How lucky we are to live in these times with the railways stretching from one end of the country to the other."

"We are lucky," Emily agreed. "I went up to London to see the Royal Wedding!"

"That must have been an experience." Mrs Tatin looked across the yard, to the stables and outhouses, but it seemed as if she were seeing the crowded streets of London, the parade of carriages and Princess Mary of Teck in her wedding dress.

"I had better empty those chamber pots," Emily reminded her, wondering if it was polite to scuttle off.

"Of course. And, Emily, don't forget that we close the hotel at Christmas, so you'll have plenty of time to see your family then."

Emily took her leave and, as she pulled the chamber pots from under the bed, she could only be grateful that Mrs Tatin had heard nothing of the long walk to Denge in the company of John and Sarah.

The Dolphin Hotel
Lydd
5th October 1893

Dear Ma,

It has been a month now since I went off. I thought it was time to show you all that I can look after myself. It's not right, a woman of twenty-two years living at home and having to share a room with her sister. I've got myself a good job in a respectable hotel. I do all sorts of jobs from the cleaning and laundry to working behind the reception.

There are live-in rooms at the hotel, but I found myself a lovely big room nearby. James Roberts has let me stay in his hotel. It's smaller than the one I work in, but it is still a hotel, not a beerhouse. There's a housekeeper, called Hattie, and she makes me dinner and supper when I am not at work.

I am not coming back to Ashford to live, but perhaps I could come to visit for Christmas? Or whenever I am allowed a few days off work. Then I can pack up my clothes and books. So please tell Molly to keep her hands off them. Perhaps you wouldn't mind sending my green tweed dress and shawl before then? They say the winds are terrible here over the winter.

I hope you are all keeping well. Please tell Jacob and Molly and the boys that I miss them and will be visiting soon.

Love from your daughter, Emily

"I think that will be all right," Emily muttered as she took an envelope from the bureau. "I know Ma won't be best pleased to know that I am living here with Mr James, but she should be happy about me working in a posh hotel." She grinned and raised her eyebrows. "Listen to you talking to yourself, Emily Parkins!"

It was early evening, and the letter would have to wait to be posted in the morning. Emily took it through to her bedroom, placing it in her handbag. On her return to the living room, James was there, reading a newspaper under the light of an oil lamp.

"I've written a letter," Emily began, "to tell Ma where I am. Look at me nicely settled with a good job and a decent room here. I hope she's pleased for me."

"I am sure she will be," he replied. "It's a step up from serving in a bakery, and you have your own room here. No need to be sharing an attic with a kitchen or laundry maid." He set the paper aside, as if pleased to have her company.

Emily reflected on meeting James in Ashford, both in the town and at his parents' home. She had often wondered what brought him to there for such an extended time. Memories of seeing him during past visits were vague, going back to her childhood, although she knew he visited his parents occasionally. "Are you going to Ashford again soon?" she asked. "You said you had business there?"

"My business is complete," he told her, now folding the newspaper, as if to indicate he would prefer to talk with her than learn about the news of the day.

Emily left her basket of mending untouched, sensing he had more to say.

"I was considering buying a hotel in the town," James announced. "I had been negotiating the price and looking into the details for some time but decided not to take the matter any further."

"Oh." Suddenly Emily's new life seemed less secure. She saw him leaving the Dolphin, perhaps in the hands of a manager, and her, with bags packed, heading up the narrow staircase to a shared room in the attics of the George Hotel. Once living and working in the hotel, she would only be safe all the time the chamber pots were emptied, and the rooms left immaculate. "Are you still thinking of moving to Ashford?" she dared to ask.

"Not at all!" his reply came quickly, and his tone was bright. "I've decided to stay right here at the Dolphin. I have a good little business, and now you are here I wouldn't expect you to go back to Ashford with me, not when you have made a home in Lydd."

"If you wanted to move somewhere else, then I'd have to get a room like I planned to when I arrived," Emily pointed out.

"No need to think of it." James leaned forward, his attention completely on her. "You and I have become such firm friends that I hope you wouldn't think of leaving me. We are like a little family here at the

Dolphin and you, Emily, are very much a part of it." He reached out, taking her hand, moving his thumbs gently in a circular motion on the pale skin of her palm. "I'll tell you a secret, shall I? I would be in Ashford now if it weren't for you. How could I leave when a beautiful woman came needing my help? To have you living here, and sharing these little chats gives me such pleasure that I no longer dream of those plans to move away. And if one day I were to consider it – I often think of the appeal of a seafront hotel, perhaps in Hastings – then you would come with me. At least I hope you would!"

A seafront hotel! My that would be something! And me, Emily who was working in a bakery just a month ago, me behind reception perhaps all the time, and telling someone else to empty the chamber pots! "Of course, I would!" she responded with glee.

He rose, letting go of her hand, "I hoped you would feel like that, but don't say a word to the others. Perhaps in the spring we'll go to Hastings and see what we think of it. And if that doesn't suit, then perhaps Eastbourne! With a few pounds in the bank, there are always opportunities." Without waiting for her reply, he left the room, and she heard him bounding down the stairs.

Sitting at the doorway of his smokery, Ed pondered on events from the past weeks: *We shouldn't have made that figure of the coastguard. It's making them think about it. Making them come here and wonder if it's a clue to something.*

It wasn't just the three from the Dolphin Hotel who had ventured along the rough tracks to Denge. There had been others, mostly sightseers from Lydd. *Sightseers*! Ed smiled at the word which had come to mind. *Sightseers - here at Denge! That will be a first, and most likely a last too. Perhaps if we placed more figures then Helen could earn a few pennies by making cups of tea and Victoria sponge cake! Victoria sponge - I might be a man but even I know you can't make a sponge cake over an open fire. Maybe some drop scones - with a few currants in them?*

While the first pieces of driftwood smouldered in the brand new smokery, Ed wondered how to keep them smoking, rather than burning fiercely, and visualised the day trippers descending on Denge. What other figures would Jake choose to create?

Never free of Jake for long, his cousin chose this moment to stroll by, disturbing a rare moment of peace for Ed. "There's been a robbery," he announced. "The post wagon on the Hastings to Ashford line has been raided. I don't know what's got into people nowadays, taking stuff that don't belong to them and causing all sorts of trouble."

Chapter Fifteen

Emily buffed the mahogany chest of drawers and the curved back of her bedroom chair until the wood shone a reddish brown. It was a task she usually enjoyed, but on this occasion her thoughts roamed to Ashford. Two weeks had passed with no word from her mother. *It's only November, too early to blame the weather for the post being delayed. They just can't be bothered with writing a letter to me. That's how it is. They've got a new daughter now – that May with all her smiles and friendly talk.*

She glanced around the room, taking no pleasure from the scent of the polish or everything being spick and span, gathered the cleaning rags with the brush and pan, then proceeded to return them to the scullery. Before reaching the hallway, she was alerted to a raised voice.

"I've told you not to come snivelling around here – if you have things to flog then try your luck on the streets. You'll put a few shillings in your pockets before the sergeant catches up with you," James was saying, his words tinged with contempt.

The second voice was low, and although she heard it fall and rise, Emily could decipher none of the words. She paused, ready to retreat if necessary, but curious to know more. It was two hours before opening, and she had never witnessed James speaking to Alf or John with such distaste.

"Coffee?" There was surprise in the landlord's tone now. "People round here don't have a taste for that!"

More explanations followed, but again not one word uttered by the second man could be interpreted.

"Sit yourself down then," James responded. "I'll hear you out, but I'm telling you – a few casks of brandy, or a box of tobacco, that's one thing. But don't you dare try to cajole me into shifting fifty sacks of anything dubious."

Gracious! What can he mean? Fifty sacks of coffee! It must be them beans I've seen pictures of, but what's a sack? Is it a sack of flour we see at the grocers, or like a paper bag with a few handfuls? And Mister James is right – I don't know no one who drinks the stuff. There was some movement in the bar area, and when James spoke again his voice was lower. *He must have been by the door before. Well, I'm curious and there's no denying it, but I can't go listening and I've forgotten my smalls!* Emily retraced her steps to her bedroom, gathered her collection of delicates and hurried along to the scullery to pop the items in a bucket of warm water to soak.

It was not often that Emily was at the Dolphin to help on a washday, it being a rare Monday free of work, but now she asked Hattie if there was anything she could do to help. The housekeeper nodded to a basket of towels. "If you could hang them out in the yard, I'd be grateful."

The last towel was being pegged on the line, and already the wind was catching them, when Emily heard movement at the back door. On seeing Jake Brooks striding out, she cowered a little behind the wet laundry. He left without spotting her.

Seated at the table, with a dinner of cold meat and fried potatoes with cabbage, James ate with haste.

"I'm sorry Hattie," he explained the rush, "I need to get to Denge and back before dusk." Then he turned to Alf, "Can you saddle my gelding, please?"

No one asked why he was going to the remote settlement, but no doubt Emily was not the only one who had witnessed Jake Brooks' presence in the hotel earlier. They ate in near silence, before the landlord made a further request, this time to Sarah: "Mr Blackmore will be returning as soon as he is able – prepare his room, please." He continued, almost to himself, "He won't be here unless he knows to come." This time James turned to Emily, "I need word to go to Mr Blackmore immediately, and don't want to delay my departure. Could you write a letter asking him to come?"

"A letter?" Emily repeated, immediately feeling a little foolish.

"A letter!" He smiled at her. "You'll find everything you need in my desk. His address is in a slim notebook, and there are stamps in a small wallet."

"How shall I sign it?"

James considered this, then said, "On behalf of Mr James Roberts."

"Should I give him a reason?" As she asked, Emily sensed the others perk up, as if sure there was to be some revelation.

They were disappointed. "No, no. Mr Blackmore understands my business." With those words, James was pushing his plate away and thanking Hattie for the meal. He clattered upstairs, and Alf scurried out to the yard, with a backward glance at the last forkfuls of food on his plate. Moments later, James had returned wearing riding boots and calling out that he expected to be back within a couple of hours.

"You best get it written," Hattie instructed Emily. "Don't you go worrying about clearing up here."

With assurances she would be back, Emily left the table and was soon opening the dark oak bureau. There was a selection of dip pens in a clay pot, and she eyed the wooden turned handles, then lifted a couple before selecting one with a standard writing tip. The ink was a rich black, sticking to the sides of the glass pot as Emily moved it towards her. Having extracted a piece of headed paper from a drawer, she dipped the pen, shook off the excess ink and wrote *Dear Mr Blackmore* before dunking the nib again. Now she considered her next words, feeling both nervous and gratified to be given this task, while aware that no advice had been given as to exactly what to write.

"Dear Mr Blackmore," Emily murmured, as she began to write, "Please can you come to the Dolphin Hotel at… at your greatest convenience – I don't think I can spell that – as soon as possible. That's not much of a letter, is it? Your room has been prepared. With respect, Miss Emily Parkins – on behalf of Mr James Roberts. Well, fancy that – me a secretary now!" Then Emily let out a laugh, realising she had been talking out loud all the time.

A leather-bound book contained the information 'Mr Edward Blackmore, Accountant'. *Ah! A money man. I thought he was something like that – it looked like ledgers he was working at when I saw him.* It seemed like an age ago when Emily had peeped through an open doorway and seen the bent figure of the elderly man at work. *How long ago was it?* She considered the matter, counting on her fingers – *six weeks!* Then, having selected an envelope, she wrote the address, and added a stamp. The ink was dry, so the letter was folded and slipped into the envelope.

Emily, wrapped with a warm feeling of being useful to James, fetched her coat and left for the post office.

The following afternoon, a low wagon rumbled into Lydd and pulled into the yard of the Dolphin Hotel. Dinner had just finished, and James leapt to his feet, leaving the kitchen with barely a thank you thrown in Hattie's direction. Seconds later he returned calling out, "Come and have a look at this, Emily!"

Hessian sacks, each one stamped with the same combination of letters and numbers, were lined up on the low-sided wagon. There must have been fifty or more of them filling every space.

"Don't you want to know what it is?" James challenged, his voice as eager as a schoolboy's. "Come on…" He was lifting one of the bags out and balancing it on an old bench.

Caught up in the excitement, Emily retorted, "You've hardly given me a chance!" *So, this is what a sack of coffee looks like – I can't tell him I was eavesdropping yesterday, but there's still plenty I don't know. For a start, I've never seen a coffee bean in my life!*

This was soon to be remedied as the ties were released, and James was pulling at the opening. It was the smell which first caught Emily unawares, being so different to anything ever encountered. Not spicy, or tart – not floral, or savoury – it was all new, and she leaned forward breathing deeply, not yet knowing if it was an aroma she appreciated.

"What's it for?" Emily asked. "All this – it is coffee, isn't it?"

"What's it for?" James half-smiled, a bemused expression on his face.

"For drinking – I know!" she grinned. "Not that I enjoyed it. I had it from a stall," she admitted. "And it weren't very nice. We always kept to tea at home."

"You just can't trust what's been mixed with the beans if it's not come from a reputable coffee house,"

James informed her. "For a start there's chicory, and that's not too bad at all, but sometimes they dry and grind all manner of other roots into the sacks. You might think you are drinking coffee, but you've got roasted carrot in there! And then there is the milk which may be none too fresh or watered down."

"Oh my!" Emily eyed the mass of raw beans, as if expecting a carrot or turnip to be nestled amongst them. "I don't fancy that!"

"There's nothing to worry about at all," he assured her. "But if you are to try it again, then just be sure it is from a respectable establishment. I'll take you on a train to Rye one day – what do you think of that? We shall have a hot drink in a little place I know of, a stroll around the cobbled streets, and dinner in one of the many fine eateries."

Surprised by this offer of such a glorious day out, and honoured that James would put aside his many responsibilities, Emily was unsure of how to respond, so she asked, "Are you setting up a coffee shop?"

"No!" He let out a guffaw, seemingly intoxicated by the arrival of the wagon brimming with the precious commodity – or perhaps delighting in showing Emily new things, and his offer of a day out. "I shall sell it!"

"Sell it?" *Who's going to want a sack of beans? Or will it be in little bags and Lord knows how long it will take to shift them all.*

"No – not like that," he replied, as if reading her thoughts. "It will be advertised throughout Kent and Sussex – Mr Blackmore can see to that, sending word of it to the newspapers. There will be two sales: one for the coffee and one for general goods. We do this two or three times a year, and if you're lucky then you'll be able to see Mr Blackmore in action – the sales take place in the upstairs meeting room."

Emily could picture it all: Mr Blackmore at the end table, taking charge of the room with a gavel in his hand; a bunch of men anxious not to be outbid but not wanting to spend more than necessary; a cloud of tobacco smoke hanging in the eaves of the vaulted ceiling; Hattie, in the kitchen, busily preparing cups of tea – or even coffee! *But why would they come here – all this way – for our beans?*

"James…" she began, not knowing if it was her place to question, but he always seemed so free sharing the news with her. "These people… these people who come to buy the beans – why aren't they having it from their usual places? Why would they come here for this?"

"The price!" he replied with relish. "Our coffee is a third of the price, perhaps less – and if they were to acquire several sacks it would still be a saving even if they travel and stay here overnight. Others will send their bids by post. These men who buy the beans will be looking to secure large quantities."

So many questions – life at the Dolphin offered unexpected moments, and Emily felt James' excitement rubbing off on her. Now he was looking about, calling for John to help Alf, who was already lumbering to and fro with the sacks. A disused stable had been swept and some wooden boards placed on the ground, creating a platform a few inches clear of any damp or remaining dust. Emily turned back to the kitchen, knowing it was only fair that she helped Sarah at the sink for a few minutes, but also conscious she was due back at work in the George Hotel.

"There's to be a sale of coffee at the Dolphin!" Emily told Mrs Tatin, as they studied the guest book together. The young woman wore her new dress of brown tweed, while working at the reception desk in her favourite role at the George Hotel. Every afternoon spent here increased her confidence, and there was an inward glow as new skills were learned.

"You never know what could be in the next sale," Mrs Tatin responded. "It depends on what the boats were carrying."

"It came from Denge – I mean that's where the wagon came from," Emily explained, "but then Mr Roberts was so busy. He showed me the beans and I never learned how he got them."

"There would have been a ship wrecked near Denge, and that was its cargo." Mrs Tatin closed the leather-bound book and returned to the business of work. "We are expecting thre new guests this afternoon: a salesman from Tonbridge who comes here two or three times a year, and a married couple."

"I'll look forward to meeting them," Emily replied, no wiser as to how the coffee had come to be sold at the Dolphin. Mrs Tatin was due to have her afternoon off, leaving Emily to tidy the dining room and guest lounge while keeping an eye on reception. She would have to be patient and wait if she were to learn more.

On duty until six o'clock that evening, Emily greeted the salesman first – taking him to his room and then making several trips up the stairs and along the corridor with some luggage he had deposited in the entrance hall on arrival. The bags were not heavy, and although she was curious to know what they contained, she knew better than to be inquisitive where guests were concerned. Once the new arrival, a Mr Johnstone, had everything just as he wanted, Emily escorted him to the lounge where she served him a pot of tea, accompanied with cook's freshly made shortbread.

During the afternoon, other guests returned, some slipping upstairs to their rooms, others to the bar or lounge. Emily provided tea as required, listening out for the ring of the reception bell, and sometimes having to scurry from one task to the next. She was always busy when on reception duties but took a pride in her job and especially enjoyed meeting new guests. Now the autumn had established itself, there were fewer visitors to the hotel, and those who did come were mainly on business.

It was six o'clock when Emily returned to the Dolphin, passing the front door as usual to enter by the kitchen. The wagon would have been sent away hours ago, and the sacks of coffee beans safely stacked in the stable, but she remained curious as to what was to be gained by selling them. Much as she liked and respected James Roberts, Emily was certain he would engage in no business unless likely to secure a healthy profit from it. Her steps slowed, and she wondered if it would matter if she were to slip into the stable, open a sack and breathe in the curious aroma. Movement at the back door prompted her to reject this idea, and she frowned, then gave a cautious smile, to see Ed walking outside with James.

Oh! It's him again. I wonder what he's doing here – it must be something to do with the coffee. If it came from Denge and had something to do with that nasty looking man, then I suppose Ed must be involved too. I can't help thinking he's handsome, although I shouldn't, of course.

"Good evening, Miss Parkins," James said, surprising her with his formal manner.

Ed gave a brief nod and uttered, "Good evening." His voice was gruff, as if he weren't used to greeting a young woman dressed in a neat brown outfit, her hair as bouncy and glossy as when first brushed that morning, and her eyes alive with curiosity.

"Good evening," Emily repeated. She stepped aside allowing them to move on from the doorway, then watched for a moment, as the two men walked across the yard to the roadside. Entering the rear of the Dolphin, she scampered up the stairs, and couldn't help herself from smiling. *There you go again, Emily Parkins, giving him a second look! There's no good that could come of it, so you best get on with some chores and put those silly thoughts away.*

In the sitting room she shared with James, Emily had left a basket of material, with a box containing her growing collection of threads, needles, buttons and hooks. She was making herself a second winter dress – a challenge which would take a couple of months to complete. As she picked it up, she mused that each one took so long to finish it would be time to start on summer costumes by the time this one was done. *Unless I write to Ma and ask for my belongings to be sent on.* A sense of resentment wrapped itself around her young shoulders. *Why didn't she answer my last letter? I know she won't be happy to know where I am, but I thought that was better than not knowing at all. If I write again, she'll think… I don't know what she'll think. And I don't want to cause upset if Johnny is about to marry. Best he gets settled down before I write again, and Ma gets herself in a state.*

Emily pictured Jacob, Cora and Molly coming to see her at the Dolphin Hotel, squeezing into a place at the dining table alongside the family of characters living or working there. She imagined Cora's confusion in trying to understand why dinner was at two o'clock in the afternoon, and supper at eight. But what Emily felt the most when she visualised the scene was her mother's unreasonable distaste for James, and how he could do no good at all in her eyes.

There was an expression Cora used about wayward characters – perhaps it was an Ashford term, founded in the town's association with the railway. *Off the rails.* Emily considered the saying. *I don't know if Ma thinks that James is a bit unreliable, but I know exactly what she would have to say about me running off and coming here. Off the rails – that's what she'd say about me. And she'd be right, I suppose.*

When she heard familiar footsteps on the stairs, Emily was glad to be distracted from her thoughts and smiled as James entered the room.

"That was Ed Brooks," he said without preamble.

"I know," she responded. "I've seen him about the town."

"You met him here – in Lydd?"

"It was on the High Street and in the churchyard." Emily concentrated on her stitching, aware that his expression was curious.

"Anyway, he was here about the coffee – checking it had arrived and was all put away safely. If he'd come earlier, he could have helped unload the cart. That was heavy work, but all done now, and John has a bed there in the loft. Those beans are worth a lot of money, so I won't take any chances."

"Where's it come from?" Emily took her opportunity to learn more.

"The coffee? All the way from the Ivory Coast in Africa." James looked into the distance as if imagining the ship's journey. "Imagine voyaging all that way only to be shipwrecked at Denge."

"Those beans must belong to someone though. Are you selling them for them people from the Ivory Coast?"

"Oh no! That's all over. They belong to whoever managed to salvage them, and I've got to admit that Jake Brooks, Ed and the rest of them down at Denge did a good job of getting the sacks before they were soaked in seawater and good for nothing. The beans belong to them now."

Emily couldn't help noticing the glee in James' voice and she could only hope that it was admiration for his neighbours in Denge, not taking pleasure in thinking of the ship sinking, and the traders losing both their goods and, most likely, several lives. "But they are yours now?" she asked.

"Not at all!" He took a couple of long strides and seated himself at the writing bureau. "I will sell the coffee on behalf of our friends at Denge and take a hefty commission. They have neither the brains nor the contacts to arrange a sale, and they know it. We shall do very well indeed."

Emily tried to ignore the pride in his voice. She had always admired James for his confidence, but this was a little more and it unsettled her. "Is that you and Mr Blackmore?"

"Mr Blackmore?"

"You said 'we'."

"No…not Mr Blackmore. I pay him a wage." James ran a hand through his hair, then shuffled some papers about. "Did I say we? I meant me of course, but if I earn a little extra money then we all gain from it, don't we? And you, Emily… you will benefit if I were to treat you to some ribbons or a length of flowery material – and that is exactly what I will do!"

"Oh! Thank you. I didn't mean to be asking…"

"Not at all!" Having achieved nothing for all his moving papers about, James leapt to his feet. "I'm going downstairs for a brandy. It's that kind of day! Would you care for a port?"

Emily considered this and, caught up in the excitement of the moment, she answered, "I would like that very much – just a small one, mind."

It looks like she's living there at the Dolphin. She wouldn't be just visiting – not for all those weeks since I first saw her. Ed considered how much time had passed since he gazed at Emily walking through the cemetery. *It was when I fixed the cross in place at Ma's grave. When was that? ...About six weeks ago. She arrived from the station that day with a bag and a basket.* He recalled the summer dress, her curls tumbling about in the breeze, and his heart ached with a rare yearning. *What brings her to the Dolphin – she's no skivvy, so perhaps a relation. I've heard Mr Roberts has family in Ashford. Plenty of time to find out.* Ed Brooks was a man who was used to waiting – for the tide, the fish, the fair weather. None of these would change their pace for him. He would learn more about Emily over the next few weeks and that was good enough for him.

We did well to secure all that coffee. His mind wandered to the recent events at sea, and he wondered if the money earned would be enough to repair their boat. Jake had plans to extend his shack, and if this offered some extra comfort to Helen, then it would be money well spent. A moment later and his mind was, yet again, filled with Emily. *Well, Ed Brooks, if you can't get her out of your mind then you'll have to do something about it before she's off courting another man. And if she says no – which most likely she will – then at least you'll have tried.*

Chapter Sixteen

The following day Mr Blackmore arrived and was greeted with some ceremony. Hattie presented him with a slice of fruit cake, which appeared to be bulging with more than the usual selection of dried and candied fruit, and John gave him a generous glass of whisky. There was an air of excitement about the Dolphin – a knowledge that Mr Blackmore's arrival heralded a time of greater activity: rooms filled with men keen to scoop a bargain sack of coffee or other items; extra meals to be cooked; competition amongst those men, perhaps leading to a rowdiness that, no doubt, James could handle with ease.

Emily watched all this from a distance, while she pressed the heavy iron over one apron after the next or ran piles of laundered and ironed clothes to the cupboard on the landing and various rooms, as directed by Hattie. She was standing on a low stool before the shelves of bedding, towels, and aprons when James and Mr Blackmore ascended the staircase and walked along the landing to the huge back room.

"Fifty sacks!" Mr Blackmore was saying. "I had to see them to believe it to be true! You did well to secure them." His voice was low, but Emily heard every word and was curious to learn more. "And loathe as I am to admit it – those scoundrels at Denge did well to save them."

"Just two boats, three old men and the two younger ones," James told him.

"And not a sack lost?" the older man asked.

"They say not."

"And no doubt a few other items for their efforts?"

"You'll see for yourself. I suspect they kept a few pieces for themselves, and why not? They have so little."

"I can't see them grinding coffee beans at Denge though!" Mr Blackmore gave a slight snigger.

Emily scowled. *I haven't ever ground a bean either. They've got a difficult life down there, but from what I see, Ed Brooks is hard-working, and he makes the effort to smarten himself up when he comes to town. You can't do much better than that, not when life is so hard. I don't like Mr Blackmore sneering in that way and would never say a word to Mr James, but I can't say I think much of him.*

She returned to the ironing. Although not going to the George Hotel that afternoon, Emily's duties at home often mirrored those at work. *Not that I can complain. If I still lived with Ma and the others, then I would come home and carry on with the chores. I'll still get a break before I'm back in the George to help serve supper.*

It was almost nine o'clock when Emily returned to the Dolphin, weary from a long day. She yearned to slip into bed and was determined that nothing would hinder her. Yet James remained buoyant since the arrival of Mr Blackmore and, despite the bar being busy, he seemed to sense her return, bursting through into the house before Emily had placed one step on the stairs.

"Emily! I must just show you…" Then appearing to note her despair, he continued, "Just for a moment."

Bounding up the stairs, encouraging her to follow to the back room, he indicated sheets of paper laid out on the long table. "I knew he would understand just how to word it…"

Emily read aloud:

"To be sold by auction.
On Thursday 16th November, 12 o'clock precisely,
At the Dolphin Hotel, Lydd.
Approx. 7000 pounds of finest coffee beans from the Ivory Coast.
Saved at sea, with no water damage.
Sold in 140lb sacks in lots of two or five.
Bids by post accepted before 15th November."

"And the next…" James demanded.

Emily pushed another paper towards the lone oil lamp on the table and read:

"To be sold by auction.
On Thursday 16th November, 1 o'clock precisely,
At the Dolphin Hotel, Lydd.
Various lots to include:
Three one-inch ropes of twenty yards long, unused.
A dozen pairs of working men's boots in various sizes.
Forty 2oz pouches of tobacco, sold in lots of ten.
French brass carriage clock, dating from 1890, in good working order.
Five 18 inch silver platters, sold as one lot.
Miscellaneous tools, overalls and sealed jars of spices."

"They've been sent to the papers already!" James announced. "There's nothing more fun than an auction. It's a bit like a day at the races but every lot is a winner."

Emily frowned, failing to understand how an auction could be likened to a day at the races, never having been to either. However, she imagined the men placing bets as to which horse would win, and the rising excitement as the race progressed. But for every winner there would be numerous losses. In an auction, there would be those who secured the lot and many who didn't. "I'm tired," she told him. "It's all a bit complicated for me, but I can see Mr Blackmore has a lovely, neat hand, and won't it look fine in a newspaper with the Dolphin Hotel written all fancy!"

"It's been a long day for you," James put an arm around Emily's waist, pulling her closer. She leaned into him for a moment, exhausted and thinking of sinking into her welcoming bed. "These will be in papers all over Kent and Sussex by the day after tomorrow, and the auction is next week. People will act fast if they want a bargain – there will be no opportunity to dither over it."

"They won't have much time," she agreed, pulling away and turning to leave. "Ta for showing me."

James' fingers strayed to the curve of her small breasts as Emily turned. She shuddered, knowing it was her fault for twisting as she did, when he would have expected her to stay and admire the adverts for a moment longer. *I doubt whether he noticed. His mind is full of them sales.* But just in case he was feeling a little awkward, she asked, "Where have all those other things come from? The rope and clock and everything…"

"The same as the coffee – these things fall off ships every so often. Some will be from the same ship and some from others. All perfectly normal around here."

"Oh. I suppose there is all sorts of things to learn when you go to live somewhere else."

"There is!" He extinguished the lamp, leaving them in near darkness. "Sleep well, Emily. I must have a word with Hattie and tell her not to work you so hard. You're not her skivvy, although I know you like to help."

"She's nice to me," Emily replied. "I don't mind." She went through to her bedroom. Someone had already lit the lamp and drawn the curtains. A small fire burned in the grate. Emily felt herself relax. *It's good to be home and have this room all for me.* She busied herself, preparing for bed and laying her clothes out on the back of a chair, taking care to leave no creases.

Every lot is a winner. Emily considered these words while drifting off to sleep. *Of course! It's not the bidders winning – it's Mr James. He'll be earning from every sale.*

Two days later, the advertisements were in local and regional newspapers, and each one of them was revealed to Emily by James who sought her company to share the latest developments. Wrongly believing that once one or two had been viewed, then it was unnecessary to see any more, she had each new advert pressed upon her. James made a show of taking her to the meeting room, spreading the newspapers on the table and showing her the position of each advert.

"Which will bring the most interest, do you think?" he insisted, seeming to be eager to hear her opinions.

Never before asked about such a thing, Emily faltered, then considered the matter. "This one here is next to a local news story, so perhaps it will gain more attention," she suggested. "No. No, the coffee beans are for business people who will go directly to the sales pages to look for a bargain. They may not want to know about Princess Mary, or where Mr Gladstone opened a public building. The adverts for the beans are best with others of their type, but the extra items could appeal to anyone, so I can't say…"

"I think you are right!" James declared. "Won't it be interesting to see how far men will travel to come to our auction?"

Two days after that, Emily was again called to the meeting room, and this time it was to study the letters arriving from interested parties.

"Look at this!" James spoke with glee. "There is no time to dawdle, and these people know that. There are seven bids for the beans, and no doubt more will come tomorrow."

"You mean not everyone will come to the sale?" Emily asked.

"No, Mr Blackmore will have the bids to hand and keep a close eye on them as the sales begin."

On the day before the auction, the brass clock, tobacco and silver platters were displayed in pride of place on tables set to the side of the lofty room. The more mundane items, such as boots and rope, were laid out on the floor. Chairs were placed in rows to face the large mahogany table, behind which Mr Blackmore with his gavel would preside.

Ushered upstairs to view the changed scene, Emily could only stay for a moment as she was due back at work. "Very nice," she said, knowing her words were rather ineffectual.

I can't say I understand what Mr James is so excited about. He must be going to make a lot of money, and I can't help hoping those poor fishermen at Denge get a few coins for all their trouble. It seems to me that they did all the hard work, and maybe some money should go in a fund for those poor souls who were on the sinking ship. Emily's thoughts flew to the tragic day when her father was drowned at sea, while her and Cora were some of the few survivors. She had no clear recollection of the event, but her mother's memories had been shared over the years. A memorial to some of the victims stood in the churchyard, and at times she went there to reflect on fragmented images of Stanley Parkins, and those early days when Jacob and his three sons came into her life.

No time to dwell on that. She told herself sternly, while walking briskly through Wheeler's Green and around the corner to the High Street.

To Emily's surprise, the activities at the Dolphin Hotel melded with her work at the George that afternoon. She had only been on reception for an hour when a portly man entered with a travelling bag and, on his heels, came a taller gentleman, his eyes roaming about the place as he waited at the desk.

"Good afternoon, sirs," Emily greeted them, unused to two arrivals at once. To the second, she said, "Would you like a seat, sir, while I book in this gentleman?"

After showing the first to his room, he asked, "Could you direct me to the Dolphin Hotel, please. I have some business there tomorrow."

"Certainly." Mrs Tatin had instructed Emily never to offer a reaction or opinion on anything a guest asked, unless invited to do so. "You turn right onto the High Street, and right again..."

No sooner had he been settled, than the second offered his purpose for being in the town while signing in at the reception desk. "I am here on the business of securing coffee beans," he told Emily.

"How interesting," she replied. "I heard there was to be a sale."

"They should sell for a good price," he responded. "By that I mean good for me! Not many will bother to travel here at this time of year. There is always one trouble or another on the railway once autumn comes, and then winter is even worse."

"I imagine it's awfully hard to keep it all running." Emily had nothing else to offer on the workings of the railway, which she always found to be impressive.

The day ended with three businessmen booked into the George, and the two spare rooms at the Dolphin taken. There were other inns and hotels in the town offering beds to travellers, and the auction promised to be as well-supported as James predicted.

That evening, Emily returned home at seven o'clock to find Hattie bustling about between the kitchen and a small dining room reserved for guests. "Mr Roberts is as pleased as anything," she said. "There's been quite a flow of men coming through the bar all afternoon, and Mr Blackmore has been taking them upstairs to view the goods for sale, or even out to the stables to look at the beans. I thought one coffee bean would look no different to the next, but I suppose it's different for them in the trade."

"They'll be wanting to check the sacks are dry," Emily suggested. "After all, they have come off a sinking ship." But her words were lost to Hattie, who was now in the scullery giving orders to Sarah.

Thursday 16th November came – a day of high clouds and a brisk breeze whipping across the Rype and through the High Street.

"By the time you return from work, it will all be over," James said, as he stood at the kitchen table gulping down a cup of tea. "What a shame."

For a man of more than forty years, he sometimes looks like a child who didn't get enough jam on his bread. And I can't say I like that in a grown man. "You can tell me about it," Emily attempted to console him. *I don't know why he's so worried about me being in the thick of it all. I can't say it matters to me.*

"I'm just sorry that I didn't think of giving you a job here," James said, taking Emily by surprise.

"A job here?" Her voice was a little sharp. "I'm very happy at the George, and speaking of work, I had better get along there now."

But it seemed that her words went unnoticed. As Emily left the room, he was murmuring, "A job here – I'll have to think about it."

On her return from work at two o'clock, Emily would usually find her new family seated at the kitchen table with Hattie serving the meal. But on this day, both James and Mr Blackmore were missing.

"The men are doing all the paperwork and say they'll be with us within the half hour," Hattie informed her. "We are to eat as usual, then John and Alf can help load the carts which are bound to come shortly. It's heavy work, so best they get food in their bellies while they can."

"Did the sale go well?" Emily asked, despite her being more interested in sitting down and savouring Hattie's meat pie.

"From the way Mr Roberts is strutting about, I'd say it went very well," Hattie replied.

Conversation flowing about the table followed the usual topics – talk of local news and snippets of information gleaned from the newspapers. *I hardly like to think it, but I'm glad I don't have to hear how much each bag of beans sold for.* Emily tucked into her meal with relish, joining in with the idle chatter.

"I've said I don't want to do business with that no-good Jake Brooks," Emily heard James say as she began to clear plates from the table. He was standing in the hallway with Mr Blackmore.

"I think you've made it clear enough that I will hand their share over to his cousin," Mr Blackmore stated. "Although it would be best if neither of them was sniffing about the place. Ask your potman to look out, so we are alerted to his arrival."

They moved through to the kitchen, and Hattie busied herself with loading their plates with steaming meat pie and vegetables. "Alf, keep a sharp eye out for Ed Brooks. Let me know when you spot him," James ordered, as he pulled out a chair and flopped down on it. "And call me as soon as the carts start arriving. Let's get these beans away as soon as we can."

For once, James didn't seem compelled to draw Emily into the news of the sale. Instead he exchanged a few polite words but continued speaking about the business of the day with Mr Blackmore. Spotting some damp towels and cleaning rags, Emily sidled outside to hang them on the line, curious to watch the arrival of carts and the loading of beans. Perhaps, although she did not admit it to herself, she was awaiting the arrival of Ed from Denge. Or perhaps, as she had already spent the morning toiling at The George, she wanted some time to herself away from the rushed atmosphere in the kitchen. Whatever the reason, James had insisted she was not to do chores at the Dolphin but must enjoy a break after dinner. So, Emily lingered, and it was only when the tall figure of Ed was spotted walking across the Rype that she scuttled back inside. Not to her room and a book she was reading, but to a window where she could look down upon the back yard.

From here she watched James leave through the kitchen door and shake Ed's hand. Emily smiled her approval to see the fisherman from Denge being treated with some decency. They spoke a little, no doubt of the sale, and James pointed towards the stable holding the beans, then indicated the arrival of carts. Finally, a small packet was pulled from the pocket of James' tweed jacket and handed to Ed, who in turn slipped it into his pocket. They shook hands again and parted. Emily moved away from the window.

That night, Emily drifted into a deep sleep, but within minutes she was roused by shouting on the street below. "You're a cheating scoundrel, James Roberts!" The words rang through the crisp night air.

At first befuddled by the sudden awakening, she wrapped her blanket around her shoulders and, stumbling, moved to the window, opening the curtains a little. Below her, standing against the front wall of the Dolphin, she saw the landlord. Across the road there was the indistinct shape of a tall, wiry man. As she watched, this figure swung away, putting his back to her and beginning his lurching journey across the Rype. More words flew from him, now unclear. Emily watched from the window for a minute or two. Unaware of her presence, James remained on the pavement, before they both moved away, she returning to the warmth of her bed, and he to his business of running the bars.

Ed folded the pound note he had extracted from the envelope handed to him at the Dolphin. He placed it in a small metal tin, opened a cupboard beside the chimney breast and slipped the tin through a gap in the base. The pine door closed with a satisfying clunk, and Ed straightened before seating himself at the small central table.

He felt no guilt – Jake would have done the same to him. The money earned from the sale was to go on repairs to both the boats at Denge, and any change would, most likely, find its way into Jake's pocket, and then to the landlord of the Hope and Anchor. Ed hoped that a few shillings could be used to make Helen's life more comfortable. The baby was due within a week or so, and it didn't matter to Ed if he lived in a one-roomed shack, but Jake's family needed a bit more space. *They used the planks from my mother's home to make theirs good.* Ed reminded himself. *Without asking me.*

Next, he reached into his pocket to extract the coins given to him by James Roberts by way of a tip and placed them in a row within the pool of light cast by the oil lamp. There were three shillings, a couple of farthings and a sixpence – riches to Ed and all the more appreciated because they belonged to him alone. He moved them in the light while pondering on possibilities open to him. "I'll do it now," he murmured. "Before it's gone."

Chapter Seventeen

"I was wondering, Emily... I mean I know it's not the weather for it, but there's a train that goes to New Romney and a nice tearoom there ... or so I hear," Ed paused, seemingly relieved to have finally approached Emily with his offer.

Emily had just left the George and was scurrying back for dinner when she had spotted Ed standing on the corner near the post office. His tall figure had been appreciated, but she hadn't expected more than a nod of recognition. Now he looked at his hands, rough for their twenty-eight years, and awaited her response.

"Are you asking me to go walking out with you, Mr Brooks?" Emily asked. *Oh Lord, I don't know what to say - I can't deny he's handsome. And he's always been so polite whenever I see him, but I don't know that we should be going to a tearoom.*

"I'm… I'm asking you to share a pot of tea and a crumpet or a piece of sponge cake. I don't mean to share the cake. You'd have your own!"

Emily let out a laugh. "I like a bit of Victoria sponge."

"If it was summertime then I'd suggest a stroll to the seafront at Littlestone – it's a different world there with tall houses and places where people go to stay on holiday, and greens to go walking on."

"It sounds lovely." Emily pictured the seafront at Hythe and wondered if Littlestone was similar. "But not in November. I've never been to New Romney and it's only ten minutes on the train, so that will be nice."

"You'll come then?"

"Oh!" Emily frowned, then smiled. "I suppose I just said I would!"

"Perhaps on a Saturday afternoon? I don't go fishing on a Saturday."

"I'm off this weekend!"

"Shall we meet at the station then? Or I can call for you at the Dolphin, but James Roberts isn't your guardian, is he?"

Memories of Frederick Brown having to knock and meet her parents came to mind. Emily almost shuddered to think of Ed Brooks presenting himself at the hotel. "Oh no! Mr Roberts is a friend of the family. I don't need no guardian – I'm twenty-three. At least I will be on Friday. I would prefer to meet at the station, ta."

"It's your birthday?" He seemed pleased. "You're not planning anything special?"

"Oh no. I don't want a fuss. This can be my birthday outing!" Then she looked away, realising he might have thought she was hinting for a gift. "I don't like a fuss on my birthday," she stated, although this was not entirely true.

"There's not many trains running. Is the one forty-two all right for you?" Ed asked. "The next one isn't until almost three o'clock." He sounded apologetic for the lack of choice.

Emily brushed aside the routines of the Dolphin and the dinner being at two o'clock. *I can make do with a slice of bread and some cheese. It's no one's business where I'm going, but they'll ask anyway, so I'll have to think of something.* "That suits me, thank you." Her tone was now formal, and she tried to soften it, "I'd better go now. See you on Saturday. Ta very much."

"Bye then."

They exchanged awkward smiles, and Emily walked home, her step light and the smile still on her face.

No word of the arrangement to go for a trip out with Ed Brooks passed Emily's lips. She knew how gossip spread and would not allow herself to be a part of it. While James was busy in the bar, Emily told Hattie she wouldn't be there for dinner. "It's a lovely day, isn't it? Not so windy, and it looks like the sun wants to show its face. I'm going to treat myself to a train ride to New Romney and back. No harm in having a proper afternoon out, is there?"

"Well, I don't know what there is to see in New Romney that we haven't got in Lydd," Hattie pondered. "If it were summertime I'd say go to the coast, but not in November."

"There will be different shops to look in, and I'll buy a cup of tea somewhere," Emily suggested.

"As I say, it's got nothing that Lydd hasn't, but go and take a look and you'll see for yourself."

"I'll have a bit of bread and cheese now, if that's all right?" Emily sidled towards the pantry.

"Of course it is, and I'll save some dinner for you. No need to go all day without a hot meal inside you."

Not wanting to eat at the kitchen table under Hattie's watchful eye, Emily scampered up to the bedroom with her plate. *I shouldn't really eat up here, but I'll be careful. I'm keen to see why Hattie has no time for New Romney. Never heard much about the place before.*

Emily had two good winter dresses, using one for church on Sunday and the other for her work at the reception desk. She thought longingly of her favourite green dress, no doubt hanging in the shared wardrobe back in her Albert Road bedroom. For a moment, a double dose of sadness struck her – first that there had been no word from her family since she had written home a month beforehand, and then that she could not wear her favourite outfit for the trip to New Romney. However, Emily was never downcast for long and while eating her bread, then re-pinning her hair, she wondered if there would be another afternoon out with Ed, or perhaps a chance to venture further afield.

Not long after, Emily managed to slip out of the Dolphin unnoticed and she walked briskly past cottages and the smock mill, then through the cemetery and towards the station. Ed Brooks hadn't kept her waiting – a point Emily was pleased to note. He was standing at the picket fencing to watch her approach.

"Hello, nice to see you," Emily spoke first.

"I'm glad you came," he replied. "I thought you might not…"

"It's a lovely day and I'm looking forward to an outing," she declared. They walked side-by-side to the office where Ed bought two return tickets. By now the engine could be heard in the distance and there was the first tell-tale sign of smoke from the chimney. "I came here by train two months ago," Emily told him.

"I saw you," he said, catching her by surprise.

"Saw me?"

"I was in the cemetery tending my mother's grave, and you walked past with your bags."

Emily considered this for a moment. "I'm sorry you've lost your Ma." Her words were almost missed by the arrival of the train, but he gave a nod to indicate they were heard.

As the engine came to a halt and released steam, carriage doors opened and passengers stepped out, then hurried away. *They don't stop to take it all in,* Emily noticed. *Not like when we were at Charing Cross, or even when I first came here. They know it already and this station is nothing special to them.* It had faded since her arrival in September; the chrysanthemums, once so rich in colour, were now washed out, and even the orange bricks of the main buildings seemed to be lacking in warmth. Yet the guard stood, as proud as ever, his whistle at the ready and uniform neatly pressed. He indicated where a young porter might be of assistance and answered a query from an elderly gentleman.

For Emily, there was still a thrill to be had from being at the railway station. She loved the powerful engines and all the sounds and smells which brought them to life. Stepping into a compartment, she was both pleased to see that they had it to themselves, and aware it would be more respectable had a matronly woman, complete with shopping basket, been there to accompany them. But she could hardly go seeking such a person, and no one joined them before the guard was closing doors and announcing that the train to New Romney was about to leave.

No sooner had they settled and exchanged nervous smiles, than Ed raised the subject of his mother. "She died recently – back in September. It was time for her to go, so I was glad for her in some ways. No one wants to watch someone suffer like she did and another winter down in Denge would have been more than she could have endured."

Emily waited, knowing he had more to share. She thought nothing of rubbing the window clear of condensation and craning her neck to see the view. All her attention was on the man sitting opposite her, their knees almost touching.

"She was a good woman, Ma was. Hard working but always had a smile on her face. I think you would have liked her." Ed reached into his pocket and withdrew a clean handkerchief. "I don't have much, but when you said it was your birthday, I thought you might like this. It was hers, you see."

As he unwrapped the brooch, it lay nestled in the folds of white cotton on the palm of his hand. The design was a simple silver bar, parting to become an oval in the centre. Set within the slender curves there were four green stones, equally spaced with four seed pearls between each. It was neither showy nor extravagant, but there was an elegance in its shape, and on this November day the sun shone between the clouds, through the murky window, allowing the gemstones to sparkle.

"It's beautiful," Emily gasped. "But you can't… You hardly know me…"

"You like it though?" He reached out, offering her the piece of jewellery on his upturned hand.

"I love it," she said, her words hushed. Taking it, Emily turned the brooch this way and that, admiring its shape and the way each pearl and gem was held in its own silver cup. She thought of protesting more about Ed's generosity, but instead gave a smile and looked straight into his dark eyes. "Thank you. It's kind of you. Very kind."

They fell silent, Ed watching as she pinned the brooch to her coat, and then both gazed out of the windows, after he had rubbed them clean with the handkerchief. It was a day of low clouds, with weak sunlight forcing its way through where possible. The railway line had already split, and Emily travelled past new places, seeing the swathes of shingle banks and undulating scrubland, stretching further than she expected from the point at Dungeness. The sea was no more than an uninspiring band of grey beyond this, and the train took them parallel, although at some distance, from the coastline.

"Look at that!" Emily suddenly exclaimed. "Sandhills! I've never seen so much sand in all my life – there's just a small bay at Folkestone, and a strip when it's low tide at Hythe."

"That's Greatstone," Ed told her.

"Greatstone! I've never heard of such a place. I know about Littlestone, but never visited. Has it got posh hotels and boarding houses as well?"

"There's nothing there at all. Just sand and all those stones before that."

"Nothing at all? But don't people want to go there for an ice, and perhaps get in a bathing carriage and have a swim? How nice to go swimming without all them stones hurting your feet."

"Have you been in a bathing carriage?" He looked at her in wonder.

"No! But my ma made sure I could swim, and we got changed under our towels. Me and the boys, and later my sister, Molly."

"There's none of that at Greatstone," Ed confirmed.

"Why not?"

Unused to such lively conversation, Ed pondered over this for a moment. "I suppose because there's no road there, just a track. And no railway station either. You can walk from New Romney, but those people you are thinking of – they don't want to walk all that way to find no tearoom, or even a cart with ices."

"Well, it seems like a waste of all that lovely sand," Emily declared. "I'd like to go there."

"You could, as long as you didn't expect anything more than the sand," Ed responded. Then, as an afterthought, he added, "There's a beerhouse – The Jolly Fisherman."

"A beerhouse!" She let out a burst of laughter. "It doesn't sound all that jolly stuck there on its own." But this was soon forgotten with new scenes opening up in the form of a body of water, grey and still, enclosed by the land, fringed with reeds and ragged grass.

"Do people go swimming there?" Emily asked, her mind alive to possibilities, despite it being a miserable-looking place.

"I don't know," he replied. "It's called Romney Hoy, and they say that's where the sea used to come in – all over this land here and up to the town. Now it's all silted up and there's all the mudflats between the Hoy and the coast. A mucky old place to go swimming."

By now the train was approaching the station, and they stood, bracing themselves as the engine nudged the buffers, this being the end of the line. The red brick building was typical of that found in a small country town, with space for both ticket sales and a waiting room, and a deep canopy covering the width of the platform. Emily and Ed trailed through the gates and onto a rough road with the few passengers who had journeyed to Romney.

Almost immediately, they found themselves standing midway along a wide tree-lined avenue, and although these trees were now bare of leaves and not yet achieving their full potential in height or breadth, it was still an impressive sight. A sign indicated the sea was to their right, and the town to the left, and now she was torn, for although a trip to New Romney was on offer, she was tempted by thoughts of the grand buildings on the Littlestone seafront, and a view of the sea.

As if reading her thoughts, Ed said, "There's no wind at all, and that's rare around here, would you prefer to walk to the coast? It won't be pretty like in summertime, but I am sure the hotels are still serving teas."

"I'd like that very much, ta!" Emily grinned and slipped her arm through his as they stepped out under the bare branches of the elms.

Had they ventured to New Romney, the avenue would have been flanked to one side by terraces of railway workers' homes and, to the other, by an occasional cottage. The road to Littlestone seafront was bare of houses. Yet, as they ambled along the path, there was much to interest them. On either side of the avenue to the coast, new roads were being laid parallel with the main thoroughfare, and it appeared that plots of land were marked out, giving a hint of changes to come. However, on this November day in 1893, the land was mostly given over to sheep, and the various waterways extending from the Hoy were still free to meander as they wished.

The walk was pleasant, with the promise of grand sights once they reached the promenade. Already, hints of wealthy people giving patronage to Littlestone, while enjoying their leisure time, were revealed by a golf course to the north, and the distant terraces of homes and guest houses facing the sea, along with large hotels. Ed pointed out the red-brick water tower to the north, and the Methodist chapel to the south. On reaching the coast, the road was for the first time bordered by the tall, terraced buildings, with bay windows directed to the sea, each with steps leading up to the ground floor and down to the basement. Balconies and decorative iron railings all added to the air of opulence. The avenue had come to an end, and now they were able to cross the coast road, stand on the greens with their backs to the sea and admire these properties parading in either direction.

"It's lovely," Emily spoke in awe. "Imagine staying in one of those hotels or guest houses and standing right up there," she pointed to the upper floors, "and being able to look out – maybe all the way to France."

"When we go for tea, I'll ask for a window table and there will still be a fine view," Ed told her. "There's a break in the clouds over there, so perhaps we'll get a bit of sunshine too."

They turned to face a water fountain created from smooth brown marble with rounded features, then stepped past, walking across the strip of grass until they stood at the top of the sands and looked out at the grey sea. It was no surprise, given the lack of wind, that the waters were sluggish, rolling back and forth midway down the beach. But for Emily, it was still a treat and she breathed deeply, appreciating the salty tang.

They continued, first to the south, where in no time the limits of Littlestone had been reached. Here the greens merged with menacing mudflats. A construction of wooden stakes and planks spanned this forbidding wasteland, preventing the sea from encroaching the Hoy on a high tide. Here there were a few huts used by fishermen, and some boats pulled up on the bank.

"Shall we go for tea?" Ed asked, nodding towards a guest house with a board in the window offering refreshments.

Emily glanced at The Grand Hotel but knew it would be unfair to expect such luxury, so turned towards the mid-terraced property indicated by Ed. "That would be lovely."

Once a table with a view had been claimed, they gazed through glazed doors and across the green, the wet sands and flat grey waters. "Wouldn't it be glorious in the summer with these doors open?" Emily commented. "Do you think they put chairs out there?"

"Probably," Ed replied, appreciating his companion's enthusiasm. He eyed the stuffed seabirds on the mantelpiece, preferring to see them flying free, but didn't like to seek Emily's opinion, so instead he asked, "Are you warm enough?"

"Oh yes. There's not much of a fire, but we've had a good walk to warm us through."

At the round gate-leg table, topped with a cotton cloth and a layer of lace, they enjoyed tea and fruitcake. Conversation flowed - sometimes with ease and at times a little awkwardly. Whereas Emily was used to chatting with a variety of characters, Ed's life was a lonely one with many hours spent in the company of his cousin Jake. The view and new seaside resort were a distraction. As they drained their second cups of tea, a group of elderly women settled themselves at a corner table, but otherwise their only other company was the maid who served them.

"We've just got time to walk the other way a bit," Ed suggested, as they descended the short row of steps from the front door to the pavement.

Once more, Emily tucked her arm through his, and they strolled along the green towards the decorative water tower. Here, after the imposing new residences, the road turned to a rubble track and a row of single-storey coastguards' cottages.

"How plain they are after all these fancy houses," Emily pointed out. "I wonder if that Mr Tubbs you were telling me about – him who planned all this – I wonder if he'll knock them down and build the coastguards something else?"

"He'll be wanting this land for posh houses," Ed agreed.

"Well, I hope he keeps the watch house and the lifeboat station," Emily continued.

"I'm sure he will." Then Ed, encouraged by his companion's lively manner, suggested, "How about I have a word with Mr Tubbs and see if he'd like to build some nice houses down Denge way? Then I could have a maid and invite you to afternoon tea!"

Emily laughed, "Gosh! I don't know what he would think about that." Then she turned her attention to the water tower. "That's something special, ain't it?" It must be as tall as a lighthouse, but far more ornate."

This marked the point where it was time to retrace their steps, back to the tree-lined avenue and then the railway station. After one last glance at the sea, Ed said, "Thanks for coming out with me today. It's been lovely. I haven't got much money... and it's a rough life there at Denge, but perhaps you would walk out with me again one afternoon? Maybe to New Romney next time?"

Emily gazed at his dark eyes, thick brows and the furrows that had settled on his forehead. She saw a decent, hard-working man, who treated her nicely. He may not have the banter of the young men she was used to, but he had interesting things to tell her, and she had enjoyed every moment of their time together. "I'd like that. Ta. Ta very much."

Taking his time on the moonlit track from Lydd to Denge, Ed relished this chance to relive the afternoon with Emily.

She liked the brooch. She must have done or there would have been some excuse not to wear it. That's what women are like – they don't wear anything they haven't taken a fancy to. Besides, she tucked her arm through mine, and it was lovely having her close like that.

Closing his eyes a little, Ed breathed deeply, and although his nostrils were filled with the scents of damp grass in the fields, rotting reeds at the edge of the ditch, and a faint fragrance from the sea, he registered none of it. Instead, he recalled the aroma of Emily's floral soap, and the sweet lavender that brushed against her coat when hanging in the closet.

His feet moved with the undulations of the track, never faltering despite him paying no attention to the furrows and scattered stones underfoot. On finally spotting the weak light emitted from the shacks at Denge, he refrained from calling in at the Hope and Anchor but decided to continue reminiscing in the peace of his humble home.

Chapter Eighteen

November merged into December, and time trudged steadily forward, with nothing of particular interest to mark the weeks. The skies were dark and oppressive over Lydd as the shortest days of the year approached. It was too soon to think of brighter days ahead – the coldest months of winter were yet to descend on them.

Emily tried not to count the time since she had so enjoyed her outing to Littlestone, yet as another Saturday neared, she couldn't help but realise four weeks had passed. *It can't be easy for him to get away.* She tried to be rational, understanding that it would take an hour for Ed to walk to Lydd if he were to seek her out with a message, also knowing his days were governed by the tides. But Emily was not blessed with patience and his silence frustrated her, leading to conflicting thoughts rattling about in her mind. *I know it's not easy for him – it must be difficult at the best of times, but to go out to sea in the winter must be miserable. He'll get in touch when he can… he said he would… and he gave me the brooch that was his ma's. He gave me the brooch, but probably changed his mind about liking me and didn't think to ask for it back. That's what happened. And then he was being polite, saying we would meet up again. I suppose that's all there is to it. I'll see him about the place this week or next, and he'll offer me a nod and walk on by, because he won't want to come and say that he changed his mind. It's for the best. Silly of me to think any different…*

Three days before Christmas, Emily stood on the corner of Wheeler's Green with her coat fully buttoned up and a shawl wrapped around her shoulders. As she scanned familiar shop fronts, the wind buffeted across the Rype and through the streets, carrying anything it could pick up on its way. Strands of straw clung to Emily's ankles and the hem of her dress; she shook them off, scowling at their audacity. Her spirits were low, as she braced herself both against the wind and the realisation that there was to be no message from Cora inviting her back home for Christmas.

"Some wool for Hattie," Emily muttered, and set off to the High Street. She needed gifts for her new family at the Dolphin, including John and Sarah who would be with their parents on the day, but may still call in for a drop of sherry after church.

An hour later, the shopping basket held a leather pouch and tobacco for James, ribbons for Sarah and wool for Hattie. Emily was already progressing with the knitting of scarves for John and Alf.

Not inclined to go home, knowing her thoughts would soon wander to the scenes in Albert Road where her mother and Molly would have the Christmas preparations in full swing, Emily slowed near the entrance to a tearoom. Soft lights at the windows beckoned her, and a string of decorative paper angels swayed gently.

"Are you coming in, Emily?" A young woman passed her and pressed on the door. "Share a table with me if you like?"

Emily flashed a smile, her mood lifting. "Oh, go on then!" She followed Ellen, a maid in one of the big houses, into the tearoom.

It was during that pleasant half hour, Emily realised how much she missed the company of the women she had grown up with, or those she met regularly around the town. She had no one to accompany her on a Sunday afternoon stroll, or to swap ribbons, wool and dress material. When she and Ellen parted on the street, the shops were all closing, and the night sky was a starless black. A light mist shifted about under the glow of gas lamps on the High Street.

"Have a happy Christmas if I don't see you before," Emily said.

"And you too," Ellen replied. "I've had a right giggle over the tea and buns. Ta very much."

I think I've made a friend! No longer as bothered by the chill, Emily stepped out, following one pool of light to the next, welcoming the overhead lamps and clutching her basket close to her. Her pleasure was short-lived though – she had walked no distance at all and was about to move aside for a man on the pavement, when he spoke, "Hello Emily, I hardly hoped to see you out here in the dark."

"Hello Ed," she responded, showing no emotion in her voice. "Fancy seeing you after all this time."

"It has been a long time," he said. "One of our boats is in Rye for repairs, and so we're all toiling hard to catch fish from the one boat and working on the homes too – trying to keep the old folk warm through the winter."

"I've been busy too with my work at the George, and I've just had a nice bit of tea with a friend."

"Well, it's been nice to see you, and…" Ed paused. "Don't think I've forgotten about us going over to Romney sometime."

"I'd like that." Emily thawed a little. "I never got to see the town, did I?"

Neither of them seemed to know what to say after that, so they parted, Emily now with a scowl on her face. *I like him. I can't deny it – but he can't expect a girl to be waiting about for a trip to Romney. If he wants to go walking out with me, then I expect to see him every week. But is that what I want? To go courting? I suppose I do, but it's a barmy idea…*

A couple of days later, after completing her work by early afternoon on Christmas Eve, Emily walked to the Dolphin with a small packet containing her Christmas bonus in her pocket. She relished the few days off work, while wondering what she was to do with herself at this time. Her pace was slower than usual, reflecting feelings of uncertainty about the days ahead. Having only ever known Christmas to be spent in the heart of her loving family, try as she might it was hard to imagine the festive season in her new home with characters who had been strangers to her only three months before.

However, on reaching the Dolphin, dinner was underway with cottage pie being dished up, and Emily found herself thrown into the hectic life of being part of the family living and working at the hotel. By the time she was scrubbing the dishes at the scullery sink, her spirits had lifted, and she had made plans for the rest of the afternoon.

Well, I'm on my holidays so I'll settle down with my book for a while.

Over the past month, James had asserted his rule over the Dolphin and made it clear she was not to slave for Hattie as well as work long hours at the George Hotel. With a cup of tea carefully balanced in its saucer, Emily moved upstairs to the welcome solitude of her bedroom and settled herself by the window. Here the grey winter light cast itself on the pages of her new book, and she was soon absorbed in the romances of Elfride Swancourt in Thomas Hardy's novel *A Pair of Blue Eyes.*

James closed the pub early on Christmas Eve. Later in the evening, they were to walk the short distance to All Saints and celebrate Midnight Mass within its ancient walls, but it was long before this time that the patrons were being ushered onto the street. From her seat by the fire in their shared sitting room, Emily heard the pub-goers leave, most likely to the smoky environs of the nearby New Inn. She frowned, unsure of why the bar would close at this early hour.

"It's my tradition here at the Dolphin," James told Emily when she asked why he closed early. "But there is no reason why you and I can't have a drink together. Something to warm us before we go to church?"

"I'll have a small port," Emily replied, glad to be distracted from her melancholy thoughts of the family in Ashford, and equally gloomy ponderings about Ed. Thomas Hardy's novel had occupied her for a while, but once the sun was setting, she had become aware of the chill in her bedroom and wandered restlessly between the warmth of the kitchen range and the comfort of the sitting room.

James returned a few minutes later, "Isn't it a treat to come here and find you to keep me company?" he said. "It's all very well being with the men in the bar, but they don't compare to having a talk with you."

Emily sipped, allowing the red liquor to caress her tongue before slipping down her throat.

"You and I will have that trip out as soon as winter has passed," James was saying. "To Hastings, or even Eastbourne. You'd like that, wouldn't you?"

"Like it?" It felt as if the port flowed through her limbs, warming and relaxing her. "I'd love it, I'm sure!" Then Emily wondered, "Don't you see your parents at Christmastime?"

"Sometimes." He stretched his legs out, so his toes almost touched the hearth – a picture of a man well satisfied with life. "But you are here, and I couldn't wish for better company."

"Oh… listen to you!" She laughed, pushing back a stray tendril of hair, then pressing the pins into the knot at the back of her head. "Think of all those interesting people that you meet from different places. Clever men like Mr Blackmore are far more remarkable than me." Emily hadn't noticed before that the bottle of port was on a side table, and now she watched as James rose to top up both their glasses. "Ta very much, I'll be nicely warmed through before church."

"That's what I was hoping." He slumped back into the chair. "The cosier the better before we head out tonight." They were silent for a moment, watching the low flames lick the coals in the grate, then James continued, "You're wrong, you know, about other people being more interesting. It's always fun when we talk. I like listening to your opinions, and you are eager to learn."

Emily was considering this when James jumped up from his chair, almost spilling his drink. "Stay there – I've got a gift for you…"

"It's not Christmas yet!" she chided as he left the room, but it was too late, so she took another sip of port. *All them miserable thoughts have gone now. I'm looking forward to going to the big church for Midnight Mass, and tomorrow will be different, but I am sure I'll enjoy it well enough.*

Reappearing within seconds, James carried a large bundle wrapped in decorative paper. "Happy Christmas!" He placed it on her lap and stood to watch her open it.

Emily loosened the string and the paper fell open to reveal a shawl knitted from a tawny coloured wool. "Oh! It's beautiful. You shouldn't have…"

"Shouldn't have bought you something special? Of course, I should!"

"It's like the colour of autumn leaves." Emily held up the shawl, turning it to and fro. "And so thick. Thank you! I'll be as warm as anything when the frost and snow come."

"Emily, I've got an idea, and I hope you think it's a good one." James remained standing before her. "We've agreed, haven't we, that you and I make a good team? You know how I want to look after you and keep you safe… and treat you to nice things."

Emily nodded but said nothing. Her world had mellowed and her troubles were nothing to her now. She wrapped his gift around her shoulders.

"You like the shawl, don't you? I went to Rye for it – I wanted something special for you."

"It's lovely. And you went to Rye for me… just for me?"

"I'd knit it myself if I thought you would appreciate it!"

Emily laughed then, to imagine James sitting at the bar with a basket of knitting. "No! You do enough – giving me a place to stay and letting me share your private sitting room."

"Have another taste of port – it's good, isn't it? One of the best in my cellar – I keep it for special people – my special friends."

She took another sip, only it became more of a gulp and raced down her throat.

"Don't worry," James soothed, as if he knew she felt a little foolish. "It's all about keeping warm for church. You'll be lovely and snug with the port and the shawl."

Emily took a small drop, a dainty one. She was warm – too warm with the fire, and the port. She took the shawl off and placed it on the back of the chair. "What was your idea?" she asked, suddenly recalling his earlier words.

"I thought we should get married!" James shuffled forwards in the chair and reached into the pocket of his waistcoat to withdraw a small box.

Stunned, Emily gazed at the large solitaire diamond nestling in navy silk. An image of Ed slammed into her mind and for a moment she saw him sitting before her, and her body swayed as if they were together in the carriage pulled behind the train bound for New Romney. Blinking, she swept it away. *No point in wondering about him.*

"I didn't think…" Emily began.

"Didn't you?" He offered her the ring. "I think of it all the time: how good it feels to share your company, how wonderful it is when we are close. I'm a little older, of course, but you're not a girl. You're a woman who appreciates what a good friend I have been."

"Oh, you have… you are." Emily recalled the small touches – a hand on her waist, the time he massaged her shoulders… the comforting hug. Her skin began to flush, knowing she had felt soothed by his care, then realising these could be construed as the gestures of a lover. She imagined more of those moments… being appreciated…wanted. Now it seemed foolish to yearn for a poor fisherman when the person who could offer her love and security had been with her all the time. *But I never even thought of it. He's older than my ma, but I can't deny he's a handsome man, and knows how to treat me nicely.*

Emily reached for the ring. It caught the light from a lamp and captivated her with its beauty. A sensation of warmth and softness coursed through her body, and she felt one of his hands resting on her knees.

"What do you say?" James reached forward and eased the ring from its box. "Will you marry me?"

"Yes," she blurted out. "Yes, I will."

Enthralled, she allowed James to slip the ring onto her slim finger. "A perfect fit," he announced, and leaning forward he kissed her gently on the lips, pressing his tongue into her mouth a little and bringing his arms up so they circled her neck. She responded, wanting to please him.

"I love you, Emily," he murmured as they parted a little. "I love you more than you could ever imagine."

"I love you too," she whispered. At that moment, with his fingertips caressing the back of her neck, she meant it.

The fire burned low while they kissed and whispered words of affection to one another. When he moved to put more coal on the embers, then flopped down in his armchair, she asked, "When will we get married?"

"As soon as possible," he stated. "We could have the banns read in January."

"January? How will we get ready in time?" Her words were rushed, and suddenly the effects of the port seemed to have left her body, only to be replaced with a feeling of unease. This sharp contrast of emotions confused her.

"What is there to do?" James asked.

"We'll have to tell our parents… and plan a nice wedding breakfast. And I'll need to make a dress."

"I thought it could be just you and me?"

What is he thinking of – just me and him. How can he not have his own dear parents at our wedding, and I must tell Ma, so she has plenty of time to make dresses for her and Molly. This will show I can be trusted to go off on my own and make something good of my life. Fancy me marrying a rich man with a hotel! I'll want them there to see it all – especially this place where I'll be Mrs James Roberts, wife of the landlord!

"No," she replied. "It won't be just us. I want it done respectable and that means having our parents sitting in the pews behind us, and everything just so…"

"How long will that take?" he groaned. "You've just made me the happiest man alive, and I want to take you as my wife as soon as possible."

"I was thinking the spring?" Emily suggested. "How about April or May?"

"March!" he demanded, reaching for the port. "It should be champagne, but I think you have a taste for this!"

"It will be too cold in March." She held her glass out, but insisted, "Just half."

"We can wrap up. March it is."

They kissed again and she liked the feeling of his hand on her back. The bewilderment eased, to be replaced once more with a warm, fuzzy feeling of contentment. His fingertips roamed towards her corseted breast. *I'll have to get used to this sort of thing now I'm engaged to be married.*

"Helen?" Ed stood in the doorway of his cousin's home.

"Shut the door and come on in. He's not here." She referred to Jake, who was probably at the beerhouse.

"I know." Ed perched on the edge of a chair and tried to keep his gaze averted from her breast. The baby was only six weeks old and seemed to be permanently attached. "How are you?"

"Tired with being cooped up in here," she replied. "And that ain't going to change any time soon." Icy winds had been gusting from the west since the new year, and snow would soon follow. It was no place to nurture a newborn. "Anyway, you didn't come here to ask how I am. What's bothering you, Ed?"

"Can you write, Helen?"

"Write! I don't have much need for that, but I can put a few words together and some numbers."

"Could you write a letter?"

"It would be more of a scribble..." Helen admitted. "What do you need it for?"

"I want to let Emily know. I want to say I won't get to Lydd much and when the snow starts, not at all. I'm praying she'll wait for me." He paused, hoping she wouldn't mock him for falling in love with a beautiful woman.

Helen moved the sleeping baby, then wiped both his chin and her breast with a cloth. While tending to her child, she was thinking how best to advise Ed, and finally she spoke, "Go to see Miss Wilkie at the school. You want a good letter – not a bit of a scrawl. She'll help."

Chapter Nineteen

Dolphin Hotel
Lydd
4th January 1894

Dear Ma and Jacob,

Happy New Year! I hope you all had a lovely Christmas. I kept thinking and wondering what you were doing. I should have sent a card and gifts but was sad you never replied to my last letter. It was a different sort of Christmas here in Lydd with Midnight Mass at the big parish church, and dinner in the Dolphin Hotel with James Roberts and the other people who live here.

I don't want there to be bad feelings, so I am writing again with good news. At least I hope you will think it is good. James asked me to marry him on Christmas Eve, and I said yes! He has been so good to me since I arrived – keeping an eye on me and making me welcome in his home. Your daughter Emily is not so little now. I'm going to be a married woman! We haven't set a date for the wedding yet. James wanted it to be straight away, but I said we must give you time to prepare and no one wants to go travelling in the winter. Next week we will go to see the vicar and look at dates in March. Ma, that gives you and Molly three months to make yourselves some fancy dresses!

Well, you can look forward to the official invitation in the post, and the same for Ada and Reuben. I expect James will write to them as well.

With love from your daughter, Emily

"I've written a letter home," Emily told James. She was sealing the envelope as he walked into their sitting room.

"Wonderful!" James took long strides across the room and placed his hands on her shoulders while she remained seated at the writing bureau. "Your family will be thrilled to have a daughter about to be married."

"Do you think so?"

"Of course!" He began to rotate his thumbs at the base of her neck, pressing gently. "Parents worry about their children, so what a relief it must be to have a daughter of twenty-three years ready to settle down. They'll know I can keep you in comfort here at the Dolphin, or wherever else we may choose to settle. Do you remember I spoke of us running a hotel in Hastings or Eastbourne?"

"We were going to go there in the spring," Emily recalled, finding herself relaxing under his touch.

"Perhaps for our honeymoon?"

"Oh!" Emily began to blush to think of the intimacies shared at that time. "That sounds very nice indeed."

James leaned forward, and Emily turned her head, ready for him to press his lips upon hers. He moved his hands, over her high collar and the pleats of material encasing her chest, cupping her breasts and squeezing a little. Releasing herself from the kiss, Emily moved forward on the chair and stood up, so he had little choice but to allow his hands to drop. They settled upon her waist as she turned to face him.

"I'll arrange something," James said, still referring to the honeymoon, and kissing her lightly.

"Are you going to write to your parents?" Emily asked. "Or shall I? Perhaps I should as I am already so fond of them."

"Let's both write." James flashed a smile at her. "We can put the two letters together. Think how pleased they will be to learn that our families will be joined by marriage!"

"They will be, won't they?" To hear those words and to know that her dear Ada and Reuben would now truly be her family filled Emily will a sense of happiness she had not yet reached since her engagement. Any doubts she had suffered for the gap in age between them flew from her mind as she pictured Ada and Reuben coming to the Dolphin, perhaps staying for a few nights and them all sharing family meals around the table. "Shall we do it now?" she asked. "Write the letters?"

"Why not?" he agreed.

"Then I'll take them to the post office, and you can have a rest – read the paper or something before the bar opens again."

"I can see you'll look after me very well!" He kissed her again, this time allowing his hands to roam to her pert bottom before releasing her.

Having posted the letters – the one to James' family being satisfyingly plump as it contained two pages of folded paper – Emily paused on the pavement and gazed up at the church tower. As she did so, the chimes of the half hour filtered out of high shuttered openings and resonated through medieval stonework. *Half-past three. It will be dark in no time, but I can do a circuit before I'm stuck in for the evening.* Emily retraced her steps, then walked past the Dolphin and picked up her pace, determined to walk the whole way around the Rype before the long evening set in.

The sky was leaden with low lying clouds, the grass withered, and those weeds bold enough to show their faces were short and ragged. It was as bleak a scene as Emily had ever encountered in the town she now called home. True, there were short terraces of brick houses, thatched farmhouses and the tithe barn fronting the green, but standing on the brink of it, these places were indistinct. *When the frosty mornings come, it will look a picture.* Emily, generally optimistic, set out at speed, soon reaching the far side.

"Hello Emily!" A young woman's voice rang out. "Can I walk with you?"

"Ellen! What are you doing over here?"

"I'm visiting my aunt." Ellen replied. "I was hoping to see you – I heard you're getting married!"

The two women stepped out alongside each other, and Emily confirmed the news, "I am! Mr Roberts – James – asked me on Christmas Eve. It was a surprise, but a nice one." She held out her hand to show off the ring.

"Is that a real diamond?" Ellen asked in hushed tones. "I've never seen… well, only on the rich folk. It's big, isn't it?"

"Of course it's real!" Emily let out a short laugh. "He's a wealthy man, is Mr James."

"I suppose he is, what with running the Dolphin Hotel, and he probably has a bank account and goes off to see the manager to have talks. He's that kind of person – important."

"I suppose he is," Emily agreed.

They walked in silence for a moment, Emily relishing the opportunity to share her news with a friend. The sky was darkening rapidly and, with the plan to circle the whole of the Rype abandoned, they took a path leading across the green, both wanting to return home before nightfall had completely settled upon the town.

"I thought you might have taken a fancy to that John who works at the bar," Ellen spoke next.

Emily, recalling James' advice that she should not encourage any familiarity with John, was quick to answer, "John! Oh no, he must be a year or two younger than me, and I don't think he has any prospect of bettering himself."

"He's not bad looking though."

"It depends on what you like." An image of Ed Brooks flashed into her mind. "John's a bit too young for me, and I like them a bit stockier."

"Well, he might be a bit older than you, but I can't help saying that Mr Roberts is a looker too! He's a real man, isn't he? I don't blame you for agreeing to marry him, and he'll look after you nicely."

"Yes, he is," Emily smiled, enjoying the chance to gossip with a friendly young woman. "He's certainly handsome, and he's been so good to me since I came here. And his parents are close friends of my family back in Ashford."

"They'll be happy for you then."

Pushing aside Cora's obvious dislike for James, Emily decided, "They will! It's going to be lovely – all one big happy family, and Ashford is no distance by train. They can come visiting and we can go there. I've just posted a letter to my parents to tell them all about it, and James wrote one to his too! They're in the post-box as we speak!"

"Will you get married in the summer?"

"James wanted to get married straight away!" Emily confided, "But it isn't right to rush into it, and I told him we must give our parents a chance to hear the news, and our mothers to get themselves posh frocks. So, we agreed on the spring, but he says March although it will still be cold, won't it?"

"May would be nicer," Ellen agreed, "but he's a man and he'll want you in his bed as soon as possible."

Emily began to colour, recalling James' obvious passion for her, and uncertain of what to expect on the wedding night. "I don't know about that... He just wants to get married, I think. Anyway, we are going to see the vicar tomorrow, and the date will be set."

The two women parted company as Emily neared the Dolphin. On reaching the hotel, a figure could be seen at a front window. Knowing it to be James she gave a wave, but the curtain fell, and the window was left in darkness.

"I would have gone with you if I'd known you wanted a walk," James said. He now sat at the bureau, with some paperwork before him.

"I only decided after I posted the letters," Emily said. "You'll be back in the bar soon, but it's a long evening for me when the winter comes."

"I suppose you are used to pleasing yourself when you are not at work," he suggested, still turned towards the papers, his pen poised to dip in the ink.

"Did Hattie need me?" Emily suddenly felt alarmed that the housekeeper may have expected her to assist with some chore, or perhaps an arrangement had been made and forgotten.

"Not that I know of." James lay his pen down and turned to face her. "It was me who missed you. I was beginning to worry. It's getting dark."

"I must have got used to only thinking about myself." Emily stood before him and offered a kiss. "I saw Ellen and was telling her how we are off to see the vicar."

"Of course, we are!" He reached and gave her bottom a slight squeeze, then grinned. "I was being foolish, thinking you had forgotten about me for a moment."

"I wouldn't do that." Emily forced a smile. *I didn't know this getting married business was going to be complicated. That's my problem, just like Ma always said – I don't think enough. There's me going for a walk like I only have to please myself and not realising that he might worry about where I've got to.*

"I know that now." James turned back to the papers in front of him. Emily picked up a pamphlet of dress designs in the newest styles and began to consider which would suit her as a wedding dress.

Despite her arm being tucked through James' and knowing she had taken care to look her best, Emily's pace slowed on reaching the rectory. "I don't know what he's going to ask me," she confided in James. "I'm worried I won't speak posh enough."

The house before her was substantial. As Emily pictured the graceful furniture, sumptuous fabrics and delicate ornaments that were, no doubt, to be discovered in such a home, her agitation reached its peak and the thoughts in her head began to swim about. Loosening her shawl, she breathed deeply and slowly, while taking in the architectural details. Sash windows, each one the same proportions as the others, stood to attention either side and above an elegant doorway, while the walls showed a smooth render framed by raised plasterwork at the corners and cornicing below the roofline.

"The vicar will be as delighted with you as I am!" James declared. "And you *have* met him at church."

"I keep myself to myself in church," Emily admitted. Awed by the ancient All Saints and the vastness of the building, she suffered the loss of all that was familiar in her modern Methodist chapel in Ashford. "I'm worried that God will be confused by me being Methodist one day and going to regular church the next."

"As long as you worship, He will think nothing of it." James tugged on her arm, encouraging those last steps as they moved from the pavement, onto the short front path, and stood under the shallow porch. He raised his hand and gave a couple of sharp raps with the door knocker.

The couple were soon being ushered through the hallway and into the study where the vicar stood to greet them. When she considered it afterwards, it seemed to Emily that she remembered nothing of the first few minutes of conversation, while seated in an upright chair, with James close by and the vicar opposite. All pleasantries were exchanged between the two men, while she had a recollection of making some obliging noises, which seemed to be all that was necessary. She recalled floor to ceiling bookshelves, a desk of mahogany, and the vicar relaxed on a chair which had brass castors on each of its three feet, allowing him to move about in an intriguing manner. It would have been pleasant to look out on the garden, but the curtains were so full, and her position made it awkward to appreciate the view.

Once tea was served by the maid, Emily's nerves began to subside, and she became aware that the men were speaking of banns being read. "Three Sundays before the ceremony..." the vicar was saying. "When were you thinking of getting married?"

"As soon as possible!" James was quick in his response.

"Then you should apply for a special licence if it's a matter of urgency."

"It's not urgent," Emily retorted, her tone a little sharp. "Sorry… it's just that we spoke of March..." She felt her cheeks begin to burn and looked down at her hands, then twisted her ring to and fro.

"March it is then?" the vicar queried. "Shall we say the end of the month, in the hope of the weather improving a little by then?"

"Perfect." Emily couldn't bring herself to look at him. *To think of him believing that we have to marry. I'm not that sort of girl.*

"Now I must take some details." The vicar pulled forward a sheet of paper and dipped his pen in the inkwell. "Starting with your full names, dates of birth and addresses."

James gave his and they both turned to Emily.

"Emily Anne Parkins," she said, her mouth beginning to dry. "24th November 1871. The Dolphin..." A heat rose through her body. *Gracious, what will he think with my address being the same? He already mentioned me being in the family way, well close enough... He's going to think I'm one of them women with loose morals and him a religious man...* "I'm at the same address, but I'm there as a lodger, it being a hotel."

"Of course you are," the vicar clarified. "But perhaps you would prefer to use your family's address, just for the records."

Emily took a gulp of tea. "Yes, that would suit me very nicely. I'm from Albert Road in Ashford…" She shifted in her chair a little so as to have a glimpse of the garden, then added, unnecessarily, "I came here in September, but I knew Mr Roberts before then."

"Albert Road," the vicar repeated as he wrote. Opening his diary, he turned the pages, scanning dates. "Let's say Saturday 24th March at midday."

Emily glanced at James. "Splendid!" he said.

They left not long afterwards, with Emily barely recalling the details of the conversation following the wedding date being agreed. There had been discussion of commitment, and the significance of the vows to be taken, and some general information offered about each of their families. Afterwards, the men had exchanged a few comments about local matters. Unable to focus and fearing that she might say or do the wrong thing, Emily allowed her attention to wander to the view seen through the vicar's window: a robin on the bare branch of a magnolia tree, lichen spreading over an ornamental cherub, and a spider's web stretching across the dormant wisteria. Her tea chilled, and she sipped the last of it. Then they were on the doorstep and James was suggesting they stroll to the western end of the Rype and back.

"To stretch our legs," he elaborated.

"I'd like that," Emily agreed, hoping that fresh air and exercise would brush away the fog seeming to have wrapped itself around her in the time spent sitting in the rector's study.

"Two and a half months!" James exclaimed. "I don't know how I shall bear the wait."

Emily frowned a little. *I don't know what he's complaining about. We already live together and so it won't make much difference if we are married or not. I suppose he's thinking of intimate things that happen between a man and his wife, but the time will pass soon enough.* She placed her arm through his and attempted to pacify him, "You're so busy in the hotel and with all your other work, and I'll have a dress to make and all sorts to plan. The time will soon fly."

"It will," he agreed, planting a bold kiss on her lips. "And in the meantime, you can give Mrs Tatin notice that you'll be leaving your position at the George

Hotel. I think a week will suffice, or two if we are to be more considerate."

"Leaving?" the word ricocheted in Emily's mind. "But I thought… I mean I like it there."

"I know you do. But you don't need to work now, my darling." They stopped walking and James turned to face her. "I want to care for you."

"You do care for me." Emily felt a chill wash through her body. Her hands felt cold and small encased within his. "I thought I'd work until we were married, or until…" *Until the baby comes…*

"That's one of the many things I love about you," he declared, squeezing her hands in his and smiling down on her. "But I can't have it. I won't have it! You have to understand, Emily, that I have over twenty years more experience of life than you do, and so I know the ways of the world more than you… than you could hope to."

"I'd like to work until the wedding," Emily responded, choosing her words carefully. "But I hadn't thought… It's not right, is it? You the owner of a hotel, and me doing the cleaning in another. I do like my work on reception though. Perhaps I could work until the end of February, and leave three weeks before the wedding?" *He's right. Of course, he is. I'm lucky really, because if it wasn't for him, I'd go through my life making all sorts of foolish mistakes. And over twenty years between us means he knows so much more than a man of my age – they're still boys really.* Yet despite these bold thoughts, Emily was already finding the business of planning to marry utterly exhausting.

Having slipped his boots into backstays, Ed set off on the lonely path to Dungeness, the flat boards enabling him to progress at a fair pace without sinking into the shingle. There was nothing to break up the tedium of the trek – not a patch of withered grass or bedraggled seakale. His thoughts remained fully engaged with the content of the letter he hoped to pen.

On nearing the school, Ed saw he had timed his journey to perfection. Trails of boys and girls were leaving – bound for their homes, and a hot dinner if they were lucky. A substantial building, the school was both classroom, and church on a Sunday, as well as accommodation for teachers. Ed approached from the back and rapped on the kitchen door.

The housekeeper answered, opening the door a crack and peering suspiciously at him. "I've come to see Miss Wilkie," Ed explained. "I was hoping she could help me."

While her dinner kept warm in the oven, Miss Wilkie led the way to the schoolroom and sat at her desk, with her back straight and a piece of writing paper at the ready. She knew without having been told, this letter was of a personal nature, and not to be written under the watchful eye of the housekeeper.

"It's to Emily," Ed began. "Dear Emily..."

When she had finished, the headteacher passed the pen to Ed for him to sign his name, then offered: "I have my own letter to post tomorrow. Would you care for me to take yours as well?"

He nodded his thanks, and reached in his pocket, then passed her a penny for the stamp.

Cora's Story
Chapter Twenty
Ashford, Kent

With the letter clasped in her hand, Cora raced down Albert Road and around the corner where she reduced her pace a little. She wore no coat, despite there being a hard frost that morning and the remains of it still lurking in the shadowed corners. Her shawl, the one torn by Emily days before she fled, was hanging precariously. Cora hadn't enough hands to hold up her long skirt, secure the thick woollen wrap and keep the letter firmly in her grasp. Having rearranged herself so both shawl and letter were secured by one hand, she continued to walk briskly, breaking into a run at times.

At the gates of the cemetery, she paused, her eyes roaming to and fro, then took the central path. Frustrated by the evergreen shrubs hindering her view, she darted to each gap in the hope that she would catch sight of her husband. Time slowed, although in reality only a minute or so had passed before Jacob was spotted sweeping the paths around one of the chapels. Cora scampered onwards, not liking to call out to him, and knowing he would be alerted by her movement in this place where the rhythms of life were generally ponderous and predictable.

At first, Jacob smiled to see her. Then, having propped his broom against a wall, he moved towards Cora, his expression showing he was both eager for her news and concerned for what she may reveal. "You've heard from her. Thank God."

"It just came..." Cora's breath was ragged, as she continued, "She's in Lydd! In Lydd with James Roberts!"

"But he's over twenty years older than her..." Jacob paused to digest the news further. "You mean with him like...?"

"They're getting married. Yes. With him. How did that happen? How could it have happened without us knowing?"

"I don't know, love." Jacob reached out for his wife. Putting his arms around her and resting his chin on the top of her head, he attempted to reason with this news: "We did our best for Emily. James hardly knew her. In fact, I didn't know of them ever meeting, not in recent years anyway."

"Oh, he spotted her working in the bakery," Cora's tone was knowing, "and was full of praise for her. And remember that night she ran off – she went to Reuben and Ada's, didn't she? He was there – fussing over her no doubt."

"Come and sit down," Jacob led her to a bench. "I need to see this letter for myself, and we'll work out what's to be done."

"We'll have to go there and stop her!" The words flew from Cora.

"We'll have to think about this and be very careful," Jacob responded. "No rash decisions."

Seated side by side, they held the letter open between them and read it. This time Cora took the time to consider every line. "I hardly saw this before," she said, now subdued by the first lines. "Emily wrote before. She says so here. She wrote before, and we didn't get it. How could that be?"

"And she thought we didn't care enough to reply."

"I know." Tears began to form, as Cora imagined how Emily felt to receive nothing in return for her first letter. *No wonder she turned to the man who was, no doubt, giving her attention and flattering her every hour of the day. First there was that business with Johnny and May – she felt rejected by him. Then, when she wrote to say where she was, it seemed like we didn't care anymore.* "James Roberts had easy pickings when it came to Emily."

"I think he did," Jacob agreed. "But they're not married yet, and perhaps there's a chance of changing her mind. I have a feeling that Emily has got herself in a fix, and if we can have a chat with her, show her that we want her back home, then maybe…"

"We can go tomorrow." In her mind, Cora was already at the railway station peering at the Sunday timetable. "She'll be expecting us, won't she? Emily wrote the letter yesterday, knowing I would go to her the moment I knew."

"She won't be expecting us," Jacob reminded her. "Because she wrote before, and we didn't go to her, or even reply. Emily doesn't know we didn't get the letter. And another thing…" He paused, knowing his wife wouldn't like his next words, but they needed to be said. "Another thing… Emily will think whatever he has told her to think. It's been over three months and that's plenty of time for him to sway her thoughts to whatever suits him."

"I can't believe we didn't get her letter." The tears rolled unhindered down Cora's cheeks, and she nestled into Jacob.

Neither of them uttered a word for a few minutes, each enveloped in their own thoughts. Jacob pulled a handkerchief from his pocket and wiped her tears away. A while later he stood, encouraging Cora to rise from the bench. “It’s too cold to be sitting about,” he said. “Come on, I was about to pack up anyway. We can go home.”

“I’ve not got the dinner on!” Cora wailed.

“We’ll do it together.”

The broom was placed in a tool shed, and they began the short walk home. Before reaching Albert Road, Cora’s thoughts had shifted to the elderly couple she loved as family: “What about Ada and Reuben? They don’t know about this, do they?”

“If they do then they’ll be in the same boat as us, hearing by letter today,” Jacob suggested, “and I know they are proud of him, but we can be sure they won’t be happy about this. They love Emily and have been as worried as we were. We know she has told us about the wedding, but has James told them? I suggest we go to see them after church tomorrow and see if they’ve heard anything.”

“But we are going to Lydd tomorrow.”

“No. Let’s just think about this for a few days and give ourselves a chance to calm down. Another week won’t make a difference. I’ll take the morning off next Saturday and we can set off nice and early.”

“You’re right,” Cora admitted, using all her inner strength to think sensibly. “I need time to get used to it, and part of that is accepting she might well marry him. It’s been three months, and it seems like Emily has got herself settled into a new life.”

That afternoon Jacob and Cora went first to their eldest son, William. They sat in the kitchen of the ground floor flat, while his wife made tea and their young daughters pored over the pages of a picture book brought to absorb their attention while the adults spoke. Then they walked to Willesborough, to the narrow, terraced home where the newly married Johnny lived with May. Here they perched on the edge of a thirdhand sagging sofa and relayed the news. Back home, Frank and Molly were the last of the close family to learn of the letter, now becoming tattered as it was passed around.

Relief came first – above anything the family rejoiced to know Emily was safe and had at last been in touch with them. Lydd wasn't too far away, they all agreed, and if she couldn't be persuaded to return home, then nothing could prevent them from seeing her regularly.

"It's not like we are living in the olden days when we had to go everywhere by horse and cart, or even walking," Frank voiced their thoughts. "It's no trouble to get to Lydd by the railway."

These initial feelings of joy were replaced by sorrow that Emily's first letter had gone missing, and the family had suffered unnecessary months of distress.

"She was always bossing me about, but I miss her," Molly murmured, while she sat with Jacob's arms around her. "I thought she didn't care about us at all, that she had gone off and couldn't be bothered about us, but I was wrong. She did write and we didn't know."

Then came the curiosity about how Emily had come to be in Lydd, living with James Roberts.

"We barely saw him," William explained to May, who knew nothing of this man. "You've met his parents, of course, but not him. He was there though, staying with them at the time Emily ran off."

"He must have lured her." May was wise to the temptations open to vulnerable women. "If he's got his own hotel and is a bit flash, then it's easy to be taken in."

There were questions from the young people about what sort of place the Dolphin Hotel was. Both Jacob and Cora recalled it as being a fair-sized property, well-built, and having a decent reputation.

These topics were explored over and over, from William's flat, to Johnny's terraced house, and back to the front parlour of the home in Albert Road.

"It's exhausting, isn't it?" Cora said to Jacob, once a rushed dinner had been eaten and the plates were draining by the scullery sink. "Going over the same thing, but it's helping get it all straight in my mind."

"None of them knew of Emily meeting up with James before she left, but we can only assume that she did see him, and an offer was made for her to go to him if she wanted," Jacob concluded. "I don't believe she left us to be his… I mean to be with him as more than a family friend. She was too upset about Johnny and the wedding."

"And somehow all that changed," Cora continued. "I bet he knew what he wanted from her."

"Of course he did."

By the time they went to bed, all talk of James and Emily had been exhausted, all avenues explored. They could only wait until the next day and see what news, if any, Reuben and Ada had to share.

"We knew nothing about it," Ada said, as she opened the door to Cora and Jacob. "If we had…"

"Then you'd have told us," Jacob completed her words.

"But you know now." Cora pulled Emily's letter from her bag. "You got a letter the same as us?"

"We had two." Ada led the way to the kitchen table. "One from each of them."

At that moment Reuben entered the kitchen from the back of the house. “We were expecting you,” he said, giving Cora a brief hug and shaking Jacob’s hand. “It’s a sorry business, and there’s only one joy we can find from it – at least our Emily is safe and well.”

“We’re trying to keep that in our minds,” Jacob agreed.

They sat, the four of them, at the table with the tea brewing in the pot, while Cora and Jacob were passed the letter from James. It was written in a neat hand, with the name and address of the hotel printed at the head of the paper. James’ letters were large and well-formed, his loops and tails were generous, indicating a confidence as he told of his forthcoming marriage.

Dolphin Hotel
4th January 1894

Dear Mother and Father,

What a Christmastime it has been, and I write to you with the best of news – I am to marry Emily! She came to me last autumn and has settled well into life at the Dolphin Hotel. We soon became the best of friends and on Christmas Eve she agreed to be my wife.

As I write this joyful news, the date has not yet been set but we are eager for it to be in the spring.

What news of our plans after that? With my new wife’s comfort and interests in mind, we are to take some trips to Hastings and Eastbourne, with the view of securing ourselves a seafront hotel. Do you fancy a holiday on the coast?

With regards to you both,
Your son, James

"He's got a way with words!" Cora admitted. "A seafront hotel! She'll like that, I can't deny it."

"I'm not happy about this, not happy at all," Reuben said. "But I can't deny James has done well for himself, and Emily will never want for a warm coat or coal on the fire. He was in Ashford on business, and we thought he was going to buy a hotel here. It all seemed to be done and dusted, but he changed his mind."

"Because of Emily," Cora suggested. "He must have invited her to go to him, or suggested it, and when she turned up, he knew he had to stay there. If he wanted her for himself, then it was no good bringing her back to Ashford where she'd run off from."

Ada stood to stir the tea and pour it in the waiting cups. "It made no sense to us at the time when he sent a note to say he wouldn't be back in Ashford for a while. I just thought he'd changed his mind and decided the Dolphin suited him well enough." She passed the teacups and offered sugar. "To be honest, I hoped he'd meet a nice woman and decide to settle down, but not a girl twenty-two years younger than him. I'm ashamed that he would even think of it."

"I don't know the man, and it's clear he has a way with money, but apart from him being much older than Emily, then I always thought of him as being a bit of a ladies' man," Jacob began. "And there's no offence meant to you both when I say that. Emily is an innocent though. She might be a bit headstrong and foolish at times, but she's naïve as to how some men can be."

"She wasn't happy," Cora's voice began to rise. "We all know that, and we can say it here in the privacy of your home without Molly listening in – Emily had a thing about Johnny and ideas of them being together. She ran off, and I bet she saw James as her protector, and somehow he got her to recognise him as something different."

Jacob reached out and took his wife's hand. "It makes sense, even if we don't want to see it. If he gave her a home and treated her nicely, then she would be grateful, and it turned to something more."

Sometimes Cora felt jaded having to clean the grate, repeating the task day after day, week after week. On a Monday evening and Tuesday morning, her back would ache from lugging wet washing about, pegging it on the line, and hauling it off again. With Emily missing, she had been anxious for her daughter, often lying awake in the early hours of the morning, wishing for some news and, in her mind, replaying scenes from the days before she fled. Now the news had come, and with it the images of James coercing a young woman into feeling she needed him, and her admiring of the money and security he offered. Cora was absolutely exhausted. Her body felt cold and weak, and there was a slight ache pressing upon her forehead. "You said you had a letter from Emily as well – can we see it?" she asked.

"Of course." Ada pulled the paper from her apron pocket and slid it across the table.

Dolphin Hotel
Lydd
4th January 1894

Dear Ada and Reuben,

I hope this finds you both keeping well. If you have read the letter from James, then you will know the good news that we are getting married! He has been very kind, taking care of me since I moved to Lydd, and I know he will be a fine husband.

Tomorrow we are going to see the vicar and the date will be set. We will be getting married in the big parish church and are looking forward to you being there with us on the special day.

You have been good to me over the years, and I hope you are pleased to know that our families will soon be joined by marriage.

With love from your daughter-to-be,

Emily

"I couldn't help being shocked that this came with no apology after all these months. She must have known we'd be worried sick," Ada said once the letter had been read. "We were pleased to hear from her, but it's not much, is it? Not after going off without a word."

"It seems like a letter went missing," Cora offered her own for them to read. "Emily wrote to us last autumn and we never got it. You never heard a thing from James, at least not about this business."

"He was too ashamed," Reuben spoke with bitterness, "and so he should be."

Cora, so used to being comforted over the past months, now tried to console Reuben, "I know. I think the same thing over and over, but it won't do us any good and they don't care how we feel. Twenty-two years difference in their ages is more than I am easy with, but I am trying to think that, as your son, he'll treat Emily well. We want to go there and have a word, to see if she is happy and getting married for the right reasons, but I am trying to accept that, most likely, the wedding will go ahead."

"We know neither of you had any idea this was going on," Jacob continued. "But what I'm wondering now, is who should go to the Dolphin Hotel and find out what the situation is? I suggested to Cora that we wait a week and not go rushing into anything."

"I'd like to see them, and I know Reuben would too," Ada began, "but all four of us – what will that look like? I don't want to get them all defensive and then be rushing to the church to spite us."

After much exchanging of thoughts and adjusting of ideas around the kitchen table, the place where most of life's problems were resolved, Cora and Jacob left. Plans were made for the women to meet again during the week, and they all felt a little more at ease. They tried to place their trust that James Roberts, being the son of their dear friends, would care for Emily and hoped that, on arriving in Lydd the following weekend, they would be assured of his kind heart and commitment.

Not too far from the domestic scenes in Ashford, a fishing boat moved upriver with the incoming tide. The views beyond opposing riverbanks were taken for granted to those on-board, but to a stranger they would be almost remarkable – to the east a deep beach of golden sands and sandhills topped with spikey marram grass, and to the west, shingle ridges reminiscent of those at Dungeness.

Before long, the stones were replaced with muddy wetlands, thick with salt, and then a small settlement named Rye Harbour emerged. Here the shorelines were framed with sturdy uprights and supporting beams, as befitted an inland harbour.

The vessel came from Denge, a place with only two boats to its name, so the variety of marine craft moored bow to stern along the Rother was of constant interest to the fishermen sailing along.

"There she is!" old Alf Brooks, father to Jake and uncle to Ed, pointed to the boat he had fished from for over forty years. "She's coming home to us, as good as new! All thanks to that James Roberts who knew how to get us a few pounds for those coffee beans we salvaged."

"He's a tight-fisted blighter if ever I saw one," Jake grumbled. "I'd swear he cheated us, but he's a smart one and I don't stand a chance of getting the better of him."

Emily's Story
Chapter Twenty-One

"There's a letter for you," Hattie said, as Emily arrived home in time for dinner. "I put it in your bedroom. Don't want it getting mixed up with all the post that comes for Mr Roberts."

The fish pie had been placed on the table, and peas steamed in a separate dish, although James and Alf had not yet arrived from the bar. Emily ached to dash upstairs and read her mother's response to her own letter sent just three days before. However, she was trying to be less impetuous in her actions, so stayed to eat the meal with her new family, each morsel a struggle to swallow and digest. After the plates were cleared of food, then the dishes removed and washed up, Emily only had five minutes to change into her good frock before heading back to the George for her afternoon reception duties. Finally released from the kitchen, she shot upstairs, knowing she could only glance at the letter before leaving for work.

The yearning for contact with her mother was now unexpectedly powerful. For too long Emily had pushed all thoughts of home and family aside, reminding herself only of the petty squabbles in the home, and not of the enduring love and support given by her family. When she saw the small, cramped letters on the envelope, and the perfectly spaced lines, she was momentarily stunned to realise these were not the generous curves of her mother's hand, nor were they the ponderous characters created by Ada, or even the straggling lines written by her friend Jane. The letter taunted her from where it had been placed on her dressing table. 'Your mother hasn't the time to reply yet' it mocked.

Crushed, yet curious, Emily picked up the envelope, noting its quality in the thickness of the paper. From her dressing table drawer, she took a nail file and used it to slice open the slim packet, then pulled out a matching piece of cream writing paper.

Dengemarsh
Friday, 5th January 1894

Dear Emily,

I hope you are keeping well. Here in Denge there will be harsh days ahead with the snow coming. It makes it difficult to fish and not easy to walk all the way to Lydd. I have made myself a smokery though, so at least we all have smoked fish to keep the hunger at bay.

This letter comes because I need to let you know that I have not forgotten about our outing to New Romney. If I was there in Lydd then it would be my wish to take you for a walk, or out for tea and buns, every weekend. You are a lovely woman, and I am sure you could find a better bloke, but if you have taken a liking to me, as I have to you, then please remember that when the winter weather passes, I will be back in the town and asking you to be my girl.

With affection,
Edward Brooks

It felt as if the whole of Emily's body froze, yet she had to keep moving – to pull off her plain dress and slip into her brown tweed outfit. By some means, she must tidy her hair, then ensure her teeth and the corners of her mouth were free from crumbs. It seemed as if she looked on at another woman going through the motions in preparation for the afternoon's work, while the real Emily stood motionless staring at the words before her. Somehow the letter was refolded and replaced in its envelope, then popped into her handbag. She eased stiff feet into unyielding shoes and walked downstairs, her movements wooden.

An hour passed, and in the familiar surroundings of the George Hotel Emily became herself again. In a quiet moment, she re-read the letter to find that it was all she had remembered – a declaration from a man who led a simple life, but whose company she had enjoyed and, she had to admit, was attractive to her.

What was she to do? A commitment had been made to James and there was no doubting his ability to keep her in comfort, whilst every day he spoke of how much he enjoyed her company. Her husband-to-be was older than her, in fact older than her mother, but Emily had decided that there was no harm in that. *He's as fit and healthy as anyone ten years younger, and he'll know how to guide me. Them young men I used to go walking out with were just boys… Not that Ed is a boy – no, he's hard-working and perhaps five years older than me. He seems like a decent man, but I hardly know him, and he's left it too late. I'm not going to go breaking an engagement or sneak out to meet someone.*

Despite there being no doubt in Emily's mind that her loyalty to James was decided, over the following hours she pondered about whether she should at least reply to Ed's letter. *It's only polite, after him being so kind as to write, for me to pen him a short reply. I'll do it in a day or so.*

When Emily returned to the Dolphin, the place had once more come to life. From outside, she could hear the buzz of conversation at the bar. No one voice could be distinguished from the next, but a raucous laugh burst out, followed by an exchange of banter. She smiled, savouring the pleasure she felt at living in this lively home in the heart of the town, then turned the corner, walking across the yard and stepping through the back door.

There was no one in the kitchen, so Emily scampered upstairs, looking forward to a couple of hours peace and quiet before suppertime. However, no sooner had she hung up her coat and removed her shoes than there came the sound of James bounding up the stairs. Expecting him to go to his bedroom or the sitting room, Emily jumped up from her position on the edge of her bed as he entered without knocking or announcing his intention to come in. With all the confidence of someone who suffered no qualms about entering a woman's domain, James offered his explanation, "I missed you!" Then placing his hands on her shoulders, he pressed her backwards, forcing her to sit once more, and pressed his lips upon hers.

Wrong as it may be, Emily couldn't help appreciating his ardour, and she responded with enthusiasm, liking the taste of whisky on his tongue and the sensation of his fingers caressing her neck. "Every delicious part of you is covered up," he murmured. "This feels nice, doesn't it, but it's hardly enough." With years of experience in manipulating the tiny buttons and hooks to be found on ladies' garments, James loosened the neckline of her dress. Now his hands roamed her collarbone and reached the frill of her chemise. Fingers worked their magic on her skin, never straying into the truly forbidden areas bound by her corset but following the lacy trims.

With her head tipped back to receive his kisses, Emily's body arched a little, unknowingly presenting a provocative picture to her betrothed. He paused for a moment to savour the image before him, his fingers remaining on the pale skin previously hidden. Her lips stayed slightly open, and eyes fixed on his, while James' gaze flitted between her face and the temptation of what lay beneath the layers of tweed, boned corset and cotton chemise.

"Are you sure you want to wait until March?" James asked, his voice husky.

"I want to do it right," Emily replied, now aware that somehow he had managed to press his knee between her legs, parting them gently, and in the process lifting her skirt beyond her knees.

Now, even as they exchanged these words, James' hand roamed near her stocking tops. Helpless to wriggle away, Emily knew this was different from the innocent dalliances she had experienced before.

I know that it had ma all of a bother when I was going along on Fred's bicycle. It was silly of me, and she was right because my ankles were showing, and up to my knees when I got off, but it weren't the same as this. It was a bit of fun. I let him - and Ernie last spring - have a kiss, but they never tried anything else. And there was Walter too - he let his hands go where they shouldn't, but there was no undoing of buttons. The difference is that they were boys still, even Fred who is twenty-four. James is a man. He might be my intended, but it's not right. Not before the wedding.

"Doesn't this feel nice?" he asked, running his fingers around the top of her stockings, brushing on bare flesh.

Emily shivered.

"It does feel good, and it shows how much you love me. I need more than a kiss, however delectable they are." James pressed his lips on hers again.

Not knowing whether to concentrate on his kisses or the hand which continued to roam on forbidden flesh, Emily edged back a little on the bed, hoping to dislodge him.

"I'm not going to hurt you," James murmured, as he nuzzled into her neck, "Just show you some love."

"You show me love every day," she replied. "By giving me a home and asking me to marry you." Emily wrapped her arms around his waist and nuzzled up to him. *I never thought he would need reassuring like this. Not a man with a hotel and staff and money in the bank. But I suppose it's only right we have a few moments of… well… moments.*

While Emily tried to reason with herself, her stocking top was loosened, and James pulled away from their kiss, straightening himself. Emily, half lying on the bed was able to sit herself up in a flash, at the same time pulling her skirt down. "Now that's enough, James Roberts!"

"Oh, come on… If you're going to make me wait three months before we marry, then surely we can have a little bit of fun beforehand. The date has been set and you know I won't abandon you. No one would know."

"I'd know!" she retorted, "and I'm not having none of it. We can have a kiss and a cuddle but there will be no undoing of my stockings or anything else."

"Three months is a long wait, and I reckon a few more times like this and you'll be asking for more." With this, James placed his hand under her chin, lifting her face towards his, and gave a brief but firm kiss on the lips. Before Emily could even consider a retort, he was gone.

At suppertime, Emily was already seated when James came into the kitchen. He placed his hand on her shoulder and gave a gentle squeeze. "How was your afternoon at the George?"

"It was fine, ta," she replied.

"Mrs Tatin will be sorry to lose you."

"We haven't spoken about that yet, but I told her we were getting married, and she was very pleased for me." Emily skirted her way around the matter of her leaving before the ceremony.

That night, Emily's sleep was restless. "*You are mine and you'll do as I desire,*" James taunted in her dreams, while in the background there stood a younger man – tall, dark and silent. She woke numerous times with the memories of the increasingly passionate kisses she was receiving from her husband-to-be and could almost feel his hands on her stocking tops or tracing the skin beneath the lace trim of her chemise. *"I look after you well, don't I? A fine home… the beautiful shawl… a housekeeper and a maid… the diamond ring on your finger… All thanks to me."* In the distance, the darker man frowned and turned away.

I am lucky, Emily told herself when she woke in the dark hours. *Me, who always made mistakes, getting myself a wealthy husband. And he treats me well. He can't help it if he's getting a bit enthusiastic about things we must not be doing until we're married. I just need to tell him firmly that I'm not happy about his hands going where they shouldn't.*

Despite this being resolved, sleep was fitful. Emily rose before dawn to perch on the edge of her chair and gaze unseeingly from the window. She had a long day ahead of her: working the morning, eating a midday meal at the George, and continuing again until six o'clock in the evening. *I'll have a rest on the bed this evening before supper.* But even as Emily pictured this, she was also imagining a wedge placed under her bedroom door and being roused from her slumber by James voicing his frustrations at being kept away.

"What's the matter?" Mrs Tatin caught Emily unawares as the younger woman slumped on the chair behind the reception desk, allowing her head to rest in her hands for a moment.

Emily lifted her head and gazed at her employer. As she did so, the glass window in the front door distorted, casting a shimmering light into the hallway, and the pressure above her left eye grew. She raised a hand to shield her face from the light, but the dancing particles of light spread further than she could block them. "It's my head. My eyes. Everything has gone sparkly and it's dancing about. I don't know if I'm going to get a headache or be sick… but I can't think of anything else."

Mrs Tatin placed a hand on Emily's shoulder. "You must go home and lie in a dark room – it's the only thing to do. Don't move. I'll fetch your coat and ask Daisy to walk back with you."

"Thank you," was all Emily could say. She closed her eyes, allowing herself some respite from the kaleidoscope of swirling colours.

It was about four o'clock when Emily crept up the stairs of the Dolphin, her hand clutching at the banister rail. The hotel was usually quiet at this time of day. It was the lull between the bar closing at two o'clock and opening again at six. Hattie would be dozing on her bed, Alf would be sitting and snoozing somewhere, while James would probably be in their sitting room. *I'll tell him I am back and going to bed.* Emily turned the handle of the door but as it opened a few inches she was aware of James not being alone.

"I didn't know about that. You'll have to tell her it's off..." The words flying from the lips of the stranger, halted Emily in her tracks.

The woman facing her, yet still unaware of the door having opened, appeared to be in a desperate situation. Her eyes were wide and face flushed. Blonde hair was in disarray and lips still slightly parted. As she placed her hands on full hips while awaiting a response, and James moved a little from his position between the two women, Emily was privy to a fuller view of his visitor. Astounded by the sight before her, the young woman remained frozen.

The dishevelled image confronting Emily was no longer limited to blue eyes, fair curls and a blotchy complexion – now she was faced with the curves of full breasts, exposed by the stranger's dress being fully unbuttoned at the front, and the corset partially unlaced. Hardly knowing if this scene before her could be true, or if it was a figment of her imagination, her forehead began to pound, and she kept herself steady by reaching for the doorframe.

"We can talk about that later..." James reached out to caress the bare flesh before him.

"No! We'll talk about it now, and if I'm satisfied then you'll get your pleasure." She took his hand and placed it on the rounded curve of her belly. "I won't have you denying it. The child is yours and I want to know what you'll be doing about it."

"I was thinking of a cottage and a few pounds a year..."

"I was thinking of a ring on my finger and settling down here." She pouted a little, awaiting his response.

"Look Gracie," James murmured, while circling her waist with his hands. "Child or no child, we can still enjoy each other's company, and I'll see you right. You've not been short of a few coins over the last year, have you?"

The woman, now known as Gracie, chuckled and changed her tack, "I know you won't marry me, not when you've got an innocent young thing to warm your bed, but I'll be expecting that cottage or there'll be trouble for you." She closed her eyes and puckered up to receive his kisses.

Leaning against the doorframe, Emily felt giddy, her legs heavy and unable to carry her those few paces to the relative security of her bedroom. She took slow, deep breaths while averting her eyes from the scene before her. When she looked again, Gracie's skirt had been lifted, revealing podgy white flesh above a stocking top, but although James' attention was fully on his mistress, she had her eyes firmly locked upon Emily's face.

Pulling away from James, Gracie said, in a casual manner, "I'm sorry, love, but he's not a man to wait until his wedding night."

At these words, James pulled away and turned. As he faced Emily, a look of horror washed over his face – his mouth gaped and eyes focused on her. Stepping towards his betrothed, James then realised the extent of exposed flesh on view and reached for a shawl, handing it to Gracie, and ordered, "Cover yourself up."

Gracie, not even bothering to adjust her corset and dress, flung the shawl around herself, at least relieving Emily from any further exposure. "Look, you can marry him, and I won't cause you no bother," she said while leaning down to adjust her stockings. "You're a pretty thing and I heard you were young, so I can see why he's taken a fancy to you."

"This is for me and Emily to discuss," James responded. Reaching into his waistcoat pocket, he pulled out a pound note. "Now leave me be. You can see she's upset."

Emily pulled back from the doorway, leaving space for Gracie to swagger by, then her legs gave way and she sank to the floor. There, from her position on the floorboards, she watched the older woman leave the Dolphin, then closed her eyes.

A moment later and James was crouching beside her. "I don't know what brought you home, Em, but you don't look right. Let's get you to your room."

Almost grateful, Emily allowed him to help her stand, then offer support while they walked to her bedroom, and she was seated in a chair. James kneeled to ease her shoes from aching feet. "I'm going to be sick," she croaked, and leapt towards her washstand, using the last of her energy to pull the basin forwards. The vomit flowed immediately, and she sensed him leaving the room, only to return with a glass of cool, fresh water. Emily took it and rinsed her mouth but offered no thanks.

"You need to get into bed." James pulled back the covers.

"I hope you don't think you've come in to finish what you didn't do with her," Emily found her voice at last. Shocked by the vile words erupting, it was too late to take them away. Turning from the washstand she moved to the bed and lay so her back was to him.

"I wouldn't need her if you appreciated me more." His voice was low, but Emily heard every one of James Roberts' words.

Ed looked up at the vast sky, noting the clouds gathering to the north, hanging over Lydd. There was a purple hue to their mass - an indication of snow

She'll be good and warm working at the hotel or keeping herself busy at home. It will reach her first, and then us.

Ed hadn't been a spectator to the scene in the Dolphin. In his imagination Emily was always smiling and full of energy. He, like everyone else who knew and loved Emily, had no clue that she now lay huddled in a ball on her bed, weakened by a migraine as well as the shock of finding her husband-to-be with his pregnant mistress. Emily would not stir herself to look from the windows to see the snow clouds gathering or marvel as those first flakes drifted to the ground. Yet in Ed's mind, that is exactly what she would be doing – he saw her as a young woman who was alive to the wonder of nature.

Placing his hands on the worn handle of the winch, he set the about business of hauling the boat up the beach. Helen, with the baby bound to her body in a shawl, approached. "Did you get a good netful?" she asked. "It looks like snow's on the way."

"We did all right." Ed replied. "It's early in the year. Let's hope it doesn't hit us too hard." With his eye on the boat, he built up a slow rhythm at the winch.

Cora's Story
Chapter Twenty-Two

"Jacob was fussing about the snow, but look at the sky – all clear now," Cora said, as she met Ada on the station platform. "I don't know what I'd do if we couldn't travel today."

"It's melting already." Ada gestured to the slush swept into gutters by the porters. "Nothing to worry about."

"Just think, in an hour or so we'll be back together again!" Cora grinned. "It doesn't matter if she gets a bit cross with us, or if we have words about her running off, as long as we can spend some time with Emily. Now, shall we get a cup of tea before the train comes in?" There were twenty minutes to pass before their journey started, so before long they were in the tearoom, unable to see a thing through the condensation on the windows but glad of the warmth from the pot-bellied stove.

While the friends shared a pot of tea, then settled themselves in a carriage and began the journey to Lydd, they kept their own counsel as regards their children. There was nothing to be said that hadn't already been discussed, and no plans to be made before they saw Emily and James for themselves. It had been agreed their best hope was for Emily to return to Ashford, having admitted she had made a mistake, but both felt it unlikely the headstrong young woman would confess to being in the wrong.

Is there another way for Emily? Is there somewhere else she could go? Cora wondered. *I can see that she won't want to come back to me and Jacob, and to be sharing a room with her sister, but if she has got herself into a fix over getting married, perhaps there is another choice for her.* "What's this place like where Emily works? The George Hotel?" Cora asked as the train clattered past Hamstreet and down to the low-lying Romney Marsh.

"The George? It's a big place – lots of rooms and on the High Street. Don't you remember?"

"Oh yes," Cora recalled the substantial hotel on the main road. "She's done well for herself then. They would have rooms for maids and suchlike in the attics?"

"They would, but I imagine Emily had the offer of a lovely room in the Dolphin and felt rather pleased if she was one better than the others working at the George."

"I expect she did," Cora agreed. *But if she weren't happy… If she felt she had to marry him, then maybe a job in another big hotel… in another town… would seem like a way out. The trouble is I don't know that she isn't happy – it's just a feeling I have.* She settled down to listen to the rhythm of the train clattering over the tracks and to gaze at the fields with their icing of thin snow.

Having slowed for a couple of rural stations, passed small settlements, farmhouses and their outbuildings, the rooftops of Lydd came into view and the engine slowed to a halt in the station.

"Lydd. Lydd. All alight for Lydd. Next stop Dungeness. This train does not go to New Romney." The guard, having made the announcement, stood straight, his uniform just so, and eyes scanning the platform. He gestured to porters, anticipating the needs of the travellers and watched Cora and Ada step from the carriage.

They had no need of assistance and were soon walking past the ticket collector and out to the main road. From here they chose the path through the cemetery, following in the footsteps of Emily three months earlier.

"We'll go through the back door," Ada told Cora. She took the lead along the road, while they passed flat-fronted houses and the New Inn before walking along the front of the Dolphin Hotel.

Cora gazed up, wondering if one of the windows was her daughter's bedroom and, despite her best intentions, admitting to herself that the hotel was a solid structure of a decent size.

They rounded the end of the building and nodded to a stocky man who was mucking out the stables, then Ada pressed on the kitchen door. "There's no need to knock," she explained. "Not at my son's door."

"He won't be expecting us," Cora cautioned her.

"I long gave up trying to read his mind!" Ada gave a short chuckle. "But we'll find out soon enough what's going on."

For the first time, Cora saw the place which had been her daughter's home for the past months. There was a well-proportioned kitchen with a large table at the centre – most likely the place where Emily shared her mealtimes. The pine dresser was both tall and wide, fitted along the length of one wall, and stacked with crockery, pots and tins. The space was whitewashed throughout, not papered as you would find in a townhouse, but no doubt there was a formal dining room elsewhere. As Cora stood for those few seconds, taking in the details, a woman, alerted to the arrivals, stepped out of the pantry with a sack of flour in her hands.

"Hello Hattie," Ada greeted the housekeeper. "I'm sorry to turn up unannounced."

"Not at all Mrs Roberts. You'll have to excuse me while I start on the bread, but the kettle's on the boil." Hattie dumped the bag on the table and turned her attention to Cora. "Oh my! There's no mistaking who you are - you're the spit of Emily!"

"I'm her ma, and hoping to see her," Cora said, determined not to beat about the bush.

"I'm Hattie, as you just heard. And Emily will be so pleased, but you mustn't worry if she is looking a trifle out of sorts. She's suffered a terrible headache and taken to her bed since Thursday evening. I'll go up now and give her a call, then make you all a cup of tea. If you come through to the dining room, you can have a nice talk in private. You're lucky in some ways, because if it weren't for her being poorly then Emily would be at work, but I'm sure she must be feeling better today."

Hattie gestured for them to follow and offered seats. However, Cora was too restless to settle at the table. She looked at every painting hanging on the walls, then pulled back the curtains to gaze across the street and towards the Rype.

"She's nice enough, the housekeeper," Cora admitted to Ada. "Seems like a sensible woman. But I've never known Emily suffer from a headache or take to her bed."

"These things happen every now and then," Ada reasoned,

Cora however had darker thoughts in her mind. *I complained of headaches when I was expecting her, and the same with Molly. There'd better be no reason why they are having to marry.*

Footsteps could be heard approaching, and they turned to the door.

"Ma! Cora! You'll be just the tonic Emily needs!" James stepped into the room carrying with him all the confidence for which he was known. "How lovely to see you." He gave them both a kiss on the cheek and offered a broad smile.

Cora could barely fix a smile on her face, let alone exchange pleasantries. But it appeared that her thoughts… her opinions… her needs were of no consequence as James continued in full flow.

"Hattie has gone to fetch Emily, but you must understand that she has been ill these past days. I've not seen her myself this morning but am praying I'll find she has recovered. If she is a little pale, or overly tired, then it will be of no surprise for the headache left her quite helpless. Isn't she lucky though… to have everyone keeping an eye on her, and if she were to want for anything then Hattie or Sarah would be there to assist.

"That's all very nice, James," Ada took a chance to speak, "and it's a shame Emily has been poorly, but how do you think we feel to have had her missing all these months only to find out she is here, and not a word from you?"

"Yes, well…" James had the decency to look a little uneasy, "I left it up to Emily as it was her who came looking for a home. She wanted to get settled first.' He now looked directly at Cora, "She wanted to make you proud of her and when she was fixed up with work and doing well, the first thing she did was write and tell you all about it." He stepped towards Ada and gave her an affectionate squeeze. "But I should have written too and I'm sorry about that, Ma."

"There was no letter from Emily," Cora stated. "The first we knew was when we heard you were getting married. Getting married! And you older than her own mother!"

"That's right!" James grinned. "Who would have thought it? Aren't I the luckiest man? And when you see Emily, you'll see how happy she is. We've set the date…" He turned to the doorway, "Where is she? I presume she was asleep."

At that moment Hattie descended the stairs, and James repeated his words, a jovial ring to his tone. Later, when she knew the truth, Cora would marvel at his ability to perform as if nothing could be amiss.

There was little response from Hattie, other than a look of confusion on her face as she held out a small envelope. Cora snatched at the paper, noting the look of horror on James' face as she did so, and automatically stepping away to open it. Hattie offered no resistance, retreating to the kitchen in haste.

"What the bleedin' hell does this mean?" Cora shrieked – all her manners, refined over her years living in Ashford and trying to better herself, lost as she read the one line penned by her daughter. "'Sorry, I can't stay here any longer,' she says. What does this mean? We've come all this way to see Emily and you say she's in bed with a headache, but she's run off." The note was brandished before James, and now he took it.

"I don't know," he said. "She was happy. Happy with everything. It must have been this headache."

"Headache? You've done something. Gone and upset her." Cora moved to the doorway and called, "Hattie! Can you show me Emily's room?"

There was no attempt to stop her as Cora ascended the stairs with Hattie in her wake. Once in the bedroom, she paused and, for a moment, appreciated how Emily would have loved this spacious refuge with two large windows, a thick rug over wide floorboards and a selection of beautiful solid furniture. The bed was unmade, and there was still water in the bowl on the washstand. Cora dipped a finger in the soapy water. It was warm.

"Have you seen her this morning?" Cora almost barked at Hattie.

"She came down for a bite to eat – just some bread and butter," Hattie said. "Then she took a cup of tea back upstairs, saying she was still bad with her head."

"So, she got some food in her and ran off, but look…" Cora gestured to the shoes peeping out from under the bed, and the dress hanging from a hook on the wall, "…look at all her things still here. She didn't take much."

Hattie opened the closet. "She's got her coat and a shawl, but not the thick one Mr Roberts gave her. And I'd say she's wearing her plain dress and the others are all here. No – there's one good one missing."

Cora opened a couple of drawers. "She hasn't even taken all her delicates. It seems like she wanted to slip out and if she was seen then it would look like she had a basket for shopping and nothing more to arouse suspicion." She reached out and touched Hattie's arm. "Ta, but I'll let you go now. Best *he* doesn't think you've been too helpful. I'd like to spend a moment here on my own."

Hattie gave a nod, speaking again as she left the room, "I liked Emily. She was a lovely girl – full of life. I hope she's all right."

Cora smiled her understanding, then stood in the centre of the room. She wanted to absorb all the details of Emily's time over the past months: a book left on the seat of the chair, and a box of needles and thread told of hours at leisure; the room itself gave a sense of her having gone up in the world; new clothes and undergarments showed a new beginning and a young woman who had no intention of returning to collect her items still safely stored in the family home. Cora sighed. *She was doing well for herself. What went wrong?*

Before leaving, something led Cora to the teacup on the side. She picked it up, feeling for the warmth at the base. *We missed her by minutes, but she could be anywhere now.* She frowned. *A ring. The one he gave her.* The solitaire diamond nestled in the dip within the saucer. Tucking the ring into the palm of her hand, Cora left Emily's room.

Ada and James were standing either side of the dining table. They both faced Cora as she entered. Flinging the ring so it skittered across the table, Cora snapped, "There you go, James. There's your posh ring. Now her teacup's still warm, and there's a chance she'll still be at the station, or someone will remember seeing her get on a train, so I'm not going to wait about to hear your excuses, but you've got some questions to answer and the only good thing to come of this is that my daughter isn't marrying you anymore." With this Cora was striding towards the back door.

Ada followed without hesitation. "And don't you even think of coming with us," she warned her son before allowing the door to slam behind her.

"Please… you didn't hear it from me. If you say you did, then I'll be out of a job."

Now taking the path through the cemetery, Cora and Ada turned to see the pale young woman who had been spotted toiling in the scullery but had not spoken to them in the time they had spent at the Dolphin.

"It's Sarah, isn't it?" Ada asked, recalling her from previous visits. "Have you seen Emily today?" She placed her hand on Cora's arm, as if warning her not to overreact and scare the girl away.

"I'm sorry I couldn't say before - they would have heard me, Hattie or Mr Roberts, and that would have been me with no work and no pennies to take home for my family."

"You know where she is?" Cora asked, trying to keep her tone steady after the crushing setback of coming to Lydd only to be unable to locate her daughter.

"I don't know where she is, but I know why she's run off," Sarah gave a fearful look towards Ada, "and you, Mrs Roberts, ain't going to like hearing it, but it's only fair on Emily's ma that she hears the truth of it."

"You don't need to be frightened that I'll be angry with you," Ada attempted to calm the girl. "I care about Emily as well, and it's her I'm worried for. Now let's move away… over here… by these trees and out of sight of the path, so you can tell us."

They moved to where a thicket of bushes grew around an old oak, and although the branches were bare of leaves it offered some privacy to Sarah who had been bold enough to follow the women and to offer some news.

"You know Emily then?" Cora asked. "I mean you work in the Dolphin and got to know her? Was she happy?"

"Oh yes," Sarah smiled. "Emily was very happy in her work at the George, especially when she got to wear her best frocks if she was on the reception. I don't think she wanted to leave, but Mr Roberts was saying she must, even though they weren't married yet."

"Did she talk to you about it?" Cora queried.

"No, but if he mentioned it, she never said she had handed in her notice. But that ain't why she ran off, because if it was this month or next, she would have to leave if she was getting married to a man of money like Mr Roberts."

"Why did she run away then?" Ada questioned.

"She…" Sarah looked at the ground and pushed at the skeletons of the last year's leaves with the toe of her boot. "She…" Then with her gaze firmly on the leaves, the ragged grass, her feet – anything but meeting the eyes of the two women before her – Sarah began again, "It was him. It was Mr Roberts and his fancy woman. I came back to the Dolphin that afternoon because Hattie had given me some pie for my parents, and I forgot to take it home. I was there in the kitchen when Mr Roberts brought her in through the back door and she was giggling. They didn't see me, but I saw them go up the stairs and into his sitting room."

"Had you seen her before?" Cora wondered.

"I'd seen her plenty of times but not since he said he was going to marry Emily. What shocked me the most was… I think she was expecting. You know… expecting a child."

"His child?" Cora wasn't surprised. Perhaps she should have been, but this was just what she believed of James Roberts.

Sarah shrugged.

"Did you tell Emily?" Ada asked.

"I didn't need to," the girl admitted. "It wasn't long after when Emily came home unexpected. I suppose it was because of that headache they said about. I don't think they was lying about her feeling ill. She went upstairs and she saw Mr Roberts and that woman, and then Gracie – that's her name – was going off with her dress half undone and saying she knew Mr James wouldn't marry her, but she expected to be taken care of. After that, Emily went to her room and didn't come out – not that evening nor yesterday neither."

"Did you see her at all?" Cora asked. "You can tell us. No one is cross with you. It's been three months since I last saw Emily and if you can tell us anything then it will help ease our minds and give us hope of finding her another time."

"I saw her this morning," Sarah said. "She was putting a few things in her bag and had a packet tied up with string. Not much. Not enough to make it look like she was leaving. She said that her head was still bad, and she would take a short walk around the Rype and would be back in no time. 'No need to worry about me,' she said. 'I'm just going for a walk.' But she didn't come back, and I suppose that's when she went. There was one other thing that was a bit odd, something about a missing bank book."

"Emily left the bank book at home," Cora said. "Molly found it on the floor. If only she had it, then there would be the money to care for herself."

"Perhaps she had money saved from all those months working at the hotel?" Ada suggested.

"I think Mr James got her a bank book for that and he was keeping it safe," Sarah told them. "But she would have a few shillings, wouldn't she, and a nice dress and smart coat, and her shawl. She looked like quality, Emily did, and she'll get herself another job somewhere nice." Sarah focussed on Cora for the first time and offered a hopeful smile.

Cora returned the smile and for the first time she felt optimistic for her daughter's future. "I think you're right, Sarah. Emily must have got on a train and set off somewhere new. Once she's settled, she'll send us a letter. It will take a while, but we will hear from her and be able to visit." *This day hasn't turned out how we thought it would, but there's some good news to be taken from it – she isn't getting married and there's lessons been learned. It seems like she did well working for them at the George Hotel, so perhaps she can write for a character reference. And when we hear from Emily, the first thing I can do is send on her bank book so she can get herself nicely set up!*

"We need to get to the station," Ada reminded Cora. "Just in case..."

"Ta, Sarah." Cora reached in her bag and pulled out a few coppers and a shilling. "You've been a true friend and I won't forget that. Emily might be on the platform waiting for a train, or if not, then someone is bound to know which way she went. We'd best get a move on..."

"They will!" Sarah spoke with certainty. "If Emily has been to catch a train, then they are bound to remember her." She stepped away, back towards the cemetery gates. "Ta, Mrs Rose. Ta for the coins and I hope one day I'll hear that she has been found and got herself set up nicely somewhere."

Unseen to Ed, the steam engine pulled out of Lydd Station, its whistle vibrating through steel tubes. The sound resonated across the miles of shingle and farmland towards Denge. Carried on the breeze, its pitch was long and low. He paused, straightened his back, and, for a moment, wondered about the people on the train and what places it would take them to.

Then he frowned. It appeared that someone was walking along the track from Lydd towards Denge. *What would bring a person down here when there's more snow due, and it's the last place on earth you'd want to get trapped?*

It wasn't his business, and most likely a trick of the light. The snow was closing in on the headland, the sky a purple-grey, casting an odd hue upon the stones and scrubland. Nothing looked quite as it usually did. Ed shrugged. There was a sack to be filled with wood and it was no easy task to find scraps for the fire, but perhaps in the thicket of scraggy hawthorn...

When he emerged from the cluster of stunted trees, Ed scanned the area, noting that the snow clouds had thickened, and the light dusting cast the evening before was soon to be topped up with a thicker layer. The next thing he noted was that there was now definitely a figure walking the rough track to the coast.

Four Months Later

"When I've done our place, I'll come and give yours a going over," Emily brandished a stiff brush and called out to the old woman who was an aunt, or some kind of relative of Ed's. Then she turned to haul a rug further onto the shingle and set about beating it. The vigorous exercise put a glow in the young woman's gaunt cheeks and her grey eyes shone.

After a moment, Emily turned and grinned to see the bedsheets flapping gently with the breeze. "I don't know what Ed will say if these aren't dry by nightfall," she commented to Ida who had sidled closer.

"Ed don't know how to be anything but soft with you," the woman replied. "And a bit of damp around the hems can soon be dried by the fire."

Glancing at the wedding ring on her left hand, Emily felt a rush of warmth run through her. The band was battered and a little loose, so to keep it secure on her finger, she had wound a length of thread around it. Nothing was brand new at Denge, but this had been Ed's mother's ring and that was more than good enough for Emily. Now she scanned the sea, wondering how soon it would be before she spotted his fishing boat on its return journey. "Anyway, I mean it – I'll give yours a good turn-out tomorrow or the next fine day."

Ida gave a nod of appreciation, liking the lively young woman who had unexpectedly come to live with them. Not one for many words, she knew life at Denge was all the better since the day when Ed arrived hand-in-hand with a pretty stranger. She settled herself on the chair by the doorway of the wooden home where Emily now lived.

The winter months had been challenging. At times, when the snow hammered the headland, the inhabitants of this remote settlement had hunkered down for several days, only venturing out when absolutely necessary. Spring came, or so the calendars claimed, yet time passed, at first with no hint of warmer days to come. Now, at last, the breeze flowing from the west had lost the bitter nip it had carried through the first months of the year. With the fairer weather there came a shift in routines, a lifting of the shoulders, and tentative plans for the days ahead.

The shack, with its box bed built into the wall at one end and open fire at the other, was a far cry from the generous proportions of the room Emily had so admired in the Dolphin Hotel. The furniture was mismatched and had not seen a dab of polish since it had come to reside in the home of Ed Brooks. Yet Emily had tended her new home with love – repairing the hems on curtains, scrubbing out the cupboards, and sweeping the floor daily.

On the days he couldn't fish, Ed went scavenging for food and firewood, and had repaired all three of the chairs which fitted around the central table. His smoked fish provided a modest amount of nutrition for those living in the collection of shacks, while his chickens and goats supplied a small offering of eggs and milk. Neither the birds nor the nimble beasts were inclined to produce much during the winter months.

Ed occasionally spent an evening in the Hope and Anchor, but more often than not would choose the warmth of Emily's body under the layers of blankets on their bed.

Emily glimpsed the bare mattress and piles of bedding through the open doorway. *I'll start washing the blankets once I've given Ida a hand with her place.* To Ida she said, "Well, all this standing about isn't getting the dirt out of the rug, is it?" For the next few minutes, she thumped and brushed at tufted wool, enjoying the rhythmic beat created with the bristles.

As the grocery cart trundled the last yards towards Denge, Emily moved out of sight and into her home. Ida made no comment, knowing that the newest member of their community preferred to shy away from those who came to the area as visitors or to trade. With no words exchanged, she took Emily's basket, and the leather pouch containing a few coins, then picked her way over the stones to the rough road.

In the shack, Emily dipped a rag into a pail of warm water and heaved herself up so she stood on a chair. Raising an arm, she began to wipe the whitewashed walls, lifting years of caked-on soot and the tangled remains of spiders' webs. Drips of grimy water splashed onto the skirt of her dress, causing her to tut in despair. This was the same outfit she had worn when cleaning the bedrooms or helping with the laundry at the George Hotel. Now, if Mrs Tatin were to see her in it, ragged at the hem and faded on the front, she would not think the young woman fit to wash the doorstep. Yet Emily must still do her best to keep it clean for she had brought so little with her when making that mad dash from Lydd and the clutches of James Roberts.

No sooner had the upper part of the first wall been washed than voices could be heard. Ida was now accompanied by Jake's wife, Helen, who would, no doubt, have the tiny baby strapped to her front. Her toddler appeared to roam freely upon the shingle landscape, something which Emily found concerning, although he was, as yet, unharmed by this carefree approach adopted by his parents and extended family. She threw the cloth into the pail and went to meet the women and her basket of food.

"Ta for getting that," Emily said, as she always did, running her eye over the loaf of bread, and greaseproof packets of cheese and butter. She hoped one of the paper twists would contain some dried fruit as she planned to make drop scones that afternoon. Their chickens had provided one egg overnight, and Emily was determined to make the best use of it.

"There's news from Lydd," Helen announced.

"Oh?" Emily's heart began to pound erratically.

"He don't know about you being here," Helen was quick to say. "But Jack Jones, him who comes with the cart, he always passes on the news. He says the Dolphin has been sold and Mr Roberts has gone off to Eastbourne."

"You'll be able to come out of hiding," Ida said. "He's gone and won't be back."

Emily stared out to sea and saw the speck of a boat she knew to be Ed returning to her. She glanced back at the humble timber home, to which they had hopes of adding an extra room over the next year. "Yes. Yes, I will. Not yet though. I'll go to Lydd when I'm good and ready on a day when Ed can wear his suit and I can put on my decent dress. He can take me out for a cup of tea and a bun."

The tension, which Emily was so accustomed to carrying within her slender frame, began to disperse. To help it on its way, she picked up the brush and prepared to thrash the last of the winter's dust from the old rug.

The End

About the Author

Romney Marsh writer, Emma Batten, loves to combine her interest in local history with creative writing. It is important to her that historical details are accurate in order to give readers an authentic insight into life on Romney Marsh. She enjoys giving author talks about her journey as a writer, planning unique writing workshops and meeting her local readers.

Reckless Choices is Emma's tenth novel.

Books
Reading order and publication dates

The Dungeness Saga (also featuring Lydd and Ashford) set in late Victorian times through to WW2:

*Still Shining Bright** (2020): Cora and her daughter, Emily, are brought ashore to Dungeness by lifeboat. With no home or possessions, they rely on the kindness of strangers, and Cora must use her wit to survive.

*Reckless Choices** (2021): A chance meeting on a train upsets Emily, while on the streets of Ashford someone lurks waiting to make trouble. As tensions brew within a close family, the young woman makes a rash choice.

Secrets of the Shingle (2016 & 2020): A mystery set on the wild, windswept wastes of the Dungeness peninsula in the 19th century and seen through the eyes of a naive young teacher.

Stranger on the Point (2018): Lily sets off to discover the remote coastal village her mother called home. A wrong turning takes her to a place where her arrival brings hope. The story of a determined young woman's quest to fulfil her worth, as shadows of WW1 live on.

The Artist's Gift (2019): This tells the story of a fictional young woman, widowed through the war and living amongst real life events during the Second World War. Inspired by the bombing of Lydd Church.

*Prequels to *Secrets of the Shingle*

Stand-alone novels:

A Place Called Hope (2005, reworked 2019): Set in the 16th century, this tells the story of two young women living through the decline of a remote settlement named Hope on Romney Marsh.

But First Maintain the Wall (2019): Set in Georgian Dymchurch. Harry is passing through the village when the seawall breaches and events force him to stay. As an outsider, he struggles to be accepted and a tentative friendship is forged with a young woman who seeks answers to her past.

What the Monk Didn't See (2017 & 2021): The story of New Romney and the 1287 storm, which changed the fortunes of the town forever. As the storm breaks out, a monk climbs to the roof of the church tower. It is a superb vantage point, but what doesn't he see?

The Saxon Series introduces West Hythe, Lyminge and Aldington in 7th- century Anglo-Saxon times:

The Pendant Cross (2020): For a few days a year, the Sandtun (West Hythe) is used as a seasonal trading settlement. While they await the boats from Francia, friendships are made and hatred brews. Meanwhile four monks travel by night carrying a precious secret.

The Sacred Stone (2021): An earthquake uncovers a Roman altar buried in the foundations of an old fort. An ambitious thane and his priest are determined to secure this prize, and their actions have repercussions on the people of Aldington.

For more details take a look at Emma's website:
www.emmabattenauthor.com